VIRGINIA ANN

The Potter's Final Piece

A Pooka Women's Club Mystery

First published by Caraigh Publishing 2025

First edition

This book was professionally typeset on Reedsy.
Find out more at reedsy.com

Contents

1

Maude

I'm going to start by saying my mom was not crazy. In fact, I told everyone who believes this lie that they aren't welcome at her funeral. That's probably why no one else is here except for me. And Father Doyle. It's made the moment extra sad.

Standing next to my mother's burial plot is a clear sign that the world as I've known it has ended. However, everything else about the day is unbelievably normal for an Indiana summer. In fact, it's almost pretty. Above me, the sun passes through an oak tree, which sways in the cool breeze, causing the light to dance on the fresh dirt covering my mom. Father Doyle sees it and says it is the light from a chorus of angels coming to greet my mother. That sounds nice, but it doesn't change the fact that she is gone. The sunny day is making everyone happy. Children at the school playground behind me are laughing. The church group's cheerful voices drift out of the community room's open window next to us. My mom is dead, buried underground where she can't see the sunlight dance, and they are happy. Father Doyle and his chorus clearly haven't thought of that. I wish it were pouring buckets of rain.

"Maude," Father Doyle says gently, "do you have any final words to say? A poem or verse that you'd like to read?"

Father Doyle is a good sport. He is all dressed up in his white robes and purple stole, even though it's just him and me. He stands at my mother's head with his well-worn Bible and wire-rimmed glasses, and does his very best to use big words to make my mom's passing feel monumental. I want to do the same.

I step around her grave—careful not to step on her—and stand next to Father Doyle. I pull a folded sheet of paper out of my pocket and open it between my hands. Then, I pull my reading glasses out of my other pocket, put them on, and take a deep breath.

"With pestilence and with blood, I will enter into judgment with him; and I will rain on him and on his troops, and on the many peoples who are with him, a torrential rain, with hailstones, fire, and brimstone."

I give her grave a nod to mark the solemnity of the occasion, take off my readers, and put them back in my pocket. Then I refold the sheet of paper and tuck it in my other pocket. I glance at Father Doyle, who is staring at me, a strange look on his face.

"Ezekiel," I say. He must not recognize it. As a priest, he should, but I don't want to judge. "It was my mother's favorite."

"Well." He clears his throat. "Then I think it's time for the final blessing."

I nod, my heart broken that this is the final goodbye, and move carefully back to my place beside the grave. He opens his black leather book to a page marked with a red ribbon. A distant wooden bat in the playground cracks as it connects with a ball, which *thunks* to the ground three feet to my left. I try to ignore it.

"May God give to you and all whom you love his comfort and his peace, his light, and his joy, in this world and the next; and the blessing of God almighty, the Father, the Son and the Holy Spirit, be upon you, and remain with you this day and forever."

"Heads up." A boy runs to the ball and heaves it back to where his friends are standing in the school playground.

"Amen," I say.

"Father?" A chubby woman in a floral dress appears on the church steps. "It's about time to start the meeting."

Father Doyle sighs. "One minute."

He looks at me. I'm trying to ignore the distractions, but it's hard. Father Doyle meets my eyes and looks torn. As I said, he's a good sport. But he has an entire flock to attend to and, based on their current behavior, they certainly can use his help.

"It's okay," I say. "You can go."

"Maude…" He shifts his weight from his left foot to his right, and back again. "Are you going to be alright?"

I suck in through my nose so he doesn't have to see me cry. Unfortunately, it is rather loud and sounds more like a snort. "I'm fine."

He doesn't look like he believes this—he's a smart one—but then he turns and walks towards the church. I watch his receding figure.

This is a lie. I will not be alright. Nothing is ever going to be alright again. My mother should have been rich and famous. Her funeral should have been as big as the Queen's, with all living in the town of Pooka sobbing in the streets. It shouldn't have been this.

But, then, I realize something important. My mother's reputation depends on me. "Maude," she used to say to me all the time, "a lying tongue hates its victims." She was right. And now I see that the truth rests on my tongue, mine alone. I bend down and put my hand on the dirt. Another ball sails past my ear, but this time I don't even flinch.

The dirt is soft and fine beneath my fingers, as I rub what, as best I can guess, is the ground above her shoulder. "Don't worry, Mom," I say. "I'll prove your claims. You weren't crazy. I believe you."

2

Biddy

Under the sparkling light of a magnificent chandelier made of beautifully glazed pottery, Biddy spends the early part of the afternoon standing in her Boston estate foyer. She wears her best black low-heeled shoes and a modest new black dress purchased for the occasion, nodding to the endless line of well-wishing mourners snaking through her door. She shifts her weight from one foot to the other. She wants to take her shoes off. Actually, she wants to lie alone in a dark room and cry in peace. It's entirely possible that wakes are more a punishment to family than a comfort.

The dignitaries show up in droves, just as they should. Filmmakers and documentarists who had used Charles for research for their films, famed journalists with a passion for history, and even the Former Secretary of State all put in an appearance. Charles Bramley devoted his life to ensuring that the lives, actions, and artifacts of America are not forgotten. In return, America has come to pay its last respects to the venerable Harvard professor and has even given him an honorary portrait.

It now sits on an easel to Biddy's left, and she feels her eyes drawn towards it. Harvard commissioned it for their Wall of Deans. The thought is nice, but Biddy is glad Charles never saw it. It makes him look dead. No one should have to see that when they're dying.

"The likeness is uncanny, isn't it?" Harvard's President Elliott says, following her line of sight.

"If only we were all that peaceful," she responds.

She thanks President Elliott for coming and turns to face the next person in the receiving line. President Elliott has gotten the painting wrong. The bland-looking, but distinguished man in that portrait is nothing like the energetic, passionate person of their first forty years of marriage, nor the pain-ridden, agonized one of the last three.

"Hey Mom, look." Standing beside Biddy, Megan elbows her and points to a black suit-clad man joining the end of the line that now wraps around the fountain in the center of the circular drive. "Isn't that the Vice President? Dad said he taught him, but I can't believe he came."

Biddy looks more closely at the slim, white-haired man, flanked by two burly men in sunglasses. "If it is, I'm surprised he's here. I've been told by the Social Security Office that it can take six to eight weeks for all government offices to recognize a death in their systems. Despite my best efforts to prove otherwise, his office claims that your father is still very much alive and that we need to pay his Medicare premium. This wake must be very confusing for him."

"Oh god, Mom, how can you even think about paperwork right now? It's the Vice President of the United States," Megan hisses back.

Biddy smiles and apologizes. One day Megan will get

stuck doing all this for her, and then she will see how little supposedly important people seem at this moment. Because it isn't just grief that consumes Biddy, although she wishes it could. It's paperwork. Reams of it. For example, AT&T would not cancel Charles' phone service even after Biddy had faxed over his death certificate, so concerned they were that she was scamming them. Since Charles hadn't given her his password, she had to guess his favorite actor to get access to his account to cancel it. It was Sean Connery. She got it right on her third and final try. Sometimes she is so frustrated with Megan's naïve belief in the fairness and efficiency of the world, that Biddy thinks she should just leave the whole mess of her eventual death for her daughter to navigate herself. But then she feels bad and writes the name of her favorite actress on the sheet of paper containing all her accounts and passwords, and tucks it in the folder marked "For Megan, Upon My Death." It's Helen Mirren.

This is the bit no one tells you about all this. Besides the passwords and stacks of death certificates and gallons of tissues you will need. Besides missing your spouse like he is a body part and finding yourself turning to speak to him, only to realize that he is no longer there. Besides walking through the echoey, empty halls of a house way too big for one. The thing no one tells you is that it makes you think about your mortality, too. She now feels almost-dead at the spry age of 67. Biddy has been the supporting act. She's moved where she needed to, she's ensured that the house and grounds are maintained, she's arranged dinner parties and events, she raised funds to support Charles' good works, and raised a daughter to follow in his footsteps. Her jobs are done. That life is over. What is she supposed to do now? Who will come to her wake? On second thought, Megan will have it much easier when she dies.

"Dad sure has a lot of friends," Megan says, still eyeing the line.

"He sure does," says Biddy.

When the line has finally slowed to a trickle. Megan nudges her again.

"Hey Mom, you should probably say a few words."

Biddy nods and moves to stand next to the cold-looking portrait. All around her, her black-clad guests mill conversing in whispered voices while balancing plates full of crudites and flutes of champagne. A server notices her and silently hands her a glass of champagne. Biddy borrows a fork from a nearby guest and taps it against her glass. The murmur in the room falls silent.

"On behalf of Megan and myself, thank you for coming. Charles devoted his life to history and the importance of legacy. Looking at all of you here, he could die peacefully, knowing that he had such a solid legacy in his own life. Although Charles will no longer be with us, he will live on through his published works, his students, and his colleagues, one of whom is his own beloved daughter. Megan follows in his footsteps as a tenured professor at Harvard University. You all are his greatest pride and Megan's path his greatest joy."

The group breaks into applause and acknowledges each other, as well as Megan. Megan blushes and her eyes shine. Biddy raises her glass as the applause dies. "So today we toast Charles Bramley. May his words continue to inspire, may his heart continue to protect, and may the memory of his actions make us all more purposeful in how we spend our days. To

Charles."

"To Charles." The roomful of people hold up their glasses and take a sip.

Biddy turns and looks at the portrait. "I'll miss you," she whispers.

Out of nowhere, a burst of sunlight filters through the stained-glass transom windows, dancing colors across Charles' face.

Now it looks more like Charles, she thinks. Biddy smiles and sips her champagne, comforted for the first time that day.

* * *

By three pm, the conversation between the various crowded clusters of mourners has changed. Reminiscing exhausted, they now speak about the future. All Biddy can think about is how Charles wouldn't be there for this future. How could they speak of a time without him? How can life just carry on? And yet it must. Including her own.

Biddy moves from the foyer, filled with dark-suited men, into the living room of black-clad women and joins the circle of the seven members of the Boston Historical Society Board. Each wears a perfectly coiffed silver bob, black sheath dress, and pearls. The likeness is that of a well-aged sorority photograph, not that Biddy knows much about sororities, or even college for that matter. But that is her little secret, thank goodness.

"Muffy, I've been meaning to call you." Biddy smiles at the woman beside her. "It's just been a nightmare with all the arrangements."

"I can only imagine," Muffy rolls her eyes and looks around

the room. "A cocktail party for two hundred with only a week's notice and right after your husband died? Only a man could devise the ridiculous concept of a wake."

Biddy laughs and is surprised she can. It is nice to be back in the presence of her best friend. What with the demands of Charles' care, she has barely seen any of her friends, little less Muffy.

"It's been a long haul," she says. "But now that it's behind me, I'm excited to get back on the Historical Society Board. I know I missed my year to be president, but I want to do it now. I'm ready."

Biddy has given this much thought. And even through the intense pain of Charles' loss, it has provided that glimmer of hope. Of excitement. She has spent her entire life taking care of people. First, her siblings. Then Megan. Then Charles. This is finally a moment she can do something for herself. She has never been more ready to step out of others' shadows and make her own mark on the world.

But Muffy's beautifully blue liquid eyes dart quickly to the left and then back to the center. They dart so quickly that the average person would miss it. But Biddy Bramley does not. After all, Biddy was once the person stationed to Muffy's left to receive the look. To raise her eyebrows in understanding at the perceived gaffe.

"Biddy, darling, you took your leave of absence three years ago. Of course, we all hoped Charles would live on forever in your care, so we had to fill your place on the board. We've asked Mellie Watson to be president next year. It's a job for the young," Muffy leans closer to whisper in her ear. "Plus, it's so much easier to get donations when it's the wife of a current Harvard Professor."

Biddy bites back her shock. Mellie Watson, wife of Charles' replacement at Harvard, wouldn't know Pierre Chapo, the famous French furniture designer, from El Chapo, the drug lord.

"I'm sure Mellie would be a wonderful choice down the road," says Biddy. This is a lie. "However, there's nothing quite like experience for solid leadership. And I bring that in spades. Who chaired the annual tea for four hundred? Who got the Patriotic Shawl of Mrs. Andrew on loan for display? I have so many ideas…"

This time, Muffy's eyes slip away and don't come back. "Biddy, you know how these things work. It always goes to the current Dean of History's wife. We need someone with the platform to fundraise."

Muffy isn't gauche enough to be explicit, but she doesn't have to be. Biddy's platform is now dead. Buried in a cemetery with a portrait in the hall. However, in her heart, Biddy knows this isn't true. Biddy could create a new platform through her own hard work. Through her own great ideas. She feels anger flash through her veins and fights to control it. "Muffy, I don't care who Mellie's husband is. History to her is *The Real Housewives*, Season 1. She'd be a terrible steward of the Historical Society."

"We are past our prime to be leaders," Muffy says. "Maybe volunteer the events again…"

Biddy sets her flute of champagne down on the end table beside her. She is not some second wife asking to sit on the board of the Foxy Force, which raises funds to protect the endangered red fox and which, true to its name, tends to attract the young, the new, and scantily clad. She is the long-time wife of a History Dean at Harvard and member of the

11

esteemed Boston Historical Society, which, if anything, is supposed to venerate age. She forces herself to consider her words. "Well, whether or not you approve, I'm running against Mellie for the President's role."

"What?" Muffy's forehead creases, which Biddy didn't think it could do with all the Botox. "No one runs against the appointee. You know that!" she hisses.

Just then, a server hurries over and taps Biddy on the shoulder. Muffy exhales a breath of air worthy of a yoga class that she probably now takes with Mellie Watson. The little trollop.

"I'm sorry to interrupt," the girl says to Biddy, tugging on her black polyester dress, "but you have a phone call. Shall I just take a message?"

"No." Biddy returns her eyes to the friend she's valued for over twenty years. How have things gotten here? "I'll take the call now."

Muffy grabs her arm as she turns to go. "Think this through, Biddy. Boston will only show so much leeway for your loss of Charles. This is crossing the line. We have a way of doing things and that way does not include messy public elections."

Biddy firmly pulls her arm from Muffy's grasp. "You are my friend. Do you really think so little of me not to support me on this?"

Biddy shakes her head and turns to follow the server, wedging her way through the clusters of her guests en route to the kitchen. Messy elections? America's entire democracy is founded on the notion of messy elections. Did the British just quietly hand the Presidency to George Washington? No, George shot his way to the top. Biddy finally has the opportunity to share her talents with the world, and what?

The world wants her to curl up and die like her husband? Would that make them happy? Sadly, she realizes, it probably would. Her final act, scripted by Shakespeare himself, is to die of a broken heart. Well, she would not.

She slides between two final groupings of guests and enters the massive double island kitchen bustling with loud and indifferent catering staff. She scans the room of murmuring workers and clanging cookware until her eyes fall on a wall phone, hanging in the far left corner, near the backdoor. The receiver rests on the marble countertop.

The call is most certainly spam. Who else would call a landline? However, Biddy is so happy to have a break from the funeral events, she thinks she might just be willing to buy a reverse mortgage. At least, listen to the pitch. With a gasp, she realizes this is who says yes to these calls. She promises herself she will say no and picks up the phone.

The caller says hello and, instead of settling in for a long sales pitch, Biddy's heartbeat freezes. It's a voice from a very distant and long-forgotten past. A past she has tried to keep far away.

"Ruby?" Biddy says. It's a voice she hasn't heard since she was eighteen. Since they were eighteen.

"Biddy!" says the voice on the phone.

Tears form in Biddy's eyes. Biddy has pushed her past far from her mind. Not even her husband or daughter know of her roots. But not everything from that past is painful, she suddenly realizes. Ruby is a good part. Her voice brings joy. The comfort of a friend who hasn't forgotten her. "Ruby! Oh Ruby. It's so good to hear your voice. How did you know?"

"Know what?"

"Know that Charles just passed. That's why you're calling,

isn't it? To offer your condolences? Which would be a welcome treat as no one else is doing such a good job of it at the moment."

"Oh." Ruby's voice pitches upward with surprise. "Oh, dear. No, actually…" Her voice drifts away.

Biddy closes her eyes. She doesn't think she can handle one more problem. "What Ruby? What?"

Ruby takes a breath. "It's your sister, Biddy. It's Eileen. She's died too."

Biddy falls back against the wall. The kitchen chaos around her fades to silence as vivid memories and sounds of a long forgotten farmhouse in faraway Indiana replace it.

Eileen. Poor Eileen.

"I'm so sorry about Charles," Ruby says. "That is terrible news and I realize my timing isn't the best. But I was calling to say you really need to come home to Indiana. Eileen's daughter, Maude—I don't think you ever met her, what with your rift with your family—she isn't taking her mom's death too well. She's losing jobs right and left, and is at risk of becoming unemployed and homeless. You need to talk some sense into her."

No, Biddy thinks. No. Charles hasn't even been dead for a week and now she is to assume care for a niece she doesn't even know? "I don't think that's necessary. She's just grieving. That seems normal enough." She doesn't want to care. She can't care.

"Oh, she's not grieving," Ruby says, with a little inappropriate giggle. "That would be way too normal for Maude. She's on a rampage. She has this absolutely crazy idea that her mother is the founder of Aisling Pottery and Finn Murphy stole the business from under her. She's accusing everyone of being in on the conspiracy."

Biddy lets Ruby chuckle as she glances over at the antique hutch against the far wall of her kitchen. On its center shelf sits a white platter, with the world famous green tinted glaze and an intricate hand painted scrollwork along its edges. It is from the same collection as the magnificent chandelier in her foyer. These are the only things she owns from her hometown. And they are the only things that are beautiful about her hometown.

"Why is that so funny?" she asks. "Why should it seem so crazy that Eileen could build a successful business?"

Ruby chokes mid-laugh. "Oh Biddy, Eileen was not the founder of Aisling Pottery. Be serious."

"How do you know that?"

"Because she didn't." Ruby's voice fills with exasperation. "She never went to college. She was a cleaning woman. And she wasn't even that great at that. Then she lost all her marbles. There is no way your sister founded a million-dollar business."

Of course, there's a way Biddy wants to shout. College isn't everything. Homemakers and yes, even maids, still have brains too. Why is the world so disbelieving of the talents of those who commit their lives to careers in service? Biddy has had her fill of people and their opinions for the day. First, that she is unworthy of a leadership position without a husband and his prestigious job. Then, her poor dead sister, who could easily be the founder of a successful business. Her hometown could be sitting on one of the greatest historic discoveries of the decade and, characteristically, isn't even bothering to investigate it.

And that's when Biddy has her idea. An absolutely terrific idea. An idea that will solve everyone's problems, including her own.

3

Megan

Megan has no life.

Take care of your mother. She's never been on her own before.

These are some of the last words Megan's father spoke to her, and they replay in her mind as Megan watches her mother pull her arm from Muffy's grasp and stride towards the kitchen.

The weight of the additional responsibility for her mother's welfare feels heavy along with the rest of her father's expectations and dying wishes for her. Earning a PhD in history, just as he did. Becoming the youngest tenured professor at Harvard. Publishing at an unmatched pace so that she is on track to become the dean just as her father had. Marrying her father's protégé, a graduate of the doctoral program at Harvard and now a rising star of the faculty at MIT.

Everyone assumes she is happy. Who wouldn't be with all these blessings?But the stress of being the best, of performing never before achieved feats, has consumed her. She was so caught up in the challenges that she never stopped to ask herself if she actually wanted the prize. In fact, Megan has started to question if all the sacrifices, of time and other interests, were worth it.

Megan sighs and her eyes travel across the rest of the living room. The multitude of mourners are speaking animatedly in small groups, no one even noticing her. If her father were here, he'd be leading her from group to group to network. He'd be making sure she met all the right people. He'd be setting her up for her next success. But he isn't here. And wouldn't be again. Megan knows she should take the lead and do it herself. It's what her father would want. But she just can't force herself to find the bravery required to walk up to all those strangers. Somehow, it feels like she's an outsider at her own father's funeral.

"This whole event is just so dreary," says Mellie Watson as she walks over and leans against the wall next to Megan, waving her champagne glass as she speaks. They are two of the youngest people in the room, but that is where their similarities end. Mellie's overly perfumed scent stings Megan's nostrils. "I mean, I know it's your father's funeral, but shouldn't this be a celebration of his life? He wouldn't want everyone to be so depressed, would he?"

"I think it's possible to celebrate his life and still miss him with every fiber of our being," Megan says, and then takes a rather large gulp of champagne. "And I don't think he'd mind that."

Mellie shrugs. "Well, I would. I'm more of a fan of the Irish funeral."

Megan knows that if it were Mellie's funeral, she'd want everyone wailing in the streets.

"Where's Daniel?" Megan asks.

Mellie frowns. "Why would you think I'd know where your

fiance is?"

Jeez, this woman is sensitive.

"Because he is best friends with your husband and is a frequent guest at your house?"

"Oh." She shrugs. "That's true. I think I saw him head out to the balcony. Now, I'm going to get some more wine."

Megan exhales as she watches Mellie walk towards the bar in the foyer. The woman is a hot mess. What her husband Gene Watson, her father's replacement at Harvard, could have seen in her other than her little pin curls and pear-shape, Megan will never know. Megan sets her champagne glass down and heads out a pair of French doors to find her fiance.

The afternoon air has become humid, hinting at a storm to come. In front of her spreads the verdant green of her family's ten-acre property beneath the rolling haze. And in the corner, leaning against a stone balustrade, taking in the view, stands Daniel Sturbridge. He is handsome with dark hair and a lean physique, young for a dean at MIT, but still a decade older than Megan. By anyone's account, he is perfect. She just wished her heart could feel what her head knows.

"Hi," Megan says.

He turns and spreads his arms. "Megan, come here."

She walks into his arms, wrapping hers around his neck, and standing on her toes so that her lips meet his. She relaxes into the embrace, as if, for a minute, it might shield her from the terrible pain engulfing her life. It doesn't.

"I've thought about you often." He squeezes her even tighter and then lets her go, taking a small step back. This is oddly a relief.

"I know it's been hard." His voice is still soft. "I miss him too. He was like a father to me.

Megan wants to shout that he wasn't his father. That he was hers. That he can't even begin to feel the pain she has. But she knows this is a rude, selfish thought.

"Let's go away." Megan suddenly realizes she needs to get away from all this. To find herself again. To commit herself to this relationship so that when she takes her vows, she is telling the truth. "Tell MIT you need to spend time with me and let's go away for a few days… a week. We can go to France. See the sights of Paris. Wander the streets and go to the restaurants. We could try something crazy. Like backpacking for a few days."

"Oh, Megan." Daniel leans on the balustrade beside her, and his words sound like a sigh. "You know I can't do that. What would your father think? Our careers have always come first and I'm so close to being appointed dean. I have to finish publishing my next paper."

Megan's heart wrenches. Would there ever be a time when her feelings come first in someone's life? She's been so strong for her father, so understanding for Daniel, and so selfless in pursuing her career above all else. It seems like, just once, especially when she's lost her father, her needs could come first. Does no one realize that she occasionally needs to be cared for too?

"I can tell you're sad," Daniel faces her, and his eyes convey genuine concern. "I don't want that. Maybe I can find a day to take off? We can go to Vermont?"

"No," Megan says. His words are like a slap. A day. One day. "You are right. We should stay here and pick up all the pieces after Dad's death."

He sighs and looks back out at the misty fields. "I'm so sorry I can't go away with you." Then he turns to face her, a hopeful smile on his face. "But you won't have time to go away with me, either. I have a surprise for you. Lesley University had a last-minute speaker cancellation and asked me to recommend someone for their Boston Speaker Series. I said you. It's just what you always wanted, and I know it will help take your mind off things."

Megan's eyes widen. The Boston Speaker Series? This is only the most prestigious lecture role in the entire United States.

"This would be such an honor. You earned this. You are a fantastic professor and one that I would be proud to recommend featuring on a national stage. You are the most qualified person for this, hands down."

Megan's heart warms just the slightest. It's not exactly what she wants. More accurately, it's what her father had wanted for her. But she can see the pride in Daniel's eyes for her. For her intelligence. And that's something.

"There you are!" Mellie's voice pierces the air like a siren. Megan jumps and Daniel oddly blushes. Megan realizes he probably has never felt comfortable around any woman.

Mellie stalks up to stand beside Daniel and glares at her. "Did you know your mom is running against me for president?"

Megan frowns, a little confused. "President of what?"

"The Boston Historical Society." Mellie looks at her as if this should've been obvious. "She can't do that. Muffy says it always goes to the wife of the Dean of History at Harvard. That's me."

Is she serious? This is her father's funeral and Mellie's concerned about a charity role? With so much else on Megan's plate, this is not something she wants to deal with. She glances at Daniel, who looks uncomfortable. Damn his friendship with Mellie's husband. No one is ever fully on her side.

"I can talk to her, if you'd like," Megan says, mostly just to get her to stop speaking.

"Make sure you do. This is important to me." Mellie turns back to Daniel. "Let's find Gene and leave. I can't take much more of all this negativity. You know how easily I can get depressed."

"Of course." Daniel looks apologetically at Megan. "I drove over here with Gene and Mellie so you could have time with your mother. I'll call you soon with the details for the lecture. It's a big deal and you should be proud. I know I am." His eyes soften. "And I'm so very sorry for your loss. Our loss. My heart breaks."

Megan watches them leave and realizes that she feels no more alone now that he has left than when he was standing at her side. What is wrong with her?

But she is doing the Speaker Series. Maybe this speaking position is exactly what Megan needs now. Maybe seeing the elite of Boston rise to their feet to applaud her will make her career sacrifices worth it. She remembers the pride in Daniel's eyes. Maybe it will bring them closer together. Megan decides she will knock this lecture out of the park.

4

Biddy

Biddy sits on an old coach bus winding through the Indiana countryside. Its engine rumbles violently beneath her torn green seat, shaking her and her pocketbook in a never-ending vibration. The grease smeared windows do little to let the sun's warming light in to offset the harsh blow of the air conditioner. She wraps her arms around herself to remove the chill. No one has ever claimed it is easy to get to Pooka, Indiana. Frankly, it would have been easier to get to Europe, an unfortunate fact that has been the town's biggest impediment to gaining its footing in the world.

As Biddy stares out the smeared window at the ceaseless fields of corn, she thinks back to her last conversation with Megan. To say her daughter disapproves of Biddy's trip is an understatement. Her daughter was ridiculously concerned that her family will take her advantage of her and her wealth or that she might drop dead from the stress of the plane ride. From the moment Charles died, Megan has gone from having no time or interest in Biddy to wanting to run her life. Who does the girl think took care of everything before?

Charles, Biddy realizes. But her daughter couldn't be more wrong. Charles was so caught up in his work and travel , he probably couldn't even tell you their address, little less what bills they had, who they hired, and how everything got paid. Nonetheless, it is Biddy who is considered helpless. It is a tough load women are forced to carry.

But, despite all this, Biddy feels a frisson of anticipation. She is finally putting her wants first and her idea to do so is simple. She will help her niece prove Eileen's claims to be the true founder of the pottery, and then she will use this monumental discovery as the platform to win the presidency of the Boston Historical Society. A major historical discovery has to be a surefire way to win. The only novel discovery Mellie could ever make is that there is a kitchen somewhere in her house. Biddy can't wait to see the look on Muffy's face. She knows it will be the last time her friend doubts her capabilities.

The bus turns off the deserted two-lane highway, follows a narrow road around a green hill and… then…there it is. Even fully prepared for the view, it takes Biddy's breath away. The town appears in the distance, seemingly out of nowhere. In front of it, two giant rock formations stand sentry on either side of the only road leading to the town. Beyond the rocks is a vast field of corn, each waving its bushy top hairs in the softest of breezes. And beyond that is the old stone bridge over Bent Elbow Creek. Then, finally, on the other side, there is the town of Pooka, Indiana, its pastel colored buildings lining the creek like a pale rainbow, and a massive brown stone factory standing fortress right next to the bridge. Pooka. Indiana. Home.

A lifetime ago—Megan's lifetime, in fact—Biddy vividly remembers this view in reverse. A young girl in a tweed dress sewn herself, protective hand over her still flat stomach. Staring through the driver's rear-view mirror with a dampness in her eyes but a fire in her belly. The small multi-colored series of buildings shrinking behind her as an imagined future grew ahead. A future with taller skylines and bigger bodies of water. Of new languages and cultures. Of decision makers and influencers who conversed with her and changed the shape of the world. Of a baby to raise. How happy that girl would have been with how things turned out. Mostly.

The bus scrapes past the two sentry rocks which appear inches from the bus windows, and which also imprint a long scratch down both sides of the vehicle. If you squint at the rock on Biddy's side of the bus, it looks like a rabbit. Or maybe a deer. Or perhaps a bear. The one on the right is definitely a cat. Or a bird.

"Damn pooka," the driver mutters as the screech of rock meeting metal fills the bus.

Biddy smiles.

The man in front of Biddy looks at the driver. He is middle-aged, rather heavy, and wearing the brown polyester suit of a salesman. Likely on his way to Evansville, Biddy guesses.

"What's a pooka?" he asks.

"A benevolent trouble-maker," Biddy answers, even though the question is not addressed to her. "It's part of the Irish folklore of the original settlers. Pooka are shapeshifters. They guard the town and the town is named after them."

"Like a centaur."

Clearly, the man had never been to Pooka. Nothing so fancy.

"More like a goblin with a sense of humor. The only thing that gives them away is their golden eyes."

Both rocks have streaks of yellow coloring towards the

top. The man quickly pulls a camera out of his bag and turns around in his seat to snap a picture.

The pooka guards. Biddy has forgotten about them. They are the pride of Pooka. Indiana's version of an elaborate wall around a mansion, but a little smaller. And more destructive.

The bus continues its path through the cornfield, rumbles over the cobblestone bridge, and lands in the town with an unceremonious thump. It turns left into the town, away from the towering stone factory, and pulls to a stop in front of a pub with a final shriek of the brakes.

Looking at the town, it's as if she never left. That, of course, is also exactly why she left. It is only a very few who do. Biddy has left only twice. Once with big dreams for herself. And again when she realized she needed to have big dreams for another. She stands up and stretches her stiff limbs, reaches overhead to retrieve her carry-on and then carefully lowers herself down the bus stairs, her knees protesting every step.

"You're back!"

Biddy has just enough time to brace herself before a brightly colored figure emerges from the white-washed Tutor style pub in front of her, hurtles towards her, and throws her arms around her.

Biddy wraps her arms around this body-this warm, inviting, and still completely familiar body that, after all these years, fits hers like two pieces of a whole. She squeezes tightly and breathes in the forgotten yet immediately remembered scent of Ruby. The smells of hops and happiness.

"I told you I'd come back," Biddy says into her ear.

Ruby gives one last squeeze and then holds Biddy out at arm's length. Given her friend's girth, this isn't very far. "Yes, but that was forty-nine years ago."

"Well, who's counting?" Biddy says.

As she stares at her friend, now a little rounder, a little pinker, and clad in her father's old bar apron over her jeans and sweater, she tries to remember the last time she saw her. Biddy is pretty sure that it was Megan's baptism. Ruby had made the trip all the way to Boston for the occasion. It had thrilled Biddy to greet her initially, but then she spent the rest of the baptism making her rounds with all Charles' friends. Charles had invited everyone he knew…and then there was the screaming newborn. Now, she wonders if she'd spent enough time with her good friend. Had she even followed up with a call instead of a thank you note? She is suddenly fearful of her place in her old world. She sucks in her breath. Is she even welcome here?

"No one's counting," Ruby says. "Of course, no one's counting. It's just good to have you home."

Biddy throws her arms back around her friend and the warmth returns. However, despite the forgiving words, she senses something's shifted.

"Come on, come on." Ruby laughs and takes her friend by the hand. "Let's get your luggage off this bus before it heads to Evansville and you'll be forced to buy clothes from Walmart like the rest of us."

Biddy tugs at her Chanel jacket, thrown on over her jeans and t-shirt, and feels the words like a jab.

* * *

According to the GPS, the ride to Biddy's rental house is thankfully brief, thus increasing the odds that she will arrive at it in one piece. This is a legitimate concern. Biddy is in the passenger seat of Ruby's old pickup truck, the cab of which is approximately the size, shape, and color of an orange. Her knees are folded up as close to her chest as her sixty-seven-year-old body will allow. Adding to the discomfort, the carburetor belch's big clouds of black smoke that drift in the windows every time Ruby shifts gears, a nuance Biddy should have known from the many hours she spent in this truck as a teenager but has forgotten. She supposes it didn't bother her as much back then, seeing as they were both filling their lungs with black smoke from cigarettes, anyway.

"Are you going to see Declan?" Ruby asks, the car swerving to the right as she glances over at Biddy.

Biddy grasps the dashboard. Just the mention of her brother fills her veins with ice. "Of course not. He made it loud and clear that I was not welcome."

Ruby returns her eyes to the road in front of her and the car, thankfully, follows her lead, swerving back to the center of their lane. "That was over forty-five years ago," she says softly. "Things change. He's still your brother."

Biddy ignores the words. She's not here to change the past. She's here only to make an important historical discovery by helping her niece.

A white Victorian house with a cheerful yellow door whizzes past Ruby's window, the end in a long line of perfectly maintained historic homes. Then they drive out of town, past the stone factory, and into the surrounding farmland. Biddy studies it all, tries her hardest, but remembers none of this. What she remembers was poverty and decay. This is shockingly gorgeous.

"How does everything look so good?" Biddy asks. When Biddy left, most buildings were boarded up and struggling to remain upright.

"Oh." Ruby looks at her and again the car swerves to the right, narrowly missing a rock with an unlikely goat standing on it. "That's the work of the farming cooperative. After you left, things got even worse. The farms were all about to go under. The town looked terrible. People couldn't even afford drinks at the pub. Then, this man, Brady Hughes, comes to town and saves it all. He's some brilliant businessman and figured out that, if the farms worked together to sell their product, they'd be more profitable. He's a miracle worker."

Miracle worker is right. Biddy stares at the freshly painted white farmhouses surrounded by fields of crops, dotted with gleaming new machinery. That a cooperative could have such an impact seems unlikely to her, given that most farms across America are struggling, whether or not in cooperatives. But what does Biddy really know about farming anymore? She's just happy the town is doing well.

"So how long are you staying?" Ruby asks. "I've planned so many things for us to do. I thought we could hike out to the pooka one day and maybe go antiquing in Evansville. I know you'd like that. And—"

"Oh Ruby, I'm not staying long at all." Surprisingly, Biddy feels guilt as she says the words. Her old friend seems genuinely excited that she is here. But Biddy has more important things to take care of at the moment and a life to get back to. "I'm just here to help Maude prove her mother's claims and then I have to get back to Boston."

"What? No, Biddy!" Ruby's eyes snap towards Biddy, who reaches out for the dashboard in a preemptive bid against slamming into the door as the car inevitably swerves towards the right. "We talked about this. Eileen did not found that business. Please don't encourage Maude. Can't we just have a nice visit? It's been so long…"

Biddy is tiring of hearing this refrain.

In front of them, a terrified goat runs onto a rock as they speed toward it. Biddy punches her foot down on an imaginary break but does an admirable job of modulating her voice. She decides to change the subject.

"Where did all these goats come from?"

Maude laughs. "Oh, aren't they trendy? We voted at a town hall to look for more cost-effective ways to cut the grass on public land and Henry Galsh suggested getting goats. He'd read articles in *Farming Today* that said this was a sustainable solution and everyone was doing it. So we got a few goats to try it out. And the goats ate the grass, just like they were supposed to! But then the goats got a little randy and then there were more goats. And now…" Ruby gestured widely at the goats scattered everywhere. "I guess, we understand what they meant by sustainable now."

Good lord, is Biddy's first thought. And then she laughs. Really laughs. The Biddy of old would have loved this. It sounds exactly like something she would have voted for back in the day. If only to see this outcome. But then she stops. What is she doing laughing? Her husband is dead. She shakes her head. She's not the Biddy of old. She needs to focus.

"Oh look! Here's your street!" Ruby yanks the wheel to the left and Biddy grabs the dashboard as the pickup swerves onto a gravel road between two green fields. The car straightens with a squeal and gravel shoots up, tinging against the windows as it flies forward. With Ruby's driving skills, Biddy wonders if it won't be too long before she is reunited with Charles after all.

"Is this it?" Ruby points to a paved driveway on the right beside a gleaming black mailbox and, this time, Biddy is ready as the car roars toward Ruby's pointed finger, coming to a quick halt in front of a home, visible after the dust of the gravel cloud settles back down to the earth. Ruby twists the car key, and the car groans into silence, as if in gratitude to see its destination without mishap. Biddy knows how it feels. She releases her hold on the door, flexes her fingers, and stares.

The house is a simple Colonial matchbox, composed of a mosaic of pale brown stones worn smooth with time and partly covered with thick ivy. Two chimneys shoot through the triangular slate roof. Carving out a little yard around the full perimeter of the house is an eight-foot hedge with a stream gurgling over rocks just beyond. It is small. It is quaint. It is cozy.

"It is huge." Ruby says, eyeing it.

Biddy wonders if they are staring at the same house, for this one is a quarter the size of her Boston home, but she smiles. "It is perfect."

Biddy opens the truck door, slowly unfolds her legs, and stands still a minute to give her knees a chance to straighten. The air is cool and crisp, with just a hint of dampness that defines the farmland in her memories. The only sound that fills the silence is the bubbling brook. She'd forgotten how beautiful it could be here. So suffocatingly beautiful.

She fishes around in her handbag for the code to the door and, after entering it into the keypad six times, finally gets the thing to open. This is a relief. After a very long and heated email exchange with the owner of this AirBNB, she was one hundred percent certain that she'd been scammed, when the boy, oddly named Linc, explained there was no key, only a code. But, when she opens the door, she finds a home that not only exists, but is also as traditionally decorated as described. She walks down the slate entry hall, past a living room on her left with a stone fireplace and into a kitchen in the back with a black and white tiled floor and yellow cabinets. She drops her bag on the rustic-looking table that serves as an island and glances out the side door window at a meadow gently inclining up a hill.

"Wow." Ruby plunks down on a chair at the table, round eyes taking in the space.

"It actually is quite nice." In the pictures, Biddy was concerned it was a bit on the shabby side, but, in person, it feels approachable. Welcoming.

"It's like something out of a magazine," Ruby says.

Biddy crosses to the other side of the table and sits across from Ruby.

"Now," Biddy says, "tell me about Eileen."

Ruby takes a deep breath.

"Do you remember Old Man McGilligan?"

Biddy sighs. "Ruby…"

"—No wait. I'm getting there, I promise. Do you remember him?"

This one, Biddy remembers. Old Man McGilligan was a 92-year-old man who roamed the streets of Pooka for much of her childhood. He would impart helpful advice to anyone who would listen. Things like 'the witches will arrive tonight at eleven. Best to be inside.' Or 'the furies of the elves are going to reign upon us. Duck.' Actually, the last bit of advice still makes Biddy giggle because Ruby had asked him if ducking was such a good idea as it would put them at eye level with the angry elves. Anyway, the poor man was crazy. "I remember."

"Well, your sister Eileen…" Ruby makes a face and then rotates her finger near her head.

Crazy. Oh dear. But how could a Delancy be crazy?

"And Maude, well Maude worshipped her. So when Eileen took to telling the entire town as loudly as she could that she was the actual founder of Aisling Pottery, Maude believed her."

Aisling Pottery is one of Pooka, Indiana's few success stories. Originally founded in the mid-1800s by a potter from Ireland seeking greater religious freedom, it fell into disrepair when a future generation transferred ownership to someone who didn't know what they were doing. The large old factory sat empty and dilapidated for Biddy's entire childhood. However, in the intervening years of Biddy's departure, Finn Murphy had supposedly rejuvenated the business into a global high-end phenomenon. His craftsmanship is award winning. In fact, Biddy's Aisling Pottery platter is one of the few reminders of her roots in her Boston estate.

"I take it Finn Murphy isn't taking this well."

"Not just Finn…" Ruby says, her voice subdued. "It's the entire town. We've become a tourist destination for people touring the factory. Many people's livelihoods depend on this. Finn's threatened to have Maude arrested if she comes in again and makes a scene. The rest of the town is alienating her."

"Well," Biddy refuses to leap to conclusions. "What if she's right? Why is that so hard for everyone to consider? Eileen might have simply been creative not crazy—"

"Biddy!" Ruby takes her phone out, turns it towards Biddy, and swipes through dozens of photos saved on the camera app. Then, she hands the phone to Biddy so that she can have a closer look. "That's graffiti. Eileen painted it all over the town. It covered everything. Businesses spent a small fortune painting it back to its original condition." Ruby stabs her finger at the photo on the screen. "Look at it. It's unintelligible nonsense. Eileen kept saying this was evidence of her ownership of the business. It's gibberish."

Biddy looks closely at the photo. Jagged lines and squiggles fill the walls of the building featured. They are nonsensical. But they are also somehow attractive.

"Maybe it's one of the pottery designs."

Ruby shakes her head. "It's not. I've looked. I also spoke with Eileen's doctor. Dr. Enniskillin says that there is research showing that graffiti can be a symptom of antisocial behaviour personality disorder."

Biddy shivers. The words bring back a memory. Of her father being called to the high school and the school psychologist showing him one of Eileen's notebooks filled with odd symbols similar to these. The psychologist was worried that Eileen was developing a mental illness.

But her father denied it, didn't he? And he spoke with Eileen and she stopped the behavior. Plus, not all graffiti makers have mental illnesses. Lots of graffiti creators are now celebrated as artists. This could just be further proof of Eileen's creative genius. As usual, the town is taking an outdated view of the world. Biddy shoves the photos back towards Ruby.

"This proves nothing. Let's go see Maude and sort this out."

"Are you nuts?"

Biddy shrugs. "Well, according to you, it runs in the family." She stands up and heads to the door.

"I still think this is a terrible idea," Ruby mumbles.

5

Maude

Things aren't going as well as I hoped to get my mom the recognition she deserves. I've passed fliers out in town. I've stood in front of the pottery with a sign that says 'Made by Eileen Delancy.' I multi-task and tell my cleaning clients all about my mom's plight, the whole time I clean their house. And where has it gotten me? Fired. From many clients, in fact. It really is rather discouraging. So I'm taking a rare break from it all, relaxing on my couch, alone and away from it all. But this doesn't last very long. I watch a fancy woman walking next to Ruby towards my doorstep. She is carrying a handbag emblazoned with the name of our most blessed Saint Laurent, but her gait is that of an invading army. The woman is a wolf in sheep's clothing, if I ever saw one.

I wipe sweat from my brow—the air conditioner broke months ago—and glance quickly around the house I once shared with my mother. It's in the section of town that was once used as temporary housing for agricultural workers. The cluster of homes is deep in the woods, and the buildings are simple rectangles with dirty white siding, surrounded by a thick layer of crunchy brown pine needles. They're like trailers, without the wheels. While I know this may not sound very attractive, my mom did her best to make ours beautiful. 'We may not have much,' she'd say, 'but we have our pride.' I'm sorry to say that our pride has fallen a bit since she departed this world, but I have been rather preoccupied with more important things than cleaning. So I race to the door and crack it open, hoping to ward them off before they can enter. I don't want to give Ruby a reason to start in on another lecture about how I need to take better care of myself.

"Yes?" I say.

Ruby nudges herself in front of the other woman. "Hi Maude. I brought someone who wants to pay her condolences."

This I don't believe. No one is sorry my mom died, except maybe Ruby. And that's only because she is incapable of disliking anyone. I look at the other woman, who isn't even carrying a casserole dish like a good mourner would, and then back at Ruby. The quickest way to get rid of them is obvious.

"Thank you," I say and make to close the door.

Ruby puts a hand out to stop it. "Why don't you invite us inside for a visit? So we can reminisce about Eileen together?"

"No," I say, all pretenses dropped. "Tell me why she's really here."

The woman wedges herself back in front of Ruby. "I am really here to pay my respects, which is the proper thing to do when someone dies. Just as opening the door and welcoming your guests is the proper thing to do when they arrive."

Then she pushes the door all the way open as if I'm not standing right there, clearly not wanting her inside. She marches past me and stands still in the entry, her eyes spanning the space. As I said, it's not good. To her left is my living room with laundry preparations in process. Lot's of them. I haven't had the time to do the laundry in a month. To the right is my kitchen with an old formica table covered in my research. This I have had the time to work on. Papers are stacked so high that a few have fluttered to the floor beneath. I've been diligent.

The woman walks into the kitchen area—uninvited I might add—picks one up and looks at it. It's a photocopy of an old newspaper clipping featuring the original Aisling Estate. She sets it on the table and then walks past me again, into the living area, where she stares down at the couch, pushes some laundry to the side, and sits down. Ruby, having followed her into the house, gingerly sits beside her. Left with no real choice, I take a seat in a wooden rocking chair across from them.

"Who are you?" I say.

"Maude," Ruby says, "this is your Aunt Biddy. She was Eileen's older sister. She traveled all the way from Boston when she heard the news."

This is a name I've heard before.

"Mom hated you." I say.

The woman blinks. I'll give her that much credit. She takes the truth better than others in this town.

"You are like Jacob before his atonement. You are greedy and put yourself above your family's responsibility."

The woman looks confused. She whispers to Ruby. "Who's Jacob?"

I knew it. This is not a good Catholic. She probably doesn't know who Saint Laurent is either, even though she's carrying a bag in his honor.

"Well, maybe this is like the atonement part," Ruby says to me, ignoring her friend's question.

Ruby is a do-gooder. Normally, my mom and I don't like do-gooders. But Ruby is so genuinely good, even my mother couldn't resist her wiles.

"Shouldn't you let her atone like Jacob?" she pleads.

"I don't need to atone," the woman says. "I have nothing to atone for."

Well, that makes things easy. "Goodbye then."

I stand up to show her the door. Ruby reaches out and grabs my arm.

"Maude no."

"You left my mother with your mess," I say to the woman. "You were the eldest. It was your job to take care of your sisters and brothers when your mom died. But you didn't want to do that, did you? So you picked up and left for the fancy schmancy East Coast. Who do you think got stuck with that job after you left?" I point to a picture of mom on the end table. "My mom. My mom gave up her hopes and dreams and talents and raised your five other siblings. My mom did that. And, as a result, she was the only one who didn't get a chance to leave this place. It was all she talked about."

"That's not true," Ruby says. "She wasn't alone here. Your Uncle Declan is still here."

"This should have been you," I say to my aunt, ignoring Ruby's last comment. I gesture around the room, and the woman has the grace to flinch. Even having only known her for five minutes, I can tell this is not the type of house she would deign to live in.

"Was Eileen that unhappy?" the woman asks quietly. She looks back at the photo of my mom.

I remember my mom laughing at the tacky tchotchkes scattered around some houses we cleaned. Smiling the year, we signed twelve new customers because Annie Mae finally retired. Grinning when we smashed Mrs. Brimmady's beloved pie that beat hers in the Pie Making Contest all over the windows of her car in the middle of the night. I hate to admit it, but she wasn't always unhappy. Not even with the unfair lot she was dealt. "Not always," I admit.

"I'm glad." And the woman looks like she means it.

She looks around the house again.

"I want to help," she says.

Well, this is a surprise. I'm torn. Mom didn't like this woman, so neither do I. But in all this time—this terrible time since mom got sick to when she died, no one has said they want to help. Not even Ruby, who keeps encouraging me to forget everything and move on.

"Why?" I ask.

"Because you're right. I didn't do right by Eileen back then. And I want to see if I can fix it now."

I don't really believe her. There must be something in it for herself. I don't trust her.

"Why don't you tell me what happened?" she prods.

But it's for my mom, so I have to try.

"You know how when you get older, you tend to speak your mind more?"

"Yes." The woman says. "I do."

"That's not what really happened," Ruby says.

I ignore her. "Well, that's what happened to Mom. She told everyone in Pooka that she founded Aisling Pottery and that Finn Murphy stole it from her."

I wait for the laugh, but it doesn't come.

"And Finn Murphy denies this?"

"He had her arrested for trespassing!"

I feel my body go taut again, as I remember my mom's embarrassment. Her rage. Her anger when the police arrested her. I think the woman is going to tell me to control myself, but she just looks at me calmly, as if understanding the depth of my emotions.

She inclines her head. "Did she say why she didn't share this accusation sooner? Finn opened the pottery over forty years ago."

"She said he threatened her. But now she wasn't scared of him anymore."

"I see."

The woman looks back around the room and her eyes fall on the kitchen table covered in papers.

"Do you have any evidence? Is that what all that is?"

I nod vigorously. This is the most anyone has listened. I feel a creak in my heart. I think it's hope.

"I do. I have evidence. Lots of it."

"Biddy—" Ruby says. She also looks in the kitchen, but her eyes focus not on the mounds of newspaper clippings but on a stack of green papers. She looks back at me. "Are those more eviction notices on the table?"

"What about the town council?" Biddy asks. "Couldn't they help investigate your claims?"

"Your mother wouldn't want you to lose your house," Ruby says. "Have you been fired from more cleaning jobs?"

"The town council wouldn't listen either!" I say, focusing on Biddy and ignoring Ruby. "My mom went to one of the town meetings and demanded to be heard. They called the police to have her arrested again. I just submitted another proposal to them to investigate and possibly feature her achievements in the town museum, but I know they'll deny it."

"Well." The woman looks appropriately outraged and settles back on the couch.

I can't believe it. She just might believe me.

"Biddy, look around you," Ruby whispers. "This is not the help that Maude needs. Try to understand."

I'm just about to tell Ruby that this is exactly the help I need. That I don't care about the house or the jobs. But before I can speak, the woman shakes her head. "I think I do understand. Maude deserves to be heard and to have her claims taken seriously. Eileen does too."

I pinch myself so hard a bright red welt forms on my arm. I look down at it. This is real.

"I know a thing or two about dealing with committees," she continues in a manner that makes me confident that she does. "When is the next town hall?"

"There's a meeting tomorrow," I say, quickly. "My case is on the docket."

Ruby groans.

Biddy—Saint Biddy it turns out—stands up and nods to me. "Now let's see your evidence."

I smile. As much as I'm embarrassed by the state of the house, I'm proud of my research. I lead the way into the kitchen and leaf through the stacks on the table. They may look haphazard, but I know just where everything is. I pull a sheet out from the third stack on the left.

"I have the original Articles of Incorporation with her name on it."

"You what?" Ruby looks at me with wide-disbelieving eyes. I fight the urge to laud it over her. I told everyone the evidence was undeniable.

Biddy's smile widens, and she snatches the paper from my hands. Then her smile fades. When her eyes meet mine, it is not admiration that they hold.

"Maude, it looks like someone whited-out the original name and wrote hers in."

Ruby looks over Biddy's shoulder and her forehead creases back into a familiar wrinkle.

"Don't worry," I say quickly. I had pointed the same thing out to my mother, but she explained it. "That's just because the printer was running out of ink, so she whited out the smear and wrote it in so you can see it better."

Ruby slumps into a chair next to the table and puts her head in her hands.

Biddy frowns and holds the paper out to me. "You can't be serious. This will never do."

Ruby looks up at Biddy. "Now, do you believe me? We need to help Maude move on."

It's like I'm not even standing right here. Holding undeniable evidence of my mother's claim.

"It's my mom's name on it!"

I can tell neither of them believe me.

"Do you have anything else?" Biddy asks hopefully.

Biddy, at least, seems to have some of my mother's perseverence.

"I have this." I hold out a broken piece of pottery. "It has her initials as the artist's signature."

Biddy takes the piece of pottery, squints at the initials and smiles.

"Now this I can work with."

I smile too.

Ruby just sighs.

Biddy glances over at the Articles of Incorporation which I have set down on top of the first stack of documents. Her lips press together as she stares at it. It's the first time she's looked uncertain. I get the idea that this is not a woman who is often uncertain.

"Perhaps," she says, "it's best if we don't mention that. The Articles of Incorporation."

I nod vigorously. I mean, the Articles of Incorporation are our strongest evidence, but I'm willing to follow her lead.

"After all," she continues, "in a court of law, a person is presumed innocent until proven guilty, so all we have to do is prove that it's possible she founded the pottery, not that she actually did."

"Couldn't the same be said about Finn?" Ruby mumbles.

Biddy again ignores her. "I'll go to the town council meeting tomorrow and make sure they take your claims seriously."

I stand up and throw my arms around Biddy. This is all I've wanted. It's all I've ever wanted. Biddy feels stiff in my embrace, but that's okay. Not all saints are warm and fuzzy after all.

"That's all that I ask," I say into her stiff hair that smells like roses. "Mom was telling the truth. You'll see."

6

Megan

Megan stares out from the stage at the twinkling expansive space of Boston's Symphony Hall. Built in 1900 as the permanent home for the Boston Symphony Orchestra, the hall is a tribute to a city which prides itself in the arts, literature, and academics. Symphony Hall is one of the first auditoriums designed according to scientific acoustic principles—thanks to the consulting of a young Harvard Professor of Physics— and is considered the finest, acoustically in the United States, and one of the top three in world. The hall is long, narrow, and high, with stage walls sloping inward to pinpoint sound. Gilded side balconies are shallow so as not to trap rever- berations. A 4,800 pipe organ dominates the space above Megan's head, famed for its projection. In short, the building is engineered in such a way that no one is going to miss a word she says.

Now, row after row after row of evenly spaced bodies on the main floor line up before her like an endless army. Above them are two more tiers of gilded balconies packed with beautifully dressed patrons. And above that, stands the giant and formidable casts of sixteen Greek and Roman statues in carefully curved niches overseeing the entire accord as if to judge the performer's worthiness. Capacity is two thousand six hundred people, not including the gods. And that is exactly how many people are watching her.

Staring out at all this, Megan knows one thing for certain. She doesn't belong up here. What if they hate her? What were they thinking of inviting her? She is now standing on the same stage as other featured speakers in Lesley University's Boston Speaker Series—a group including notable alumni like Bill Clinton, Ken Burns, Gloria Steinem, and Cokie Roberts. She is not one of them. She can only hope she lives up to Daniel's, her father's, and all these people's expectations.

The lights dim over the audience and the colorful array of onlookers fades into shadowy figures. Then a bright light snaps on and completely blinds her to the crowd. She shifts uncomfortably on her stool, which sits next to a pot of white chrysanthemums, and tries to look scholar-like. It's difficult when she looks so young and she is aware of this.

The quiet hum of conversation dies, and the elegant voice of the event's host fills the silence, introducing her from the podium to her left. She smiles as the woman says her name, then again as she mentions her relationship with her father. The introduction ends, and the auditorium reverberates with applause. She takes a deep breath.

"Hello." Her voice echoes into the space, sounding deep and confident. This is good. Surprising, but good. "As Dr. Hatlichek just said, my name is Doctor Megan Bramley and I am a Professor of History at Harvard University, with a specialty in historical women. I am here tonight to share my research on the impact of women in American society."

Megan delves into the research that consumes her life. The study of the wives of early American leaders and their unrecognized impact on society. She presents case studies from various periods of history. And then she discusses how women bring many necessary skills to the new world. She can feel the audience transfixed with some examples of successful women in the White House. Of how America is becoming more welcoming to women, but how there is still room for progress. The rest of her hour-long lecture flies by and she actually starts to enjoy herself. She ends her speech with a summary of her framework for enhancing the voice of women to thunderous applause. Her body relaxes despite the adrenaline rushing through it. As she does so, she notices more of the audience. She notices it is mostly men.

Dr. Hatlichek has returned to the podium, and she gestures toward Megan. "I want to thank Dr. Bramley for her incredibly insightful lecture on women in American history. I know she has given us all a new lens through which to view leadership and diversity. We look forward to seeing you at our next speaker event when John Kerry will join us to discuss his time as Secretary of State for President Barack Obama."

Booming applause restarts at that announcement and Megan can't help but wonder if the audience feels cheated they got her instead of John Kerry, who had needed to reschedule. But then she shakes it off. She did fine. She stands and takes a final bow before following the moderator off the stage to greet an assembled mass behind the stage, waiting to congratulate her and to ask her follow-up questions.

As she is sharing her thoughts on Eleanor Roosevelt with a group of eight men, her eyes travel the dark stage wing, and there is Daniel. He is standing in the back, to the left, near an emergency exit door. He is beaming at her with pride. Warmth fills her body. She is happy to see him. This was a good idea. This relationship is going to work. She was just upset about losing her father and had no reason to question this relationship.

Megan excuses herself from the group and hurries over. She fights the unusual urge to throw her arms around him and let him spin her in celebration. This is something Daniel would never do. Instead, she settles for a quick, professional hug.

"So, what'd you think?" she asks as she pulls away.

"I couldn't be more proud of you. I only wish your father could see you now."

"Thank you. I still can't believe I was part of Leslie's Speaker Series. Should we head out for a celebratory drink?"

Daniel shakes his head. "I can't. I have a deadline for the next draft of my paper. I shouldn't even be here, but I wanted to see you."

Megan tries hard to hide her disappointment. "Well, another time then."

"How about tomorrow?" His eyes twinkle. "We can't let an accomplishment like this go unnoted. I already have something special planned."

She knows she should be happy, but this feels like he is doing her a favor rather than wanting to spend time with her. She forces a smile on her face. "It's a date."

She watches him walk back through the gap in the curtains and then she bends down to pick up her coat and handbag. Any joy that she felt in the moment has now left her and she just wants to go home.

"Oh Megan, are you leaving?" Dean Hatlichek rushes over.

"I'm exhausted." Megan hoists her bag up on her shoulder.

"Thank you for this honor. I hope I didn't disappoint anyone."

"Disappoint anyone? You were great! The contributions of the wives of presidents are often overlooked. It is a great topic. You know, if you ever want to coach underprivileged women, I work with a non-profit that could really use your expertise."

Megan feels a surge of interest, but then tamps it down. She needs to focus on publishing not non-profit work. The road to prestigious professorships is paved in articles not good deeds.

"Thank you, Dr. Hatlichek. I'm afraid it wouldn't fit into my schedule now, but I'll keep that in mind."

"Please do. You'd be a natural. Oh, and if you're going out, would you mind going out the back way and carrying a load of boxes to my car? I won't be able to handle them all on my own."

"Of course not!" Megan says her goodbyes, picks up one of the many cardboard boxes of programs, and pushes against the bar of the backdoor.

The evening air is warm. A slight breeze and the late dusk light promise the joys of summer. The start of a season known for fun and laughter. For friend and family get-togethers. But that all seems so distant now. Megan tries to shake off the memory of her father grilling at their annual Memorial Day party. Summer fun feels like it is in the past. However, it isn't in the past for everyone.

As her heels click across the parking lot pavement, she can hear a young couple giggling in between two parked cars. Good for them, she thinks, smiling. She glances towards the source of the noise—a blue SUV. Then she peers at it. It looks like her boss's car—Gene Watson. She hadn't seen him inside.

And would his wife, Mellie, really attend a history lecture? That seems a bit unlikely.

Curious now, she creeps closer to the car, shifting the bulky box in her arms so she can see better. She peers down the space between the SUV and a sedan.

"Gene?" she says.

Two bodies lead apart in the shadows. One is Mellie in a skintight red dress, more appropriate for a club than a lecture. But that oddly isn't what catches her attention. That's because the other person isn't Gene. It's Daniel.

"Oh my god," she whispers.

"Megan, wait. I can explain." He releases Mellie and moves towards her and Megan's only thought is that she needs to get away. She's been so stupid. Did she really think he was spending his nights and weekends writing? She turns on her heel and runs towards her car, leaving the stupid box of programs at the trunk of Dr. Hatlichek's on her way. She fumbles with her keys.

"Megan." Daniel is only three feet from her.

She keeps her head pointed at the car. She can't even look at him. "Please go. I don't want to see you. I just want to be alone."

"Megan…"

"I think she just asked you to leave." Dr. Hatlichek, clearly having overheard the commotion has walked up to Megan's car. Megan's cheeks burn in embarrassment.

Daniel looks irritated, but has never been one to make a scene.

"I'll call you tomorrow," he says. He walks away. Both women watch him go. Megan vaguely wonders if he is sharing yet another car ride home with Mellie.

"Are you okay?" Dr. Hatlichek asks.

Megan nods her head, willing her tears to remain in her eyes. "I'm fine. Just a quarrel about wedding details."

The dean looks at her sympathetically. Clearly, she doesn't believe Megan. "Okay then. Have a good night."

Megan yanks the car door open. She does not know where to go or what to do. The most boring man in America is cheating on her with Mellie? God. What does that say about her?

Her cellphone's ring pierces the air. Megan automatically reaches into her bag for it.

"Hello?"

"Megan? Are you okay? You sound upset."

The voice on the phone is her mother's. Her perfect mother. Who would never be in a position where a man cheated on her. Megan leans against the steering wheel, closes her eyes, and takes a deep breath of the stuffy car air.

"I'm fine, mom."

"Well, you don't sound fine."

Megan wants to cry. "Sorry about that. I'll try harder. Look, I'm really tired. I just finished my lecture and…"

And what? All Megan wants to do is crawl into a hole and never emerge. What is she supposed to do now? She can't still marry Daniel.

"Well, I don't want to keep you," her mother continues. "I just wanted to let you know that I'm staying longer in Pooka. You have a cousin who is in a bit of a bind, and I'm helping her out. I don't know how long this will take, but I extended my rental through the end of the summer."

"You what?"

How is it that, on top of everything else, her mother is also having some sort of breakdown? First, she heads out to visit some town she's never even mentioned before that is in the middle of nowhere, Indiana. Now she's reuniting with long-lost family and spending the summer with them? This is not normal behavior. Megan pulls her phone away from her ear and googles Pooka, Indiana. She flips through the results. An old article featuring a farming town on the brink of collapse pops up. Dilapidated farm houses and dirty trailer parks fill the screen. Good lord. She could only imagine what these people thought when they got a look at her mother, with her fancy jewelry and fashionable clothes, recently widowed no less. If Daniel just pulled the wool over her eyes, her mother is a sitting duck in the larger world.

"I extended my rental," her mother repeats. "It's actually quite nice here…so far away from everything else. Plus, I certainly can use a big long break from Muffy Gallagher. Although wait until she sees what I'm uncovering…"

Megan stops following the rest of her mother's tirade. She has no idea what has come between her mother and her best friend, but she also doesn't care. Her mother has always had such a simple life. An easy life, with Charles protecting her from the horrible realities of the world. Her mother wouldn't survive a day in Megan's reality if her biggest problem that she needs to escape is a fight with Muffy. Thank god, her mother isn't here to get wind of Megan's problems.

Oh god. She suddenly realizes she has to figure out how to talk to her mom about canceling her wedding.

"Mom, I'm coming to see you."

"What?" Her mother's inflection rises. "No. I'm fine here. Frankly, I'm enjoying a little time to myself. Plus, I'm sure you're too busy with your own life."

Not any longer, Megan thinks grimly. The most important thing in her life right now is to get away from it.

"I'm never too busy for you," Megan says, "and it might be nice to meet this family I didn't know I had."

"Well.." Her mother still sounds uncertain. "Maybe over a holiday? Labor Day? Perhaps it's best that we talk later and find a date."

"Actually, my schedule just freed up. I'll come as soon as I can." She says her goodbyes and hangs up the phone before her mother can protest further. Then she searches for the next flight to Pooka, which apparently involves a flight to Louisville, Kentucky and a long bus ride to the remote town. She books it. Her mother can't do anything to get rid of her once she's there. She hesitates for just one second and then does something she despises. She sends a formal email to Daniel, letting him know she will extend her bereavement leave through the summer and is going to visit family. She needs time to process these events and to make some big decisions.

7

Biddy

Biddy and Ruby stand in front of the Pooka town hall fifteen minutes before the start of the town's monthly assembly. Biddy is starting to doubt herself. What is she doing here? Eileen's graffiti scribbles are undeniably weird. And the altered articles of incorporation were a joke. Plus, her niece, Maude, also seems a tad…too intense. What if Ruby is right and she is about to make a fool of herself defending the undefendable? But Biddy is in too deep now to let it go. She doesn't want to appear the sad and confused widow to be pitied. Her only hope is to convince the town to investigate Eileen's claims. Even if they are found to be false…which they likely will be…she can tell everyone that she championed Eileen's rights. That she'd encouraged a town to give a woman a chance to prove herself. It wasn't the same as being right and making a major historical discovery, but still. It should be enough to hold her head high and maybe win the presidency of the Boston Historical Society. She pushes all this from her mind and focuses on the task ahead. To get the town's support.

The building in front of her is original to the town and reflects the cottage style architecture of the founding Irish immigrants. The structure is a shockingly white stucco, with green window frames, a green door, and a thatched roof. Where anyone found thatching in Indiana, God only knows. It looks a little ridiculous for a building in the Midwest. Nevertheless, this is her stage for the day.

Biddy turns her attention back to Ruby, who is wearing straight-legged jeans, tennis shoes, and a bright pink t-shirt. Biddy is wearing a tweed jacket and skirt with low-heeled pumps. However, it is Ruby who is eyeing Biddy as if she is the one mis-outfitted for the occasion. The world has gone upside-down, Biddy thinks.

"Biddy," Ruby says. She speaks hesitantly, as if Biddy were a landmine about to explode. "It may be best to tread lightly at first. To get the lay of the land. It's been a while since you've seen everyone."

Biddy nods. Of course, she will tread lightly. Lightly but firmly. Starting right now. She leads the way inside.

The main hall of the building is dark, with only the security lighting providing a faint glow. Unlike the cavernous museums of Boston with their massive meandering floor plans and church-like echoes, this town houses its historical artifacts in the town hall lobby. And this is what Biddy squints at in the dark. She turns her attention to an annex on the left. This is where the action is. It's brightly lit and crowded with people. They are all feasting off paper plates piled high with food. Never stand between the residents of Pooka and a pre-meeting potluck, Biddy thinks. Biddy walks in with Ruby trailing behind.

This room has a higher ceiling and brightly white-washed

walls. Long tables have been pushed aside and green plastic tablecloths sit atop them. One side has an array of hors d'oeuvres for the taking. The other is filled with plastic cups and pop bottles.

"Ooh." Ruby's eyes light up. "Deviled eggs." She hurries over to fill a plate.

Biddy ignores the loud hum and distasteful amalgamation of scents and scans the space, studying the faces. She thinks she recognizes a few, but it's hard to be sure after such a long time and harder still to adjust for the impact of aging. Eventually, she gives up with a shrug and goes to pour herself a cup of Diet Pepsi. She hasn't had a processed drink in years. She might as well live a little.

"Ladies and gentlemen." The voice shouts at the room's occupants through a microphone tuned too loud. A portly man with a mound of facial hair and a bald spot wrinkles his forehead and tries adjusting a dial on the side of the microphone. At least, he is dressed appropriately, Biddy grudgingly admits, with a button-down shirt and sweater vest atop a perfectly pressed pair of navy slacks. He taps the microphone twice and holds it back to his mouth. "Ladies and gentlemen, if you can all take a seat, it's time to get started."

Arthur Dillon. The name returns to Biddy's mind like a bullet.

"Biddy, we should grab a seat." Ruby has returned holding an overflowing plate and nods towards the last row of card-table chairs. Biddy ignores this and marches to the third row. Ruby groans but follows.

Arthur sits at a long folding table at the front, next to three other people, presumably his board.

"First order of business," he says once settled, "we need to approve the minutes from the last meeting. Any objections?"

No one says anything and the minutes are approved.

"Next on our agenda is announcements," Arthur says. "Does anyone have any announcements?"

This, too, passes without comment.

"Moving on." Arthur glances down at the stack of papers in front of him and then back up. "Let's discuss the special exhibits for our little museum. We, of course, have a few exhibits core to our history that we never change out, but each year we bring through a new rotating exhibit. Being passed to you now…"

Biddy notices that a heavier set woman in jeans and a sweatshirt that says 'Don't poo poo Pooka' is passing stapled packets down the rows. Biddy takes one and passes the rest to her neighbor. She leafs through her copy.

"…are the four exhibits we are considering for this year. As president, I recommend we move forward with the one on Cullen Dwyer's farm. It has been in his family for over six generations, making it a core feature of Pooka history. So unless there are any objections—"

Biddy shoots her hand up.

"Yes?" Arthur squints at her. Biddy stands up.

"Well, I've hardly given these proposals full due diligence since you didn't post them before the meeting." She continues to leaf through the pages looking for Maude's submission. "However, this one. Right here. On page three." She taps her paper. "Is from a woman who claims her mother founded Aisling Pottery. How is that not more important than a farm? By my count, you already have six exhibits related to farms."

Arthur's forehead creases. "And you are…"

"Biddy Bramley."

Still no recognition.

"Nee Delancy."

Arthur's face lights up. "Babs? Is that you?" Somewhere beneath all that hair, Biddy glimpses teeth in the shape of a smile. "I thought you moved to New York or something."

"Boston," Biddy says. She never did like Arthur Dillon. "And I go by Biddy now. But I'm here on behalf of my niece, who would like her mother's claims investigated by the town."

Arthur shakes his head. "Babs…Biddy, that one is a no go. I know Eileen was your sister, but you haven't been here for a few decades and that woman was short a few marbles at the end. There's no way she founded Aisling Pottery."

"He's right," Ruby mumbles, but quietly enough that only Biddy can hear.

"How on earth could you know that?" Biddy says to Arthur. "Did you look into it? After all, that is good historic research practice. I'm not saying she's right. All I'm saying is the claim deserves to be explored. The facts will take us where they will."

"I didn't need to look into it—"

"—So you think you just know things without completing a thorough research process?"

"Sometimes, yes. It's called being attuned to your community."

"I see." Biddy is beginning to remember more about why she disliked Arthur. "Is that what happened to the other women's exhibits?"

"What other 'women's exhibits'?"

"Oh no," Ruby groans, still quietly.

"Exactly my point," Biddy says. "There are no other women's exhibits. I walked the entire museum this morning and there isn't a single exhibit devoted to a woman."

Arthur's face grows red and Biddy suspects a frown is buried somewhere under his facial hair. "We just haven't found the right one yet. But trust me, Biddy, this isn't it."

"Biddy." Ruby tugs on her sleeve. "I get your point, but maybe you should listen to him," she whispers.

Biddy shakes Ruby's hand off. She keeps her eyes right on Arthur Dillon. "All Eileen and her daughter want is to be taken seriously. Do you know that there are grants if you focus on representing diversity? You are missing out on useful money and publicity. I can help you. I know about these things. If I'm wrong, I'll accept it and go quietly into the night, still willing to be a resource to you."

"We don't need you or your charity," someone in the audience grumbles.

Biddy is shocked. How could the town not want her help?

"It's hard to believe you'd go quietly into the night since you can't even go quietly to Boston," Arthur says. "Babs, your sister was a nutcase. I can't waste the town's time on this. Eileen spent the last few years barefoot in the mud near the waste management grounds, grabbing fistfuls of dirt and shoving it in our faces. Called it her riches and said that it was being destroyed."

Biddy frowns as a memory jumps into her consciousness. A young Eileen. When they were teenagers. Biddy had been sneaking out to meet a boy and spotted Eileen in an old deserted farm building. Eileen had set up a plate of dirt on a table in front of her, beakers of chemicals surrounding it. Before Biddy could ask her what she was doing, Eileen lit a match and dropped it in the dirt. The flames flashed green, and Eileen laughed with joy. Buckets of dirt had surrounded

Eileen's legs, each labelled with the place she had collected it.

"Where is the waste management site?" Biddy asks. "I don't remember one."

"I really don't see how this matters," Arthur says. "It got developed after you left. They used the old Aisling Estate. It'd been vacant for years."

Biddy had seen Eileen's dirt flash green. The same color as the tint in the world famous Aisling pottery glaze. And the dirt Arthur saw Eileen holding was at the Aisling Estate, a likely namesake for Aisling Pottery. It couldn't all be a coincidence. Biddy feels hope flutter in her chest. She'd all but given up serious belief in Eileen's claims. But what if the dirt is the key component to the pottery glaze? What if the drawings on the buildings weren't doodles but chemical symbols? What if Eileen HAD actually founded the pottery?

"Arthur, I just remembered something. There might be something to that dirt—"

"It's dirt, Biddy! There's nothing to it. This town has more important uses of its time than assuaging your guilt over deserting Eileen."

"This isn't about me! At least not anymore—"

"The woman who proposed this exhibit is off her rocker and we will not be exhibiting this preposterousness. That. Is. Final." Arthur slams his gavel down, even though there is no real procedural reason to do so.

Biddy remains standing, staring at him. The key is the dirt. What if her sister had been telling the truth? What if Maude is right? Biddy blinks and realizes that she and Arthur are still staring at each other.

Ruby tugs on her arm again. "You need to sit down."

Biddy doesn't.

"If that is your final word," Biddy says to Arthur. "Then I will stay on and investigate it myself. And since it doesn't seem like you take women's accomplishments seriously, I encourage other members of this town to join me. I'm forming a special commission. For women. I believe Eileen."

The crowd, who has been watching in silence like it is a ping-pong match, now gasps. Pooka, Indiana may not have much in the way of reputation, but what it does pride itself in is its town halls. You don't mess with those.

Arthur's eyes widen. "You're going to start your own commission?"

Biddy shrugs. "It looks like I am. I'm investigating Eileen's claims."

"You can't do that," Arthur says.

"Oh, but I can," Biddy smiles confidently. Now, she is on a firm footing. "And trust me, Arthur, I know how to run a Woman's Club."

"And who do you think is going to join? The knitting club?"

A half smile crosses Biddy's lips. "Maybe. Unlike here, they'd certainly be welcome. And valued."

Biddy looks down at her friend.

"Ruby," she says, "Let's go."

Biddy picks up her handbag and takes a step into the aisle. She is aware the rest of the attendees are glaring at her. That they don't see her as one of them. She holds her breath for a minute, wondering if her friend will join her. If things have changed so much that this relationship has splintered over years of neglect. But Ruby stands up. She looks mortified, but she stands. She follows Biddy down the aisle and out of the building. Biddy could hug her.

Night has fallen and bright stars shine in the sky. Biddy's

heart soars a little with them. Tonight couldn't be more perfect. Tonight is everything she hoped. For the first time since Charles died, Biddy has found her footing. And is helping those she cares about in the process.

"I can't believe you just did that!" Ruby shouts from the top step.

Biddy jerks to a stop in surprise.

"You alienated me from the whole town!" Ruby says. "You are ruining Maude's and my lives."

8

Maude

I might be about to do something stupid, and I really hope Biddy won't be upset about it. I'm just curious. But as they say, curiosity kills the cat.

On Fridays, I start the day by cleaning Mrs. Smilton's house. Maude, she always says, it's very important that you arrive promptly at seven am. So, I do. That way, I get done by ten and then Mrs. Smilton can host her bridge group, which is very important to her. Can you imagine your biggest concern in life is a clean house for bridge club? Some people have all the luck.

In the afternoon, I head over to Ms. Coheeney's house after she returns from Jazzercise at the Y. And when I finish there, I usually go to Mrs. Green's house to do my last cleaning job of the day and cook her dinner. Except Mrs. Green fired me last week. She said that I was more focused on talking about my mom than cleaning her house. You'd think she'd be equally outraged on my mom's behalf since mom had cleaned her house for eight years. But that's neither here nor there. What's important is that, because of this job loss, I had a little extra time on my hands. Most everyone is at the town hall—Biddy told me not to go—so I figured I'd use the opportunity to visit Aisling Pottery. Now I'm standing right across the street from it.

The historic factory housing Aisling Pottery is beautiful. It's three stories high, almost a block long, and made of river rock, which is apropos as it sits in front of Bent Elbow Creek. It's like a fort guarding the town's entrance beside the bridge. It has massive, evenly spaced windows running the width of it and the leaded panes glint in the sun even on the cloudiest of days.

Of course, I've never gone in before. I mean, why would I? It's not like I could afford anything and, when Mom went in, it got her arrested. So, I figured I wasn't very welcome either. But I remember what Biddy said about every woman deserving her day in court, and the more I look at this pretty factory and the more I think about mom, the more mad I get. Why shouldn't I be welcome? Everyone else is. Plus, I'm a little curious about what all the fuss is about.

So I go in. And I come to a screeching halt in the most beautiful place you've ever seen. The showroom is cavernous, brightly lit and modern. The walls are a blinding white, contrasting with the dark, almost black ceiling. Gleaming perfectly polished blonde wood floors shine beneath my feet. My mother couldn't have shined them better herself, and that's the highest compliment I can pay to a space. Hundreds of pinpricks of light laser down on a mix of white pedestals and wooden antique tables, all featuring various types of pottery. I take a deep breath and bring in the scent of lemon cleaner. This must be what the Taj Mahal looks like.

The sound of the large wooden door closing behind me

echoes in the space and makes me jump. In no time at all, a man comes racing out of a hallway from the opposite side of the room and his quick footsteps also echo in the space. He looks like he belongs here, in this pricey artistic place. He is short, slightly overweight, with an almost fully bald head. But the bright red frames on his glasses, a loud printed green shirt, and darker green trousers are so ridiculous it almost makes you forget he is ugly. I think this is the point. On his feet are sneakers which only rich people could make look dressy. This is the type of man who could sell you a beat up old pair of jeans for over one hundred dollars by slapping a brightly colored patch on it and telling you that you are now cool. He eyes me from head to toe and it appears he is less than impressed with my patches. I suppose I should mention I am in my torn khakis (the overused, not trendy kind), white t-shirt and work babushka as I just finished my cleaning jobs.

"Sorry, we're closed today," he says.

This is a lie because I'd seen the open sign on my way in. "Your sign would disagree." I'm pleased with this response. It sounds like something Biddy would say. "I only want to look around."

Which is entirely true. I'm not hurting anything. I'm just curious to see the pottery my mother helped create. I walk over to one of the display cases and stare at a platter. It's beautiful. It has that elegant quality that sneaks up on you. The longer you look at it, the more beautiful it gets, as if the beauty comes from somewhere inside the piece and radiates out. All depth, no flash. It's very different in that regard than the man who stands before me. He's all flash and no depth.

The pottery is coated in what must be a signature glaze as all the pieces in the place have it. The color is hard to describe. It's white with just the slightest greenish cast that changes color in different lights. On this particular piece, a forest green border has been added with teeny tiny clusters of clovers in the corners. My mother used to doodle this design. Having seen this, I can't imagine why everyone is so shocked my mother had a hand in this. I'm more shocked that anyone believes this garish man could create this beauty all by himself.

"I know who you are," the man says. "Look, perhaps it's good that you stopped in. What your mother said isn't true. But there is no reason for you and I to be at odds."

He walks across the big space towards me, his footsteps still echoing like he is a giant on the move. He extends his hand. "I'm Finn Murphy."

"Maude Delancy," I say with all the dignity I can muster whilst covered in Ms. Coheeney's dust.

"It isn't true," he says again, as if repeating it would make it so. "The chemistry alone that it took to achieve this signature glaze is mind-numbing. We found it in our archives and invested heavily to produce it at scale."

"Who found it in your archives?" I ask. That was the thing about mom. You would think she was just a cleaning woman who wouldn't know beauty if it rose from the ground and slapped her in the face, but that wasn't true at all. Think about it. Who spends more time carefully studying some of the finest works of art in the world than a cleaning woman of the rich and elegant? She dusted all of their carefully curated, expensive objects for hours a day, week after week, year after year. Her exposure to art and its teeny tiny details were pretty much unmatched. It would be just like her to see something beautiful and research how it was made, especially if she thought she could make a dollar off it. That was the other thing about my mother. If she saw a dollar to grab, she'd reach for it. When I told Biddy this, she'd called that ambition.

The man sighs. It looks like a balloon deflating. "I was really hoping that you and I could bury this hatchet. I would love for us to be friends." Then his face lights up. "Why don't I hire you? You could be on our night cleaning staff? You'd be a part of Aisling Pottery. Your mother's dreams would be realized."

Well, that is the straw that breaks the camel's back, as they say. The only thing that would have made my mother proud would be me as CEO and this man scrubbing the floors for me. My mother is the one who created all this. Dementia or not, my mother is not a liar.

Before I know what I'm doing, I sweep my arm forward and shatter the glass case and the pretty platter inside it. It crashes to the floor with a bang and explodes into a thousand pieces. Both of us are so shocked that we just stare down at it for a minute without saying anything.

I look up into the man's eyes. In truth, I think I might've gone too far with this one. All I can think is that Biddy will be so angry. But in for a penny, in for a pound.

"No, Mr. Murphy," I say. "I'm sure you could do quite better at cleaning than I. Here's a new mess for you to start with."

Now, my mother would be proud. I can hold my head high. Still, it ends with the police escorting me out of the pottery and Ms. Coheeney firing me from my next cleaning job. Thank god for Mrs. Smilton and her bridge group. She'll never fire me with that.

9

Biddy

You are ruining Maude's and my lives. Biddy freezes in place at Ruby's words. That isn't true at all. She is helping them.

Slowly, she turns back to face her oldest friend, who is still standing on the top step of the town hall. Tears run down Ruby's face and her plump arms vibrate. The only other time Biddy has seen Ruby cry was when they once hit a baby deer in Ruby's truck. They rushed the deer to the vet, spent all their allowance savings, and everything turned out okay, but Ruby had bawled as if the world were ending. That is what it is like now.

"I thought you would help Maude," she says. "Even after everything with your family, I thought you'd do what was best for her." Ruby crosses her arms across her body. "And what about me? I thought we were best friends. But you just disappeared. You left and didn't come back. And now, when you do, you're so busy being fancy and all you care about is some stupid crusade. We were partners. We used to do everything together, remember?"

Of course, Biddy remembers. Admittedly, Biddy had had a

few hairbrained ideas in her time…like when they painted all the barns in town pink to honor the Pink Ladies in Grease. But no matter how crazy the idea, Ruby had done it with her. Perhaps Biddy hasn't included her friend in this one. Perhaps she just expected that she'd follow along.

"Ruby, I'm sorry about that, but you need to listen—"

"No, you need to listen. There are no buts!" Ruby's voice quavers but remains loud. "You hurt me and there is no acceptable reason for that."

"I'm sorry."

"Well, that isn't enough!"

Biddy takes a step back as if slapped. Never…never in all their years…has Ruby fought with Biddy.

"You missed my dad's funeral. The rest of the town was there, and you weren't. Even Eileen bothered to come and she hated us growing up. You didn't even send a card."

Oh, no. Biddy had meant to. She thought she had. She must've been so busy…

"And then I almost lost the pub during Pooka's bad days. It is my father's legacy, and I almost lost that. Where were you then to tell me it would all work out and to hang in there?"

This isn't fair. Biddy hadn't known this. If she had…well. Biddy suddenly realizes she wouldn't have done anything differently.

"I loved you like a sister." The tears stream unstopped down Ruby's face. "I still do. You are so smart and so accomplished. I would do anything for you. And I don't regret that. But it just..well..it just would've been nice if you'd do the same for me."

Biddy stares at Ruby's red face. Her watery eyes. Her dripping nose. She realizes that it's one of the most beautiful faces in the world. For it is a face filled with unconditional love.

She has been stupid. So stupid. Ruby's words are the words she's been longing to hear. Except she's been listening in all the wrong places. She's cared more about what Muffy Gallagher thinks of her than her oldest and dearest of friends. The friend who came back in her life just when she needed her most. The friend who forgave her for a forty-seven-year absence, without even being asked. The friend who had disagreed with her decisions over the last few days but who had still stood by her. The friend who had followed her out of the town hall, knowing that it would anger every other person in it.

"I'm so sorry." Biddy whispers. This time, when she says the words, she means it. "I've been a terrible friend and you don't deserve this."

"I don't!" Ruby's hands curl into fists. "I watch Dr. Phil. I know all about boundaries. And I think it's time we have some."

"You're right." Biddy cringes as she tacitly agrees with Dr. Phil, but this isn't the time to voice that discomfort. "You're absolutely right about everything. I haven't valued our friendship and there is no excuse. No acceptable reason. Honestly, you are the only person in my life who has made me feel better since Charles died. I can't believe I hurt you. Please forgive me."

And then Biddy starts to cry. It shocks Ruby so much it stops her own tears. It shocks Biddy so much; it makes her cry harder. She hadn't even cried over the baby deer.

Ruby runs down the steps and throws her arms around Biddy. "Of course I forgive you. Don't cry. I forgive you."

Biddy clutches her friend and lets the tears fall. She doesn't know how long she's had them in her. She cries for Ruby and the rift in their friendship that is all her fault. She cries for the loss of Charles, a wound that can't be repaired. She cries for Eileen and her daughter Maude, both of whom she has also neglected. She cries for the cruelness of the world and the women just doing their best to get by.

"You're going to be okay," Ruby says.

Biddy doesn't think she will. She has screwed everything up. She has hurt people she loves. She's prioritized herself and her own needs. She's been selfish. She's even stealing this moment from Ruby, who should be the one crying. She is the victim of Biddy's neglect after all.

"I've done everything wrong."

Ruby grips her shoulders and pulls back slightly so that Biddy can see the encouraging smile on her tear-stained face.

"Maybe. But now you can do everything right. We'll fix this. We can talk to Maude tomorrow."

"But that's the thing…" Biddy digs in her purse for a tissue, and blots her eyes. She hands the tissue to Ruby, who does the same, and then blows her nose loudly into it. They both laugh.

It thrills Biddy to hear her friend's laugh. She doesn't want to ruin the moment, but she knows she has to. For this is the right thing to do.

"Ruby…I honestly believe Eileen may have founded Aisling Pottery."

Biddy waits for Ruby to tell her she is crazy. That she needs to let this go. That she couldn't possibly know Eileen better than everyone else. That she hasn't seen her in almost fifty years.

But that doesn't happen. Instead, Ruby takes her friend's

hands and looks in her eyes.

"Tell me why."

So Biddy tells Ruby her thoughts. Standing in the parking lot, against the backdrop of muted voices emerging through town hall's open windows and the swirly red and blue flash of police lights in front of the pottery across the street, Biddy talks about the memory of Eileen running some sort of scientific experiment with dirt. The memory of the dirt mixture flashing green. That she wonders if this could be the making of the pottery's signature glaze. That she wonders if the doodles might actually be chemical formulas.

Ruby listens carefully. She doesn't interrupt. She doesn't object. She just listens. She waits until Biddy finishes and then she still listens, this time to her own thoughts. Biddy suddenly realizes what a gift this is. To listen so carefully and to consider words before speaking. To make someone feel heard and valued.

When Ruby finishes thinking, her eyes meet Biddy's. "You really believe this is true?"

Biddy wants to say yes, unequivocally yes. But then tells the truth. "I don't know, but I think it could be."

Ruby falls silent, yet again, to think again. But this time she looks down as she does so. For this time, Ruby isn't thinking with her head. She is thinking with her heart. And it is a rare person who can hear those most difficult to be heard thoughts. So Biddy waits patiently as she watches Ruby's eyes shift down to look at her heart as she listens. As she thinks.

Then her eyes lift back up to meet Biddy's.

"If that's the case, then I think we need to help Maude investigate Eileen's claims," Ruby says.

Biddy exhales a breath she hadn't realized she'd been holding and smiles. Ruby smiles back. This carefully considered decision is why Biddy has always relied on Ruby in the past. Why she always included Ruby in her crusades. For Ruby was never some mindless sidekick following Biddy's every move. Ruby is the leader of the pair. She is the moral compass. When they had painted the town's barns pink, Biddy may have done it to honor the Pink Ladies, but Ruby had done it to honor women in general. Biddy may be smart, but it is Ruby who is the wisest person in the world. Her brain is her heart. And now, by some gift from the heavens above, the team is back together again.

Just then, her cell-phone rings. Biddy answers, and the voice on the phone tells Biddy she needs to come to the police station. Biddy's eyes are pulled in the direction of the flashing police lights in front of the pottery across the street. What was happening over there?

10

Megan

It doesn't take long to navigate what Louisville considers an airport, and Megan quickly finds her way to arrivals to collect her suitcase. As she races through the terminal to catch the one and only bus to Pooka of the day, she locates a stand with chips and a rather sad looking cheese sandwich in plastic. She buys it, runs to the bus area, and slides into an open seat. Just before the bus doors close, a man runs up the bus steps, down the aisle, and sits beside her, despite many other open seats. Apparently, nothing is going to be luxurious about this trip.

She slides closer to the window to make room for him, takes a bite of the sandwich and questions how she came to be here, squished into this seat, instead of safely tucked into her Boston apartment, ordering takeout and preparing for the lecture she was supposed to give tomorrow. She'd given up two of her speaking appointments. And Daniel. She pulls her cellphone from her bag and checks her text messages again. There are 28. All unanswered and all from him.

The bus rumbles out of Louisville and turns onto the entry ramp of a two-lane highway, which, unknown to her at the moment, marks the last time she will see a building for two hours. As the corn and soy fields spread before her like a giant all green patchwork quilt, she thinks, this—this, here—is what failure looks like. Running away to a place like this. In the middle of nowhere. Why her mother would ever return here is beyond her. But was this also where she belongs now? After all, she's doing the same thing.

She knows she should be happy that Daniel cares enough to want to fix things. But somehow she finds she doesn't want to. If she is honest, she is a little relieved he cheated on her. She'd read a few of Daniel's messages and while they were apologetic, they also claimed that she had been distant and secretly wanted the relationship to fail. Was that true? She checks the message count on her cellphone again. Now it's 29. She lets it fall to her lap and stares out the window at the flat green fields until she drifts to sleep.

"Next stop Pooka," the driver finally announces.

Megan rubs her eyes, shivers from the cold air emanating from the air conditioner, and looks out the window again. The sun is just beginning to wane beyond emerald green hills. Although the earlier part of the trip had been through flat land, here there is just enough roll to the hills that it is impossible to make out much beyond them. Reluctantly, Megan notes it is rather pretty. There are even random goats wandering rock outcroppings, which seems unusual, but what does Megan know about farming?

The bus makes a sharp turn to the right and the town of Pooka spreads before her. Beyond a field of corn with the tassels waving gently in the sun's golden light, beyond a little creek with a stone bridge crossing its banks, sits a rainbow colored town with a large stone factory standing guard beside the bridge. Megan stares at it. Perhaps Pooka, Indiana, is America's best kept secret paradise? It's nothing like the poverty-stricken town in the article she read online.

The bus grates between two rock configurations that appear to guard the road like an ancient version of gates. The one on the left looks like a rabbit, or maybe a cat. The one on the right is definitely a horse. Or a pig. Megan doesn't know why she is thinking this. In fact, she's pretty sure that the only other person who thinks they look like anything is the bus's insurance adjuster who will think they look like a thousand dollars given the large scrapes they leave on both sides of the bus.

"Those are the pooka of Pooka," her seatmate says, nodding at the rocks. Thankfully, it's the first words he's spoken to her. "Pooka are said to cause all sorts of mischief in this town."

The man appears far too normal to be declaring rocks to be mischievous. He is about her age, scruffy, but in a polished way. He gives off an aura that is more Cape Cod than cornfields. His appearance might even be considered attractive, if he weren't clearly delusional.

"Rocks don't cause mischief," Megan says. "People do."

"No, the rocks don't cause mischief," the man agrees, much to Megan's relief. "The pooka do." He leans over to whisper. "They're just pretending to be rocks."

Oh dear. She picks her phone back up and checks her messages, hoping this might discourage further conversation. Plus, if she were to be honest, she wants to see if Daniel has reached out again. He has.

"Pooka are shapeshifters and good natured tricksters. They must've come with the settlers from Ireland." He leans over her and points out the window. "The only way you can tell they're pooka is their eyes. They always have a streak of yellow. Just like yours, in fact."

Despite herself, Megan looks at the rocks and sees two slashes of yellow near the top of each.

"I hope you aren't calling me a pooka."

He shrugs. "You never know. A good pooka would never own up to its real identity. Consider your secret safe with me."

Megan rolls her eyes. She inherited the glint of yellow in her pupils from her mother, not a pooka. And she certainly couldn't imagine her polished and refined mother running around these fields, pulling pranks.

She glances back at her phone.

"Why do you keep checking your phone?"

"Why do you think that's your business?"

She thinks the words will offend him into silence. Instead, he shrugs. "I'm the curious sort. You get a funny expression on your face when you check it. I can't tell if you're hoping to get a message or hoping not to."

Doesn't that sum up her life? "Me neither."

Thankfully, the man settles back in his seat and the town grows larger as the bus passes through the cornfields and approaches the bridge. Beautifully smooth stones, almost like giant pebbles in shades of brown, compose the bridge and what looks to be a factory beside it. The bus crosses the bridge, and Megan can see the creek bubbling beneath them. On the other side, they come to a fork in the road. To the right sits the factory with a now visible working water mill. To the left sits the town, a colorful array of painted buildings on both sides of the street, standing in rows like a box of Crayola crayons. The bus turns to the left and pulls in front of a white building with wooden crossbeams, Tudor in style. The chiseled sign in front declares it to be the Shillelagh Inn and Pub. The driver puts the bus in park and announces they have arrived in Pooka. Megan and her seatmate are the only two getting off at the stop, and they both follow the bus driver out. They each pick up their bag—Megan, a hardcovered small white suitcase with leather handles and him a faded LL Bean duffle bag.

"Do you need a ride somewhere?" he says.

Only if she wants to be kidnapped and end up in a ditch with a stake through her heart, she thinks.

"No. I'll just morph into a car and drive myself."

He laughs, unfortunately pleased with her joke. "That's what I'd do too if I were a pooka." He gives her a small casual salute. "I hope the text message turns out the way you want. See you around, Proteus."

He walks away, slings his bag into the back of an old Ford pickup, and drives off. Annoyed to not understand his comment, Megan pulls out her phone and googles Proteus. The Greek shape-shifting sea god. Well, at least the man is educated…and single, according to the lack of a ring on his left hand. No matter. She has bigger worries than a slightly off academic. She has to find her mother because she's lied. She does need a ride.

Megan has left multiple messages on her mother's cell both via text and voicemail and has yet to hear from the woman. She can't imagine what has kept Biddy so busy all morning and afternoon that she hasn't checked her phone. Biddy has stranded Megan in the dark in the center of town with no idea where she should go. Megan pulls up the extender on the suitcase handle, cinches her handbag up her shoulder, and wheels the bag onto the sidewalk.

The sidewalk is remarkably devoid of people for the early evening. To her right, she hears what sounds to be a large assembly in a white-washed building with bright green trim and a thatched roof. It looks like a Disney interpretation of Ireland. Maybe the town has leprechauns as well as pooka and the town is meeting to figure out how to catch them. She smiles at her own joke.

Yet, all joking aside, the town does seem off. A little detached from reality. Although much prettier and better kept than the article led her to believe, she can't help but feel it shouldn't be. Farming does not make one rich. And this is not a town with the old money of Boston. She wonders how they got it. She can only hope no one has been taking advantage of her grieving mother. For Charles Bramley had money. Lots of it.

To her left, she sees two people emerge out of a building that looks like a police station. She heads in that direction. Maybe they can give her directions. And, if not, maybe the police have a registry of Airbnb rentals and can help her out.

The building is at the very end of the block. As Megan draws closer, the women remain standing on the sidewalk in front of it, deep in conversation. She gets closer and the woman on the right looks more and more like her mother. Megan knows she is likely hallucinating this. It's like when you go through a breakup and then you think you see your ex everywhere. No one can will a person into existence. But then she gets within a few feet of the women and she sees that it's true. It really is her mother, wearing her signature tweed jacket and skirt with low-heeled pumps.

"Mom?"

Her mother's head snaps in her direction. The other woman

also looks over. Up close, Megan can see she must be a street person in torn, dirty cotton pants and a white t-shirt coated in dust. Her stringy hair hangs loose. In her hand is a clear plastic bag holding a scarf and the rest of her possessions. It is entirely possible Megan has just saved her mother from getting accosted.

"Megan?" Biddy looks surprisingly unhappy to see her. However, she hurries over and gives Megan a tight hug. "What on earth are you doing here?" She pulls back, still holding Megan's arms. "I told you there was no need to come. But even then, you should have told me. I would've picked you up."

"I did tell you." Megan can't keep the annoyance out of her voice. "I must've left you ten messages."

"Oh. Oh dear." Biddy pulls her phone out of her bag and looks at the multitude of stripes on the screen announcing Megan's messages. "Well, I guess it's been a very long day. I've been too busy to check."

Megan realizes Biddy has acknowledged missing the calls but hasn't apologized. This is very unlike her mother—Both not apologizing and missing the calls in the first place.

"Are you okay? Is this woman bothering you?"

The other woman is still standing just behind her mother, shifting her weight awkwardly from one foot to the other, watching them.

"I'm fine," Biddy says. "I told you that last time we spoke."

"I got arrested." The homeless looking person shares this tidbit. She wanders over to stand beside Megan's mother. "And she bailed me out."

Megan feels her eyes go wide. This is so much worse than she thought.

"Megan," Biddy says to her, not meeting her gaze, "meet Maude Delancy. Maude, this is my daughter Megan."

Before Megan can say anything, like 'why should that mean anything to me' or 'what do you want' or 'get away from my mother,' the girl's eyes light up.

"Cousin," she screams, runs over, and throws her arms around Megan.

Oh. Dear. God.

Biddy

Okay, there were probably better ways for Megan to meet Maude, Biddy thinks the next morning. Biddy has parked her rental car on the far side of the town bridge and is hiking through the cornfield towards the pooka rocks to get some much needed alone time after listening to Megan chide her for being too trusting all night. The sun shines brightly above her and the cornstalks brush against her legs, scratching her navy slacks. They are a brilliant green and carry the sweet smell of sugary kernel formation. When she was a child, Biddy often hiked through these fields when she needed some time alone. It was one of the few places she could let down. To be still and just think. Now, she hopes the place still possesses the special power to calm her. She pushes through the last few stalks of corn, which thankfully are only waist high as it is just the start of summer. Then, she looks into the two slashes of yellow on the nearest rock, towering above her.

"You probably think Megan and Maude's encounter is funny, don't you?" she asks the pooka.

It doesn't answer, of course. It'd be downright silly to expect a pooka to answer. But the eyes look like they are laughing.

The thing is, it is a little funny. The look on Megan's face when she found out that Maude was her cousin. Oh, it was comical. Biddy has always worried that Megan grew up in too small a world. That Charles had sheltered her from normal people with normal problems. People like Maude. Both Charles and Megan would thoroughly disagree with this assessment, claiming to be worldly. But still. A little time in Pooka may not be the worst thing for Megan. Except.

Except something seems off with Megan. Why on earth would she leave Boston to come here, even if she is worried about Biddy? Biddy knows she had many lectures scheduled this summer and a wedding to plan. Her daughter has a full life, one that would be hard to leave, even for a few weeks. Sure, her daughter loves her and is concerned about her… unnecessarily so…but why would she leave her career and fiance over mild concern for her mother? What has really brought her here?

Well, she will have to wait for Megan to tell her in her own time. Biddy bends down and pulls weeds from the base of the pooka rocks. She'd noticed them on her bus ride into Pooka and they were unsightly. The Boston Garden Club would be appalled if they saw this.

As she weeds, she shifts her thoughts to her plan to help Maude. She has just finished hanging fliers all over town advertising the new women's club to investigate Maude's claims. The town has ignored women's contributions for too long and she expects women to join in droves.

Megan will at least be useful as a member of the club, she thinks. That is, if Megan deigns to take Biddy's quest seriously. How ironic that her daughter thinks this silly when her entire career celebrates the dead wives of past presidents. How is this any different? Eileen may not be the wife of a president, but she is dead and her contributions to society are overlooked. Instead, Megan seems to have an unnatural desire to get Biddy to drop her interest in this cause.

Biddy's cellphone rings, interrupting her thoughts. Her pocket muffles the tone, but she feels its vibration. Surprised that she has any signal at all, Biddy pulls it out and sees Muffy's name in the middle of the dark screen.

"So much for a quiet place to think," she says to the nearest pooka.

However, she has made a decision and perhaps it is best to share it now. After her conversation with Ruby, she's ready to put this silly fight with Muffy behind her and focus on what matters: helping Maude. Biddy will withdraw her name from consideration for the Boston Historical Society presidency. That should please both Megan and Muffy. She accepts the call and walks over to the base of a nearby oak tree, sinking to the ground beneath it.

"Biddy, I'm glad I caught you. We need to talk."

Muffy delivers the words in the clipped cadence of a person too busy to speak at a normal pace. Biddy smiles at her friend's familiar tone.

"I'm glad we've connected, too. I have something to tell you."

"Me first."

"Of course." Biddy rolls her eyes. She pictures her friend sitting in her floral wallpapered office, tapping her pen while they speak.

"Today is the last day to submit applications for the presidency, and we need to discuss a few things before I submit yours to the group."

"That's what I want to talk about, too. I—"

"Here's the thing, Biddy." Muffy's voice drops as if they are at a table in the Fairmont Copley Plaza and she doesn't want to be overheard. "Things could come out during your campaign."

"Oh, for god's sake, Muffy. I told you this is ridiculous. What things?"

"Charles had an affair."

Biddy flinches, but then realizes this couldn't possibly be true. Charles would never do that.

"Muffy, someone must've made it up. You know how people talk."

"I saw him. Saw him with my own eyes. He was with Serena Von Staadt in the lobby of the Parker House. He held her hand, kissed her on the lips, and then they headed towards the elevator banks. He was holding a room key."

Biddy's heart freezes. No. It simply wasn't possible. There was no way. Sure, Charles traveled a lot and went to many dinners, but that was for his job. Megan's fiance was just as busy. It was the nature of the job.

"Muffy! I don't know why you'd say something like that."

"I'm just trying to protect you! I didn't tell you sooner because there was no reason to hurt you. But Serena is on the board and she really doesn't like you. You were her competition. You can't run for office. She would not be happy to work with you again and she might talk. I'm telling you this to help you."

Jesus. Biddy thinks back to all the occasions Charles cancelled plans last minute on her. She thinks of Serena, preening as if she owned Biddy's house at the wake. Is this true? Had she just given up three years of her life to take care of Charles full-time after he had been unfaithful? Muffy should've told her this sooner. Biddy would've told Serena she could have him.

"You need to drop out of running for office in the Historical Society or she could tell everyone. It will ruin Charles and yours reputation."

So this is why Muffy felt so strongly against her running for office. It had nothing to do with Biddy's capabilities. It is because Serena is a woman scorned and Muffy doesn't want to damage their friendship. Well, too bad.

She suddenly wants to laugh. She is suddenly free of grief over Charles' death. She is free of her old obligations. She looks at the pooka in front of her. It seems to laugh, too. The painted yellow slashes tilt up as if in a grin.

"That's a shame," Biddy says to Muffy, her path forward now clear. "Because, I'm still running for President. You and Serena can tell anyone anything you want. I'm not the same person as my husband. And his actions don't reflect on me. Please submit my application."

And then she hangs up. Biddy stares up at the sunlight filtering through the tree and closes her eyes. She listens to the corn rustling in the breeze. She breathes in the sweet, earthy scented air. She is surprisingly happy to be here.

She tries to tell herself that her words were crazy. That she needs to call Muffy back and retract her application. She tries to tell herself that she should care about her family's reputation and that she's just going through a phase right now. That it will pass and then she'll be angry with herself.

But she can't seem to care. Compared with her friendship with Ruby and the problems of Maude and Eileen, Boston society's whispering about her husband doesn't seem that important. Plus, how dare Charles! She feels like her old self.

Then Biddy thinks of Megan and her heart falls. Megan idolized her father. She'd never dream he was capable of such a terrible, unforgivable thing. How will Biddy tell her daughter?

12

Biddy

It's been days and Biddy still hasn't found the right moment to tell Megan about her father's infidelity. Biddy tells herself that she's just been busy. She will definitely tell Megan after the inaugural Pooka Women's Club meeting. Then she'll have more time to deal with Megan's emotional fallout. Her daughter has idolized her father and will have such a difficult time with this revelation. But now she has a much larger problem.

Biddy sits in her living room with Megan, Ruby, a young woman covered in a thick layer of pureed carrots,—and ten empty chairs.

"Do you think more people will come?" Biddy whispers to Ruby.

"I'm sure they will." Ruby pats her hand. "Traffic and all. Here…" Ruby reaches forward and picks up a tray of petit fours on the coffee table. Compliments of Ruby, there is enough food to feed fifty. "Have a cake." The platter glistens with the faintest of green casts.

Biddy stares at the beautiful platter. How come no one cares her sister may have made it? Biddy isn't at all hungry, but she won't hurt Ruby's feelings, so she takes a petit four off the platter and chews it slowly. Ruby is a great best friend but a terrible liar. Pooka has a population of 703 and the last time there had been a traffic jam is never.

Amelia—that would be the one with the carrot puree—checks her watch. "Are we going to start soon?" She smiles apologetically, notices a spot of puree on her pants and takes a napkin off the coffee table to wipe at it. "I've got to get home to feed my youngest at six. I'm really excited about this, though."

Funny, Biddy thinks, that would make her the only person in the room to feel this way. Ruby is grinning, but with massive effort. Megan looks like she's been forced to take a driver's education class after receiving a ticket. And Biddy's own heart is gripped with regret, knowing that Muffy would be smug with faux pity if she could see this. Suddenly, she sees headlights pull into the drive, briefly blinding her. A car door slams and footsteps follow. Another person. Thank God. At this point, every one matters.

The doorbell rings. Biddy answers it and, on the other side of the door, is a young woman, about Amelia's age. She is a little chubby, incredibly well-endowed, and wears a tank top that descends far enough to expose the vast majority of her cleavage but also somehow creeps above her navel. A very short plaid skirt and plastic stilettos complete her ensemble. All she is missing is a for sale sign. Biddy's heart falls. This idea is not going to work.

"Yes?" Biddy says.

"Is this the Pooka Women's Club meeting?" the girl asks.

"No." Biddy starts to close the door.

"Don't be silly!" Biddy turns to see Ruby looking at her in confusion, and then Ruby leaps off the couch and hurries to reopen the door, her legs jiggling in excitement. "Of course it is. It absolutely is. Come on in!"

With Ruby standing beside her, a huge welcoming smile plastered on her face, Biddy has no choice but to allow the girl entry.

"Wow," Ruby says, looking at the girl, "you must really be cold."

The girl looks at her angrily and then must realize that Ruby means the observation kindly. Her expression turns to surprise as if she's never encountered such innocence, which, Biddy guesses, she likely has not. "Yes. It's a bit chilly this evening. Thank you for noticing."

Her eyes shift back to Biddy. "So, are you going to invite me in?"

Biddy sighs. "Take a seat. There are plenty."

The girl snorts and walks into the sitting area. She selects a card table chair away from the others, sits down and blessedly crosses her legs. It doesn't look like a natural position for her. She fidgets uncomfortably.

Biddy and Ruby resume their seats and everyone stares at the newcomer.

"My name is Sheila Ryan," the girl says and gives a small wave.

Ruby waves back. "Ruby."

Amelia extends her hand. "Amelia. Pleased to meet you."

Megan nods at her. Then her eyes shift to her mother, filled with a look of horror.

Biddy can't imagine what Sheila is doing here. Then again, she is starting to wonder what any of them are doing here.

"Well," Biddy says. She checks her watch one more time. It's not worth waiting any longer. "Welcome to the inaugural meeting of the Pooka Women's Club."

Ruby puts down her teacup and starts clapping. Amelia follows suit and Megan rolls her eyes.

"I have a question." Sheila rifles through her sizable bag.

"And what's that?" Biddy asks.

"Can you sign this form for me?" She holds out the wrinkled form. "I need community service hours for my last arrest."

And so Biddy discovers the reason for her presence.

"You were arrested?" Megan asks, as if she isn't sure she heard correctly.

Sheila's face turns red. "Is that a problem?"

"Not at all," Ruby says quickly. "I'm sure it was just a misunderstanding."

"Right?" Sheila looks over at Ruby. "Since when did recognizing a monetary value for providing an enjoyable experience become a threat to society?"

"Never," Ruby says. "I do that every night. I own the pub in town."

"Not the same thing," Megan whispers.

"How do you have the energy for it?" Amelia asks Sheila. Her eyes are wide circles.

"Ladies." Biddy snatches the form from Sheila, signs it, and passes it back. "We are here for a larger purpose than ourselves. Following in the footsteps of the world's greatest feminists, including Gloria Steinem—"

"Who's that?" Amelia asks.

"She's an activist who wrote for New York Magazine and then founded Ms.," Sheila says.

Biddy chokes on her tea and studies the unlikely bearer

of the correct answer. She pauses until she finally stopped coughing. "—And Helen Gurley Brown—"

"—I know her," Ruby says excitedly. "She wrote a cook-book!"

"Among other things." Biddy prays for patience. "We are going to make sure that women in our community receive the same attention and space in the Pooka Historical Museum as men. Many of their stories remain untold while space is given to much less productive residents. And I have the perfect first project for us."

She pulls out Maude's chip of pottery glazed in its greenish-white sheen. She sets it on the table.

"This is our starting point…And now, I'd like to welcome our guest speaker, Maude Delancy."

Except Maude, of course, isn't sitting with them. Biddy stands up and walks to the front door. She'd seen Maude walk up to the doorstep five minutes ago, but, for some reason that Biddy can't begin to guess, she hasn't rung the doorbell. Biddy swings the door open and there, on the other side, is Maude, staring at her and the rest of the house through wide eyes.

Biddy sighs, rather loudly, and if she were to be honest, rudely. Of all the times for this girl to get nervous, this has to be it? What else can go wrong today?

"We're waiting on you in the living room," she says. She pulls the girl into the house and then pushes her towards the living room. All eyes shift towards them. Thankfully, Maude gets her fight back, squares her shoulders and raises her head a bit. She slides into one of the many empty chairs right next to Ruby.

Biddy sits across from her and nods at Maude. "This is our guest of honor."

Maude blushes. The others smile awkwardly at her and then uncomfortably look at each other as if trying to understand what to do.

Maude's eyes fall on the coffee table and she sees the pottery chip. Her eyes tear.

"Maude's mom recently passed." Biddy says to the group.

"I'm so sorry for your loss," Amelia says.

"I lost my mom when I was three," Sheila says. "I get it."

"How did she die?" Amelia asks.

"She didn't die. She just left. But the feeling's not all that different, is it?" Sheila says.

"Gosh, I suppose not," Amelia says.

Maude nods her thanks and looks like she's trying hard not to cry.

Biddy takes back control of the conversation. "Maude's mom's name was Eileen, and she had a tough life but a great spirit. Maude has shared with me how Eileen cleaned houses and took care of her four siblings, but also found time to pursue her dream of running a business. She founded Aisling Pottery, but her co-founder stole it from under her. Maude said that Eileen kept this chip of pottery as proof. It has her initial on it. We think it's a signature from an early piece."

Maude picks up the chip and holds it up for them. "Mom used to pull this out and tell me it reminded her of a time when the world was at her feet."

"So you think her mom actually was the founder of Aisling Pottery and the current owner stole it from her?" Amelia says.

"That's exactly what I think," Biddy says.

Maude looks like she's holding her breath. For such a pushy girl, Biddy thinks, she really needs to exude a little more self-confidence.

Sheila cocks her head. "Wouldn't be the first time a man stole credit."

"But why didn't she say anything sooner?" Amelia asks. "Why wait until right before she died?"

"Well, that's the thing," Maude says uncomfortably. Even Biddy has to admit this is a sticky point. "My mom never mentioned it when I was growing up, but then she got older, and age loosened her lips a bit and it became all she could talk about. I think age made her more retrospective."

Biddy is impressed. This sounds good and is near the truth. It also excludes use of the word 'dementia'.

"I suppose age might do that," Ruby says, bless her soul.

Biddy smiles at her gratefully.

"I still don't understand why she'd hide it for so long," Sheila says. "If I was supposed to have a slice of a multi-million-dollar company, I'd be shouting it from the rooftops."

"Well," Maude says. "She seemed…scared. I'm not sure if someone threatened her or what, but she always said that she needed to be brave to get what was hers. That was the word she used. That she needed to be brave."

Sheila leans forward to take a petit four and her skirt rides up to a level that would make Boston society faint. She sits back, tugs the skirt back down, and pops the petit four in her mouth. "I can see that," she says, while chewing. "Who wants to share a couple million dollars if they don't have to?"

"Maybe she started talking about it at the end of her life because she wanted you to have the money." This came from Amelia. "If I were dying, I'd want to see my kids set for life and would risk my life for it."

Biddy instantly knows this to be true about Amelia. She looks meek and exhausted, but those are always the people who surprise you.

"Well," Biddy says. "Now it's our job to prove it to the world and set history right."

Ruby reaches forward and picks up the pottery piece. She flips it over in her hands. "It looks like two initials—FM and ED."

"Let me see." Sheila reaches across the table and takes the piece from Ruby. She studies it. "It does look like FM and ED. but there is no space between them." She passes the piece to Amelia.

"You think the ED stands for Eileen Delancy." Amelia says to Biddy. "Then who is the FM?"

"FM would likely be Finn Murphy," Biddy says. She doesn't need to say more than that. Everyone knows Finn is the man who restarted the old factory twenty-five years ago and made it a success.

"This is pretty strong evidence," Amelia says.

"I've been arrested on worse," Sheila agrees.

"You've got to be kidding me," Megan says, her eyes looking at each of them. "This wouldn't hold up anywhere."

Biddy gives Megan a dirty look and clasps her hands. "This is strong evidence, but Megan is right. We need more. I think we need to prove that Eileen created the signature glaze. Eileen was always strong at chemistry and there is no way Finn created the glaze on his own. There has to be evidence of her work on this. I know she did experiments using dirt to create color. Her notes on this must be saved somewhere. How about we each pick a place to search for it?"

Amelia raises her hand timidly. "I've been working on our family's genealogy. I'd be happy to research Maude's family tree, talk to remaining family, and see if she hid anything at her childhood house."

Biddy smiles. "That's great. Eileen's brother still lives in the farmhouse."

"Wouldn't that also make him your brother?" Megan asks.

"What you two are related?" Amelia looks from Biddy to Maude.

"Why don't you go with Amelia?" Megan says, her eyes drifting up from her silent cellphone resting on the coffee table.

"What?" This is a horrible idea. The last time Biddy spoke with her brother, he'd screamed at her she should never show her face on his doorstep again.

"Well, if you're so bent on reuniting with your family," Megan says,

"why don't you go see your brother?"

Ruby looks from mother to daughter. "That may not be the best idea…"

"Fine," Biddy snaps at Megan. "Then why don't you go to the old Aisling estate and look around there? That's where the dirt came from."

"Biddy," Ruby says, "the Aisling estate is now a waste management dump."

"I'm aware." Biddy says.

"So," Megan says, "to get even with me suggesting you spend time with your long-lost brother, you are sending me to a garbage dump."

"Toxic waste dump," Ruby corrects.

"No," Biddy says, "I'm sending you to the dump because Eileen was seen wandering around there, digging up mud, and calling it gold. The name of the pottery also bears the name of the old estate. I'm wondering if this isn't where she found the materials and formula to make the glaze that defines Aisling pottery."

"That sounds like a real clue," Sheila says. "Plus, it's an hour commute outside of town which will knock off lots of community service hours. I'll go with Megan and investigate."

Whatever Sheila's motivations may be, Biddy is confident she won't let Megan bully her or rush her. This is a perfect plan. Biddy nods.

Amelia notes the assignment in a notebook she has pulled out of her bag.

"You know what?" Megan says. "We should look into Eileen's health history."

Maude's face blanches.

"Megan," Biddy says, "I really don't see how that will help us prove Eileen founded the pottery."

"It could remove the biggest argument against it. If you really believe she is telling the truth, then we should prove she wasn't crazy. Her doctor can do that. Or are you afraid of what I'll find?"

Biddy is, in fact, a little afraid of what she'd find, however her daughter has a point. They should know what they are up against. "Alright," she says, "but Ruby will work with you."

She needs someone she trusts with Megan.

"Fantastic!" Ruby leans over and rubs Megan's leg. "It'll give me a chance to get to know my goddaughter better."

"Maude, are you okay releasing your mom's records to them?" Biddy says.

Maude looks anything but okay with it, making Biddy even more terrified about what Megan will find, but she nods tentatively. Well, nothing Biddy can do about it now.

Suddenly, Megan's phone rings. They all look at the phone

resting on the coffee table and see Daniel's name light up on the screen.

"Aren't you going to answer it?" Biddy asks.

"I don't want to miss the meeting," Megan says.

"Nonsense," Biddy says, excited at the chance to get her unusually disagreeable daughter out of the room. "You've been more than helpful. Why don't you go speak to your fiance?"

Megan is silent for a minute. The phone continues to ring. "Fine." She snatches up the phone and stalks out of the room.

"It's settled then," Biddy says to the rest of the group, despite a sinking feeling in her gut. This is hardly the most skilled or motivated group of women she's ever led and even she has to admit that Eileen's case is a difficult one to argue. And why is her daughter suddenly seeing the worst in everyone to the point of rudeness?

"We all have our marching orders," she says. "Meeting adjourned."

13

Megan

Megan replays her conversation with Daniel in her head as she drives to pick up Ruby the next morning. The call had only confused her more.

"Meggie," he'd said. "I miss you. I made a big mistake and I've been trying to be respectful of your need to mourn your father, but I just had to hear your voice."

"Oh Daniel. How could you? And with Mellie?" She finds herself disappointed in his behavior, but not angry or hurt. Why is she not feeling emotions? Is it because her father died and she's feeling numb? Or is she just not a normal, lovable person?

"I don't know. It was a silly thing to do. I want you back, Megan. I'll do anything to win you back. You haven't told your mother, have you? You haven't canceled wedding plans?"

Megan wonders if he is more concerned about the break-up of their wedding than losing her.

"No, Daniel. I haven't mentioned anything. Yet."

"Please don't. Think on it. Sleep on it. Take the time you need before you do anything drastic."

Megan is so emotionally exhausted, it feels like more work to cancel a wedding than just go through with it. But on some level, she knows this is not a good reason to get married. Then again, she also doesn't want to turn out like her mother grasping at ridiculous straws to prove her self worth without a husband."

"I need more time."

"Fine. Fine. Take the time." Daniel says. "I'll hang up now. I love you. And it was so good to hear your voice."

Megan doesn't know what to do. She can only hope that the right answer will become clear with more time. Perhaps helping her mother is the only good that can come out of this situation. She has to show her mother how crazy she's acting and to convince her that Maude is using her to get at her money. The people here are all nuts. And if Daniel cheated on Megan, imagine what these people who don't even know her mother would be willing to lie about to get rich. Megan only hopes the word of a doctor will help convince her mother Eileen was lying. Or too far gone to know the truth.

She pulls the car to a stop in front of the pub, sees the lights go off in the apartment above it, and then Ruby waddles out a door on the side of the building with a little wave. As Ruby walks towards her, Megan sees she is wearing a t-shirt with a picture of Angela Lansbury on it that says, 'I couldn't help but notice…' Oh, if only her peers in Boston could see Megan now.

"Did your mom tell you not to let me drive?" Ruby says as she lowers her considerable weight into the passenger seat.

"Yes." Megan doesn't even care if this hurts her feelings. She puts the car in drive and follows the GPS voice directions on her phone back onto the main street.

"I don't know why your mom says that. I'm really not that bad a driver. I've been doing it fifty years with only a few very minor mishaps." Ruby glances down at the phone in the cupholder. "Can you believe phones can talk now? Well, not mine. I could never figure out how to use those things. But, I'm not surprised your phone can. Your mom tells me you're really smart. Something of a celebrity."

"I wouldn't go that far." Megan's frustration with her mother thaws slightly. "But I've gotten on TV a few times. In fact, 60 Minutes is doing an episode and asked me to speak."

"60 Minutes?" Ruby's eyes light up. "Well, that is something. You'll have to let me know if Leslie Stahl is as pretty in person."

Megan is surprised Ruby knows who Leslie Stahl is.

Ruby looks back out the window as town passes by. "Your mom was something of a local icon back in the day, too. You must be so proud of her for starting a women's club here," she says. "Who knows? Maybe her research will also be featured on 60 Minutes. Then there'll be two stars in the family."

"Oh!" Megan laughs. She can't even picture her mother speaking to a leading journalist. "I doubt that. Besides, there are already two stars. My dad was on a few times."

"Well," Ruby says. "Then imagine a family with three."

Megan shrugs and stays silent. Ruby is naïve and a little nutty, but, on the upside, Ruby genuinely seems to care about her mother. Megan drives up a hill, past an old white-washed church, and then looks over at Ruby. "You know, I'm actually glad we have an excuse to talk."

"Me too!" Ruby squeezes her leg. "I always thought it was such a shame your mom and I fell out of touch. She's very important to me and you're very important to her, so that makes you important to me too!"

"Oh, well, there's that." Megan feels the slightest twinge of guilt. This is a feeling that is not returned. "But I'm also worried about Mom."

"Whatever for?" Ruby looks as perplexed as if Megan had just given her a complicated math problem to solve.

"Well, she's never been on her own before. My dad always took care of her. I'm afraid she's being taken advantage of while mourning him."

Ruby stares at Megan, and her eyes grow larger and larger. They grow so large, Megan wonders if she might see their convection point. Then Ruby laughs. And laughs. And laughs. "Oh, you're serious?" Ruby wipes at a tear that slipped from her eye. "You are serious! Oh honey, this is why we need to get to know each other. You really don't know your mother at all. Did you ever wonder why you never met your grandparents?"

"Mom said they died."

"Well, they did. Eventually. But before that, her father disowned her. Biddy's mother had just died, and her father gave her an ultimatum. If she left the farm to marry a Protestant and not stay here to raise her siblings, he would cut her off and never speak to her again. Biddy still married Charles. She knew that she'd be completely on her own and move to a city she'd never seen, but she still did it."

"She wasn't alone. She had Dad to look after her." Clearly, Megan's father had rescued her from a horrible family life and a terrible future.

"Honey," Ruby's voice fell and took on a tone of seriousness Megan had not believed capable. "That marriage could have failed. It only happened because she was already pregnant with you. He could've divorced her. It was a huge risk."

Megan is shocked at the thought. "Not with my Dad. He

wouldn't ever have left her."

"No one could know that." Ruby shrugs. "I think it's pretty brave. And, as far as throwing herself into things like this, your mother's always been this way. She once got school canceled for three days by purchasing hundreds of rats to reach the legal requirement for an infestation. It was ingenious. And then there was the school's haunted house fundraiser. She made it so scary, it was deemed life threatening and they prohibited it from being held again." Ruby laughs at the memory. "A chainsaw got caught in someone's hair." Megan doesn't see how this is funny. "But," Ruby says, looking back at Megan, "the point is your mom always blew away expectations. Just let someone try to take advantage of her. They will be in for an unwelcome surprise. You have nothing to worry about...Oh look, we're here!"

The fields and bramble on the right side of the car gives way to a gravel drive that takes them behind a low stone wall and in front of a long white single story stucco building with mustard color doors in the center. The building looks like it is being refreshed with new paint and has a partially installed brick walkway.

The parking lot is so crowded, Megan is lucky to find a spot. A steady stream of people are filing to and from the door. More to than from.

"They will not be happy to see us," Ruby comments. "If your mother were here, she'd claim to have something highly contagious to get to the front of the line."

Her mother is a hooligan, Megan realizes. She climbs out of the car and slams the door shut. "That's entirely unnecessary. I'll just let them know I'm doing research on behalf of Harvard."

For some reason, Ruby looks like she's trying to bite back a smile. Megan realizes why after a brief conversation with the nurse. "Well, good for you," says the nurse. "I can only hope working there hasn't given you the impression you are more important than the rest of us." The less than impressed woman then announces that there would be an hour and a half wait while the doctor saw real patients. Megan leads a laughing Ruby to two chairs across the room and watches as Ruby immerses herself in a talk show on the TV, hanging high on a wall.

Finally, when it is their turn, they are shown down a long hallway to an exam room with two chairs. Thankfully, this time their wait is brief before a harried doctor races through a door and falls into the swivel chair on the other side of the examination table. He is on the younger side, likely in his thirties, with a shock of red hair and thick black glasses.

"I'm Dr. Enniskillin," he says, extending his hand. "I understand you wanted a consultation with me?"

Megan takes his hand in hers. "Dr. Megan Bramley, from Harvard University. I know you are busy, so we'll be quick. We are looking into a claim by Eileen Delancy that she founded Aisling Pottery."

"Well, I wouldn't know anything about that," Dr. Enniskillin says, making to stand back up.

"No," Megan says quickly, "but you would know about her state of mind. She didn't make the claims until recently and I'm concerned that she may have not been of the right mind."

Megan fishes in her handbag, pulls out the medical release form signed by Maude, and passes it to the doctor. "Her surviving daughter, Maude, has given us permission to speak with you."

"I see." The doctor glances at the release and then looks back at them. "Eileen Delancy presented with the symptoms of early onset dementia. She had significant trouble with memory before her death and a hard time navigating the world."

And here's the truth, Megan thinks. She just knew these people weren't all her mother believed them to be.

"Would dementia also lead to delusions and paranoia?" Megan asks.

The doctor nods. "Absolutely. Those are common symptoms. The person can be very convincing, as she believes these are real."

"Thank you doctor," Megan says and stands up. "That's all we needed to know."

Ruby has watched Megan's exchange like a tennis match, often looking like she wanted to speak but also not wanting to interrupt. Megan had hoped this urge toward civility would continue to overpower the urge to speak, but unfortunately, she was not to be that lucky. Ruby jumps out of her chair.

"Wait a minute." Ruby puts her hand on the doctor's arm before he can leave. "How do you know it was dementia? Did you do any tests? Did you do an autopsy?"

The doctor smiles, but it is that fake type of smile as if he is doing this only to hide his strained patience. Megan knows how he feels. "That wasn't necessary. She had the symptoms. Since there was no likelihood of foul play, we didn't do an autopsy."

Ruby doesn't let go of his arm.

"That's not how they do things on Murder She Wrote," Ruby says. "I watched it in preparation last night. Isn't there a blood test you can run?"

Megan wants to crawl back in her chair to hide in embarrassment.

Dr. Enniskillin frowns. "There's a test which can show some likely markers, but for Eileen, it didn't really matter if we proved it or not. There was no cure. What was important was treating the symptoms."

"Well, I think we should run the test," Ruby says firmly. "It isn't fair to say she was crazy without proof."

Now the doctor looks angry. "I didn't say she was crazy. I said she had early onset dementia."

"Same thing," Ruby says.

"Ruby," Megan says, "I don't think it's necessary."

Ruby frowns. "I think it's necessary."

Megan looks at the doctor, whose face is growing redder by the minute. Then she looks at Ruby, who is only getting more set in her idea.

"Okay, you know what?" Megan says. "I'm friends with someone in the science department at Harvard who specializes in blood disorder identification and treatment. I can have him run the test on an old blood sample if it would help convince you."

"Really?" Ruby's face lights up and she drops Dr. Enniskillin's arm. "Thank you."

"Okay." Megan grabs a business card out of her bag, scribbles on the back of it, and hands it to the doctor. "Could you please have Eileen's blood work and records sent to this address?"

Dr. Enniskillin takes the card, looks about to fight this idea, but then shrugs. "I don't see how it will help, but I can. Do you need anything else? I'm always happy to look at any ailments while you're here. It's amazing what drugs can do nowadays."

What an odd thing to say, Megan thinks. She shakes her head.

"Then, if you'd excuse me, I have a bunch of patients that really need me."

He hurries out the door, and it slams behind him.

"I always dislike the young doctors," Ruby says. "It's like they think it's our fault we got old."

"Ruby," Megan almost feels sorry for the woman. She is beginning to see how her mother likes her. Her intentions are so pure. "I'm happy to do this for you, but you understand the most likely scenario is that Eileen did just get old and senile, don't you?"

Ruby shrugs. "I thought that before your mom came to town. In fact, I told her to come here to talk Maude into letting this go. But your mom believes her. And if your mom believes her, then I believe her. Your mother is the smartest person I know."

Megan thinks Ruby needs to get out more. She leads Ruby out of the examination room and passes the window of the pharmacy dispensary, which has a line even longer than that at the front desk.

"Everyone gets old and forgets things," Ruby says, "but it doesn't mean they're wrong all the time. I think we should give Eileen a chance."

14

Biddy

Biddy and Amelia sit in the front seat of Amelia's minivan. They look down the long dirt road winding back through the fields to Declan Delancy's farmhouse. Biddy's farmhouse.

The home, surrounded by healthy crops, has never looked so good. In fact, Biddy had almost not recognized it. It's a two story, mostly rectangular building, with the top floor falling just shy of squaring off the bottom level, as if the builder ran out of wood and decided they were close enough. There is a narrow door in the center with a screened door hanging in front. This hasn't changed. But now, the entire house has been re-sided, the windows replaced, and it is painted a bright white. The door is a cheerful, glossy yellow. Seeing this makes Biddy wonder about her decision to choose Charles. What if she had stayed? Would she have been better off? For now, she looks a fool to everyone. Both to the people in Boston, learning of her philandering husband, and to the unimpressed people of Pooka who are laughing at her efforts to support Eileen.

Biddy looks at Amelia, who is in the driver's seat and who

is also staring at the house. "Why did you join the Women's Club?"

Biddy is a practical person, and practical people understand that you sometimes take things you get even if you get them for the wrong reasons. Ruby only joined the group because she is Biddy's best friend, leaving her no real choice. Megan did it because Biddy forced her to. And Sheila did it to get community service hours. But Amelia. Amelia joined it because she wanted to. At first, Biddy couldn't figure out why everyone didn't want to join. Now, she wonders what made this woman want it?

"Because I know what it's like not to be seen." Amelia picks the remains of a craisin off her sweater and then her eyes lift to meet Biddy's. "You're so sophisticated and worldly, people can't help but admire you. Sheila steals the limelight of any room she enters. And Ruby…Ruby is everyone's best friend. But people like me…and Eileen…I swear people would bump right into us. We are invisible. I did it because I know what it feels like to be her. And it's a rare day someone like you takes notice of someone like us. I wanted to be a part of it."

Biddy flinches in shock. She squints at Amelia and suddenly sees her, as if for the first time. She sees the person, not the food covered exhausted mom of four. Amelia immediately breaks eye contact and goes back to looking at the farmhouse. But Biddy notes the hallmarks of her daily struggles. Her greasy, stringy hair. The dark circles under her eyes. The car littered with paper, toys, and three car seats. There is a person under all this. It makes her own struggles pale in comparison.

Biddy re-buckles her seatbelt. "I appreciate you doing this with me, Amelia. I'm ready now."

Amelia squeezes her hand as if she is the one who needs

support, puts the car in drive, and pulls up the driveway.

Despite her calm words, Biddy's heart-rate speeds up. What if Declan slams the door in her face? What if he blames her, like Maude had, for leaving the family and all its problems behind? Biddy doesn't think she can take anymore blame and anger. She has never felt more alone and adrift in her life. And so she wants to run away from this visit, even if she no longer has anywhere to run towards. But instead of running, she leads the way up the now even steps to the door, ready to take whatever blame Declan delivers. She knocks with Amelia standing at her side and realizes suddenly that her presence is supportive. A few minutes later, she hears lumbering footsteps. Then the door swings open.

Declan is larger than she remembers and sloppily dressed. His trademark Delancy red hair is now more white with a pinkish tint and is sticking out in every direction. His eyes are bloodshot. He looks like their father. Funny, she thinks, she hadn't expected this. This aging and decay. She'd expected him to look more like the house…To look better.

"Yea?" he says.

"Yes," Amelia corrects automatically. She blushes. "Sorry. Habit."

Declan's eyes shift from her to Biddy. He stares, studying her as she studies him.

"Heard you were back in town. Raised a ruckus at the town hall."

"Well, someone in this family had to."

He shakes his head. "I don't really need this right now."

"I don't either. But we are going to do it for Eileen."

Biddy pushes the door the rest of the way open and brushes past Declan. The inside of the house, like Declan, does not mirror the wealth of the outside. It's like a museum. Nothing has changed. Absolutely nothing. Not the cabbage rose wallpaper lining the hallway. Not the long table in the dining room on the right, big enough to seat ten. Not the chintz couch in the living room to the left, still covered with a towel to protect the fabric. Nor the old beat up Lay-Z-Boy favored by her father. It's as if the house…and perhaps the family…are still sitting ready and waiting for their dad to return. Biddy runs her finger over a tear in the wallpaper that she'd once created while wielding a toy sword as she swung at Declan. She heads to the couch and sits on it. Amelia sits beside her, careful to remain respectfully on the towel.

"Babs, what do you want?" Declan falls into the La-Z-Boy.

Biddy feels her heartbreak, just a little more. What has become of her brother? Where is his fight? She'd expected a battle with him. Now, there is just a shell of a man, too tired to slam a door on unwanted visitors.

"It's Biddy now."

He sighs. "'Course it is."

"You have a lovely home," Amelia says.

They both look at Amelia. Then Biddy laughs. Declan joins her. Pretty soon, both have tears streaming down their faces.

"Amelia," Biddy says, "the house looks terrible."

Amelia turns beet red. "I was just trying to be polite," she mumbles.

"What d'ya want Biddy," Declan says as the laughter subsides. He overpronounces her name, but Biddy appreciates that he made the effort to get it right.

"I want to help Eileen."

"Aww, Biddy." Declan leans back in his chair. "She's dead. It doesn't matter no more."

"Her daughter isn't dead." Biddy leans forward as if to offset his actions. "And it does matter. Eileen was a Delancy. Delancy's are to be respected."

"Oh Babs…Biddy. Those days are long gone." He waives his arms around the room. "Everyone left. You were just the first. I don't blame you anymore. Eileen and I were the only fools who stayed. There's nothing left here to be respected."

"Yes, there is. Of course, there is." The words fly out of Biddy's mouth. "Just look at the place. The house looks nice on the outside and the farm is doing great."

Declan shakes his head. "All that comes at a price."

"One clearly well worth it!" Biddy can't figure out what he is talking about. Things have never looked better.

"Look," he continues, "Eileen was as crazy as they all say. And she was a fool. After she got knocked up with Maude, the guy actually proposed to her. He would've gotten her out of here. But she turned him down. She insisted on staying. Look around you. Who does that?"

"You did."

Declan laughs again. But this time it is bitter.

"Why don't I go look around Eileen's room," Amelia says quietly. "That is, if you don't mind, Declan?"

He shrugs. "Have at it. Up the stairs, second door on the right. But if you expect to find a stock certificate for the pottery, you're going to be sorely disappointed."

Biddy and Declan sit in silence as Amelia leaves the room and her footsteps pad up the stairs and down the hall. Biddy can picture her entering Eileen's bedroom. It used to be her bedroom, too. She wondered if her twin bed is still in it or if her father had been so angry as to have it moved out.

"Why are you so bitter when you are doing so well?" Biddy

asks.

"I need a beer," Declan says.

Biddy follows him into the kitchen and takes a seat at the old formica table near the window while Declan fishes in the fridge for the beer. She sits in the seat she always did. She wonders if her siblings had left the seat vacant when she left or if someone else had claimed it.

"We had four years of drought," Declan says, his back still to her, "and then one year of torrential rain that did just as much damage as the drought. Five years total without almost any edible crop. Wiped out almost every farm in the area. We all would've sold, but there were no buyers for the land. So we stayed."

Declan slides into the chair across from Biddy and pops open the beer tab. "It was after Dad passed. Glad he wasn't here to see it."

Biddy could hear the regret in his voice. Her father had been a hard man and there had been no room for failure. Declan had lived his life trying to earn his approval.

"Dad couldn't have done anything different," Biddy says quietly. "Besides, things look better now."

Declan shrugs and takes a gulp of beer. "Some goody-goody group came in and invested in all the farms in Pooka. Got us back in business. 'Course that comes with its own set of troubles."

What troubles? Does Declan simply not want to be a charity case? Maybe that's the problem. He is a proud man and never did like outsiders.

"And what happened to Eileen?"

Declan takes another sip. "After the rest of the kids left, she was barely around. That was when the crazy started. People saw her at all hours, digging holes in fields and burning mud in fires. Then she got knocked up. Came begging me to give her money. 'Course I couldn't. I didn't have any to give her. She was spitting mad and said she'd never speak to me again. And you know Eileen—she's always good for her word. That's the last time she did speak to me. Saw her around town and she wouldn't even look at me."

"Did she say why she wanted the money?"

Declan shakes his head. "Only that she was gonna make us rich."

Biddy leans forward and grabs his hands. Forces him to look at her. "Declan, what if she did? What if she did get rich?"

"Oh Babs." Declan smiles, a sad smile full of pain. "Eileen wasn't rich. And I'm not rich. Clearly, you got rich, but that isn't as easy a feat as you think. You can't make your past fit your present. Leave this alone. Go home and forget about us again."

"No."

Biddy hadn't thought this was how the conversation would proceed. She'd envisioned yelling, screaming, blaming. Maybe a few threats. Never resignation. Never capitulation. Her brother is a fighter, not a quitter. Her sister, while perhaps a bit mean, was smart. Her family, while now splintered, has always been a leader in this community. Some things don't change. Some things just need faith.

"I'm not leaving."

Declan pulls his hands out from between hers. "Biddy."

Biddy feels the distance re-develop between them. It's the name, she realizes. He used her new name.

"You don't belong here anymore. I did the best I could by Eileen, but she's dead and this town has everything it can do just to get by. Go home. I'm staying out of this."

"Biddy?" Amelia speaks tentatively from the doorway. Her handbag is slung across her shoulder, looking a little fuller than before. "Are you ready to go?"

"Did you find anything?" Biddy asks.

"No," Amelia says. But her voice inflects upwards at the end, like she's asking a question instead of giving an answer.

Amelia is decidedly the worst liar Biddy has ever seen. She wouldn't last a day with the Boston bridge group. Biddy looks back at Declan, but he doesn't meet her eyes. He doesn't care enough to contradict Amelia.

"That's too bad," she says to Amelia.

Biddy stands and pauses in the doorway. "It's good to see you, Declan."

She walks away without getting a response.

15

Megan

If Megan thought her trip to the hospital clinic with Ruby was bad, she clearly hadn't fully envisioned her day at the dump with Sheila. They are standing in the remains of the old Aisling Estate and Sheila looks like she's auditioning for a part in a mud wrestling competition sponsored by the Sports Illustrated Swimsuit Edition. She wears camouflage short shorts, a white tank, and knee high bright pink rubber boots while she stands atop a mud pile in what was previously a grazing field and now is definitely a garbage dump.

"Don't you want to put on a pair of pants?" Megan asks her, eyeing the field of chunky wet mud.

"It's summer. Why would I wear pants?" She squints back at Megan, who is dressed in an extra large black turtleneck sweater and sweats, tucked tightly into her black rubber boots. "You know, you could be really pretty if you tried harder. I could give you some tips."

"Thank you, but no."

The day has been even longer than Megan feared. The car ride alone took over an hour. Sheila never went above twenty-five miles an hour, mumbling something about knocking hours off her timesheet so fast she barely noticed how much service work she was doing. Megan's time didn't feel like it was moving at all.

Yesterday afternoon, she'd gotten a text from the Dean of Harvard's History Department—her boss—asking her to call him. And then…when she hadn't responded because what could she possibly say…she'd gotten another. Then she'd gotten a third text, telling her that Dean Havlichek had called him and felt obligated to tell him that his wife was cheating on him with Megan's fiance. So the truth was out, whether Daniel wanted it to be or not.

Megan now surveys what was previously the Aisling Estate. It sits just on the edge of town and looks to have once been a fine home and grounds. Two stone columns flank the driveway and the remnants of the stone mansion still stand on the hill behind Sheila. However, that is all that remains of its former glory. Now wet, clumpy mud cakes the drive and fields surrounding the old home. It's looks just like her life. A complete sewage pit. She tells this to Sheila—the bit about it looking like a sewage pit, not about it resembling her life.

"That's because it basically is," Sheila shouts cheerfully back. "Berbrine Manufacturing bought it to dump their toxic manufacturing waste. Your mom told you that."

"I thought she was exaggerating," Megan shrieks. She starts wading back to their car, parked safely on one of the few remaining bits of solid ground under a tree. As she does so, she slips and slides into the muck. She slips twice more, trying to stand up.

Sheila somehow finds this funny. "Relax. Some co-operative came in and treated it so it's non-toxic. They've won all sorts of awards for the technology. Hey, do you think Eileen found treasure buried in here?" She squats down to peer into the muck.

The only treasure Megan has found is a new appreciation for penicillin, which she will take proactively the moment she gets back to town. She's also found further very convincing evidence that her aunt was in fact nuts, if she was digging around in this. Now, she wonders if it's hereditary. Is her mother losing her mind, too? Would Megan devolve into this?

Megan spits to rid herself of any possible mud that may have gotten into her mouth. "I've seen enough. Let's go." She tugs open the door of the car.

"Wait, we can't." Sheila pops up from her crouch and starts digging around in her pocket. "We have to get a sample of the mud for your mother."

Megan glances down at her ruined clothing. "I think I've seen enough mud for a lifetime. Let's go."

"No." Sheila pulls a test tube with a cork out of her pocket. Megan can only imagine that it is a prop that came with a nurse's costume.

"We said we were going to do this, so we're going to do it. Don't you have any professional ethics?" Sheila squats back down and scoops some mud into it. Megan taps her foot impatiently, waiting for the hooker, who somehow has an ethics code when it comes to dirt.

Suddenly, a beat-up pickup truck splattered in mud flies down the drive and skids to a stop about thirty feet away, still on solid ground. Clearly, it has been here before. A man jumps out and starts waving his arms at them.

"What do you think you're doing?" he screams.

"Collecting a sample," Sheila screams back. She pops the cork on her sample and then takes a long look at the new arrival. "Well, hello there," she says with a purr. "You want to sample it with me? I'm sensing we might create some chemistry together."

"Oh dear god," Megan mumbles. She walks toward the new arrival. As she gets closer, she recognizes the scruffy face, flannel shirt, and khakis. The recognition must be mutual because his eyes widen and a smile slowly forms on his lips.

"It's my yellow-eyed Pooka," he says.

"Hi again." Megan wants to roll her eyes at the ridiculous reference but realizes she has little high ground to stand on at the moment. Both literally and figuratively.

"What are you doing here?" he asks.

"You wouldn't believe me if I told you."

"Well, I know I told you that your kind thrives on getting into trouble, but this isn't a good place to do it. You really shouldn't be here. It isn't safe."

"That's what I said," Megan says.

Sheila skids down from her mud hill, somehow doing so without falling. In fact, she even looks good doing it.

"It's perfectly safe," Sheila says. "Some group cleaned it all up." She comes to a stop next to Megan, kicks her hip out, and smiles. "And, trust me, her kind doesn't know trouble anywhere near as well as my kind."

Surprisingly, the man ignores the thinly veiled reference and his eyes focus on the test tube in Sheila's hand. "I'm afraid I'll need to take that."

"My shirt?" Sheila bats her eyes.

"The test tube."

He makes to snatch it but Sheila pulls it away.

"No."

"It's just mud," Megan says. "Give it to him."

"No," Sheila says louder.

"Oh, for heaven's sakes." Megan blows out some air and looks at the man. "Let her have it and we'll be out of your hair. Trust me, it'll put to rest a stupid idea and you'll never have to hear from us again."

He sighs and looks at her. "I'm afraid I can't do that. I'm the 'group' who cleaned this all up. Remember how I told you I run a farmer's co-operative? I'm also a scientist. And one way that I raise funds to support the farmers is to treat chemical waste. It's a win-win. We neutralize chemical waste and fund the farmers it would have damaged. But that means I'm responsible for rigorous protocols. Those rigorous protocols include containing waste to the approved site and keeping people out."

Megan looks at him in a new light. She would've never guessed this man—a man who believes in mythical creatures— also developed such a ground-breaking technology, used it for good, and took his responsibility for the community so seriously. She suddenly realizes that it is she, not he, who is the fool, standing here without permission, covered in mud, and making terrible, terrible life choices.

"Of course, I understand. Sheila, give him the test tube."

"But—"

"Just do it. Not everything is a lark."

Sheila silently passes him the test tube.

The man's body relaxes. "Thank you." He turns back to face Megan. "I just realized I don't know your name."

"Sheila," says Sheila. She reaches in her pocket, pulls out a business card, and thrusts it into his hand. "All my contact information is on there."

"Oh." He turns back to Megan. "And you are…"

"Megan. Megan Bramley."

"Megan Bramley." He smiles. "It's nice to meet you. I'm Brady Hughes."

"Nice to meet you, too." Against all odds, she finds herself smiling back.

"You've got to be kidding me." Sheila rolls her eyes as she looks back and forth at them. "I'll wait in the car."

"Is she your friend?" Brady asks as they both watch her stomp off through the mud, towards the car.

"What? No." Megan suddenly realizes what all this must look like. "No. No. Definitely not. She knows my mom somehow. I'm just here to make sure an idiotic quest doesn't get out of hand."

"Ah." He laughs. "If you don't mind me saying, it doesn't look like you're doing too well with that."

Megan wants to die as she looks down at her mud soaked clothing.

Brady puts the test tube in his pocket and then scratches his head. "Listen, if you really are curious about our treatment of the soil and what we're doing to help farmers, I could give you a tour sometime. An authorized one."

Oh goodness. Was he asking her on a date? No, probably not. Definitely not.

"I shouldn't," she says, just in case he is. She's in a relationship with Daniel. At least she guesses that's still true.

"Just as friends," he clarifies. "You look like you could use one right now."

Megan wants to sink further into the mudhole and never be seen again. How could she have thought anyone would be attracted to her? Of course, he isn't hitting on her, just look at her! She exudes the very definition of one who is pathetic. But he's right. She could use a friend. Plus, it never hurt to learn more about science. And it'd make her mom happy.

"I'd like that. Love that, actually."

"Great. I'll give you a call. Uh…" He fishes in his pocket. "You don't happen to have a business card, too? Like your friend? I can't seem to find a pen."

Megan laughs. "I do." She fishes hers out of her pocket and passes it over. The sight of the Harvard logo cheers her. At least she has that accomplishment to boost her confidence. "My cell number is on that."

He looks at it and grins. "From Harvard to the mud fields. You truly are a shapeshifter. I'll call you."

"I look forward to it." She heads toward the car, trying to do so without slipping and falling again in the muck.

"Don't forget to wash that muck off when you get home," he calls after her. "It's treated, but mud is still mud!"

"I promise it will be the first thing I do." Megan climbs in the passenger seat and shuts the door.

"Here," Sheila wrinkles her nose and thrusts a towel at her. "Sit on that. You're going to ruin my car."

"You were the one who insisted on driving." Still, Megan acquiesces and slides the towel under herself.

Sheila puts the car in drive, and Megan hopes that the stench of the mud might motivate Sheila to drive home faster. The car turns around and Megan puts up a hand to say farewell to Brady, who is standing where she left him, watching their departure.

"Well done," Sheila says.

Megan rolls her eyes. "Having a man be friendly to you is

not an achievement, Sheila."

"Oh, I wasn't talking about that." Sheila cocks her head and looks over at Megan. "Although getting a man interested in you while looking like that is a bit of an achievement. But, still, that isn't what I was talking about. While you were distracting him with your mud-coated turtleneck, I got another sample. Someone's mother will be very proud."

She reaches into her pocket and holds up another test tube of mud.

16

Maude

To say that things aren't going well is an understatement. I know it's wrong to eavesdrop, but when I get to the graveyard to visit Mom, I find Biddy and Megan arguing in front of Biddy's mother's grave. Megan is covered in mud, which is not the look I would've chosen to meet my dead grandmother the first time, but I'm trying really hard not to judge my new family members. Anyway, Megan wipes at dirt covering her face and screams at Biddy that we are a family of cuckoos and that her cousin is Exhibit A. That would be me. She says she now has statements from scientists and doctors to prove it.

Biddy is calmer and tells Megan she isn't to talk like that about her family and that even scientists and doctors are occasionally wrong. Biddy is right. Everyone makes mistakes. I mean Biddy became a protestant! But I don't think Megan sees it that way. She says that the two of them are now the laughingstock of town, alongside me. That hurt a little.

After they both leave, I wander out from behind Jonah McCreetin's grave and find Mom's. It's easy to spot, as it's still a mound of rich, black dirt. The dirt is reassuring. As if she's somehow not as dead and gone as the others, with grass covering their graves. As if her death hasn't taken root yet, just like the grass seed.

"Mom," I say. "I'm doing my best by you. I'm trying so hard."

I hope she realizes this. I can't imagine how maddening it would be to sit in heaven and listen to all these people say awful things about you.

"I'm going to get you the recognition you deserve. I swear it. Your sister is even helping me. Turns out, she isn't as bad as we thought. Although, the same can't be said for her daughter."

I bend down and sit on the grass beside her headstone and run my fingers over the bumpy surface. I could only afford to have Mom's name and dates engraved on the stone, but I would've put 'loving mother' and 'she walked in beauty' if I could. Doesn't that sound nice?

"You know, Mom," I say tentatively, "not everyone will just take you at your word. It might be helpful if you pointed me toward some proof."

I wait for a sign from heaven, but nothing happens other than a bird singing while it hops from branch to branch in the tree. I stroke the grass around the headstone. I have to try real hard to imagine it's her hair.

"I can't help but think if you founded a business, you must have something to show for it. Drawings of the products or records of sales?"

Silence.

"Why did you let Finn Murphy steal it? Was it because of me?"

I whisper the last part because this is my greatest fear. That my mother had given up her fortune because I'd come along and she'd done right by me. Why else would someone give up running a business to become a cleaning lady? My mother was a great mother, but I always fear that her greatest regret in life was becoming one.

"I may have done something stupid, Mom." I look away from the grave. I find it hard to make eye contact with her when she's going to be angry, even when she's dead. "You have to understand that I needed some sort of evidence that you founded Aisling Pottery. Not even Biddy would have taken on our case without it. So I made something up."

This is my secret, and it's a big one. The piece of pottery that I said my mom had held on to and that it had her initials on it? Well, that isn't really true. One night, very late, after the pottery had been closed for hours, I went to their receiving docks. In front of the large garage doors were multiple dumpsters. I climbed in them and started sifting through the garbage. Inside were dozens of pieces of pottery with this scroll work lining the edges. It must've been a design Aisling Pottery had discontinued. When seen on a whole plate or platter, or even lining a mug, the scroll didn't look like initials at all. It just looked like a loopy design. But, when broken just right, with just four loops showing, it looked like initials. So that's what I did. I smashed about five pieces of pottery, and finally I smashed a piece perfectly, with just the four loops. I put this piece in my pocket and put the rest of the pieces back in the dumpster to get picked up the next day.

To be clear, it really could be my mom's initials. One loop looks just like an E and another looks just like a D. Everyone in Biddy's group thought so, too. There's no reason in the world that this isn't evidence of my mom's involvement founding Aisling Pottery. It just isn't a signature, nor a piece treasured by my mom.

I look back at her grave. "Don't worry Mom. I'm pretty sure I won't get caught. And in the end, when everyone knows you were telling the truth, it won't matter. The ends always justify the means. Isn't that what you always said?"

I stand up and dust off my bottom. I feel better now that I've told the truth. Now, I have to get over to Mrs. Simmon's house for her Thursday afternoon cleaning. She's the type who meets me at the door with a list a mile long and specific instructions on how to do each item correctly. If a perfectionist walks into a bar, then it wasn't set high enough, she always says.

"I love you, Mom," I say, kiss my hand and touch it to her headstone. As I walk away, my heart feels lighter, just as I knew it would. Like Jesus said, I feel better having confessed.

17

Biddy

"I now call to order the second meeting of the Pooka Women's Club."

Sitting on a folding chair in her living room, Biddy is second guessing her decision to have Megan join the group. Optically, it brings the club a certain respectability to have someone of Megan's pedigree in the organization. But, she'd also hoped it would make Megan take the people of this town more seriously. At the moment, she isn't sure this goal is being met. Megan glances at the others as if they are carrying a contagious disease she might catch, and is staring at her cellphone on the coffee table as if afraid of it. Biddy sees notices of many texts and calls pop up on the phone, but Megan doesn't react. She also has no interest in the others in the room. It doesn't help that Sheila had handed Biddy her timesheet the moment she walked in the room, asking for ten hours to be noted for time spent with Megan last week because Megan smelled so bad she deserved time and a half.

Biddy reminds herself that many of history's most celebrated achievements had unaustere beginnings. The Civil

War's first battle of Bull Run. The British evacuation of Dunkirk in the Second World War. The dual between Aaron Burr and Alexander Hamilton. Well, maybe not that one. That one was just stupid. But the learning from most of these is that change requires fortitude, perseverance, education, and patience. Lots and lots of patience.

"Let's start by appointing officers," Biddy says. "We will need a President."

"Oh, that should be you," Ruby says quickly.

"Fine with me," Sheila says. "It's not like I get extra credit from the judge for holding office."

Amelia nods her approval. Megan looks like she is about to make a snarky comment to Sheila. Thankfully, Sheila is looking more normal today, not having changed into her 'work clothes' yet.

"I'd be delighted," Biddy says, before her daughter can speak. "Now, who wants to second Ruby's motion?"

Four confused faces stare back. Megan looks back at the notices flashing on her phone.

"Seconding the motion," Biddy says, exuding the aforementioned patience, "is required before having the vote."

"But we just had the vote," Sheila says. "Were you not paying attention? Because if you weren't, I may need to reconsider my support."

"This does seem a bit silly," Ruby says.

Megan smirks, eyes still glued to her phone.

"It's not silly and, of course, I was paying attention," Biddy says. "Official voting is proper etiquette. Robert's Rules of Order clearly dictate—"

"Seconded!" Megan says, briefly looking up from her phone.

Biddy feels like she should continue to educate everyone on

the proper procedures, but sometimes you need to take a win when it presents itself. "All in favor, say aye."

Megan puts her hand up and says aye. "Just do it," she says to everyone else. The others stick their hands up and say aye.

Megan goes back to her phone.

"I love this," Amelia says. "It feels so official."

Biddy appreciates the support. Procedures exist for a reason. "Now we need a secretary to take notes at each meeting."

"I'll do it," Amelia says. "I've already started and I keep schedules for four kids and a husband. It can't be harder than that."

"It certainly can't," Ruby says.

They go through the voting procedure again and Amelia turns pink with pride when she hears the unanimous 'ayes'.

"Next up is a treasurer," Biddy says.

"I'll do that," Sheila says. "I'm great with figures and negotiating. It's a requirement of my job."

Biddy thinks about it and shrugs. She has a point. "Sounds good. Seconded?"

And with that, Sheila is voted in. Biddy looks around the room. Amelia has pulled a notebook and pen out of her handbag to take notes. Sheila is making a to do list on her phone. Megan still isn't paying the slightest bit of attention, but she'll take care of that in a moment and Ruby...is staring at her fingers, looking the way she had when Biddy had told her she was leaving all those years ago.

"I guess that makes you Vice President, Ruby," Biddy says.

Ruby looks up, surprise and delight written across her lovely, open face. "Really? Do you really mean it?"

"I really mean it. I can't imagine anyone better." Biddy says. "Any objections?"

The group has none.

"Good for you," Amelia says. "I think you'll make a great Vice President."

Ruby blushes with a pride Biddy has never seen.

"Okay," Biddy says. "Given the nature of our work, I think it is important that we have one more elected officer. A Chief Historian. I nominate Megan."

"What?" Megan's head shoots up from her phone.

"Oooh, I second," says Ruby.

"Aye," says Sheila prematurely. She looks around, embarrassed. "Sorry, got ahead of myself."

"No, quite right," Biddy says. "Anyone else in favor, along with Sheila?"

"Wait!" Megan loses complete interest in her phone. "I can't be Chief Historian," Megan says.

"Why ever not?" Biddy says. "If you don't want to be a historian in Boston right now, you can be one here."

"Don't be intimidated," Ruby says. "You'd be perfect. The rest of us are new to our jobs, too."

Really, this is going even better than Biddy thought. Perhaps she'd been hasty to judge.

"I'm not intimidated," Megan snaps. Then she has the decency to look apologetic. "I mean, of course, it is an honor and a lot of responsibility…"

Everyone relaxes a bit and nods.

"…But that's exactly why I shouldn't do it. I'm not staying forever. You need someone who can devote their full attention to this."

"Oh, but dear," Biddy says. "You said you weren't leaving without me and I'm staying until this project finishes. So which is it?"

This wins her a dirty look.

"Even if you leave, you can do it remotely," Sheila says. "A quarter of my clients are remote these days and there has been no reduction in satisfaction."

How interesting, Biddy thinks. Just imagine.

"I love the idea," Amelia says, nodding along. "We can record our meetings for you if you are gone, and that way we'll have an audio and video record as well as my notes."

"Then it's settled," Biddy says. She looks at her daughter. "All in favor?"

Before Megan can say nay, everyone else says "aye" and Amelia records the four yeses and one no. That the objection came from the person elected to the position seems to matter little to the group.

"Now," Biddy says. She notes with satisfaction that Megan is still so shocked by her leadership role that she's forgotten to stare at her blasted phone again. "Let's move on to updates."

Megan speaks first. "We now have the word of a doctor that Eileen had dementia and also of a scientist who says there is nothing other than treated dirt at the old Aisling Estate. Do we have a single shred of evidence supporting this investigation?"

"We don't know for a fact that Eileen had dementia," Ruby says. "We are still waiting to have the blood test verify it. Has that specialist gotten back to you yet?"

Megan glances back at her phone. Even from across the room, Biddy can see there are a pile of unread message notices on the screen. Is she hiding evidence? And, why hasn't she read her messages? Megan is usually a person who keeps her inbox clean.

"I might have evidence," Amelia says. "I found a notebook hidden in Eileen's mattress." She turns to face Biddy. "I didn't want to get your hopes up until I had a chance to look at it. It has a list of names, dates, and dollar amounts. It could be early sales. Maybe we can find a few people and verify it that way?"

"Can I see that?" Biddy asks.

Amelia passes the notebook to Sheila, who passes it to Biddy, who opens it and studies the first few pages. She closes it without a word. She knows what it is. Eileen had gotten suspended from high school once for blackmailing students with secrets she found by following them. This was the list. It has nothing to do with the pottery.

"And we have the pottery chip with her initials," Sheila says. "Don't forget that."

At least that is real evidence. But Biddy notices Maude flinch and look down when this is mentioned.

"Would you listen to yourselves?" Megan asks. "You're grasping at straws. This is stupid. We look stupid. You wanted my opinion. Well, my professional opinion is you need to quit. This is idiocy."

The entire group stares at Megan through giant orbs.

"Fine," Biddy says.

It is Megan's eyes that now snap wide. "Fine, what?"

"Fine, we'll suspend the investigation until we receive verification of these data points."

"Really?" Megan says.

"Really."

"But we just had elections," Ruby whispers.

The rest of the group is shocked into silence and, for that, Biddy is grateful.

Biddy glares at her daughter. "Now, if you're finished lending your incredibly useful expertise to us, why don't you head out on that date you mentioned while those of us who actually care say our goodbyes?" Biddy can't believe her daughter is going out with a man other than her fiance.

"It's not a date." Megan rolls her eyes. "I haven't forgotten I'm engaged! It's a tour of the cooperative. With a friend. And you don't have to be so dramatic. It's not like you can't still see each other. Maybe you can find something else to do as a group. Like lunch. Or bingo."

"You're going to meet Dr. Dirt?" Sheila asks. "It's totally a date. Not that I can understand what he sees in you."

"I thought we were doing something more important than playing cards," Amelia says. "I read one of your articles, Megan. Isn't this the type of movement you praise?"

Biddy smiles inwardly. Good for Amelia for not letting Megan diminish their efforts. Megan turns red. She looks as if she is trying to decide whether to say something or not. She must decide on not because she stands up, picks up her phone, gives a half wave goodbye, and marches out the door. The group sits silently, listening to her footsteps recede.

What has gotten into her daughter? It is rare that Biddy is disappointed in her daughter but she feels it now. Biddy's heart breaks a little. While Megan inherited many of Charles' fabulous traits, she also received a few of his bad ones, too. Such as pride. And belittling people who lack her educational pedigree. Biddy looks at the hurt faces around the room, and for one of the first times in her life, Biddy is embarrassed by her daughter.

The group listens as Megan's car drives off.

"Are we really disbanding the group?" Ruby's voice is quiet.

"Of course not," Biddy says, with a cheer she doesn't feel. "I lied. We're just disbanding a member of the group who didn't want to be here."

"Oh, yay!" Ruby says.

"Good riddance," Sheila says.

Biddy feels the sting of their words, but it's one she can't defend. Amelia reaches over and squeezes her hand. For only another mother can truly comprehend the pain of a child turning on her.

Biddy squeezes her hand back.

"Where can we find the evidence we need?" Amelia asks.

This is the problem. Biddy knows in her heart of hearts that Eileen is telling the truth. She also feels that the answer is in the dirt collected by Sheila from Aisling Pottery. But without Megan's support, she doesn't have connections to any chemists to have it tested against the pottery glaze composition. She has to find another way.

"At the pottery," Biddy says. "Somewhere in that building, in all the old records it holds, there has to be evidence of Eileen's involvement. I think it is our last resort."

The group nods in consensus.

"But how do we get in?" Ruby asks.

"I think I have a way," Amelia says tentatively. "Lulu O'Halloran is in my knitting group. She works at the cashier's desk of the pottery on weekends. I could ask her if she has a key."

"But why would she give it to us?" Biddy asks.

Amelia softly smiles. "This group has more people cheering it on than you know. Their husbands just didn't want them to join."

"Well." Biddy thinks it through. "It's risky. Even if we use a key, we don't have Finn's permission to be there. We could get into trouble. No one here has to do this. It's completely up to you."

"I'm in," Sheila says. "What's one more arrest?"

"Jail time?" Biddy says.

Sheila shrugs. "What can I say? I'm a sucker for standing up for women's right to conduct business."

She says this laughingly, but for the first time, Biddy wonders if there isn't a little truth to it.

"I'll do it," Ruby says.

"Count me in," Maude says.

Amelia fiddles with her wedding ring.

"You really don't need to come," Biddy says. "I wouldn't think any less of you. You're already getting us the key, and you have a family to think about."

Amelia looks up at Biddy. "I think that's exactly why I need to do it. They need to know that they should stand up for other people."

It's a risk for all of them, but Biddy doesn't see any choice. She's never been more proud of her little group. The Boston Historical Society didn't hold a candle to them. There is just one other thing she needs to say.

"Maude, you aren't coming."

Maude opens her mouth to speak but Biddy cuts her off.

"You've already gotten in trouble once and would draw attention to the rest of us. Also, any evidence we find needs to be unbiased. You can't be involved or people will think you did something deceitful. You see that, don't you?"

Maude looks uncertain. "I suppose."

Biddy pats her leg. "It's for the best. For the rest of you… Let's meet at the Pub tonight at ten. Wear dark colors."

Ruby hugs her shoulders to her chin and grins. "This is so exciting."

Biddy isn't sure exciting is the right word to describe the sinking feeling in her gut. But she nods and leans forward in her seat. "Just, let's not mention this to Megan."

18

Megan

After leaving her mother's ridiculous meeting, Megan drives out to meet Brady at his farmer's co-op. As she follows the GPS directions down a very long road between endless fields of corn and soy, she replays in her head the latest text she received from Daniel. Daniel wants her back and loves her, but is unwilling to wait any longer. He wants to know if they are going to remain engaged or if she is leaving him.

She knows she needs to make a decision. It has been weeks since she found out about the affair. Any good feminist would tell her to leave him, but what if she never meets anyone else? She is an adult and knows the world can be unfair and cruel. Maybe she needs to grow up and put away the hope for a fairly tale love story. Maybe this infidelity is a normal adult hoop to jump through. Plus, she does need to return to reality. She has a job waiting for her that she spent her whole life working towards.

The air through the open car window ruffles her hair and she takes a deep breath. It smells surprisingly sweet. Like corn on a summer day. It calms her swirling thoughts. In a sundress and sandals, Boston feels miles away. She can put these problems out of her head a little longer, she decides, as she drives farther and farther from civilization.

Eventually, a series of red metal roofs crop up in the distance. As she grows closer, she can make out long sleek metal buildings beneath them, about five in total, arranged like legos in a complex tight-fitting design. The only nod to the historic farm buildings scattered throughout the rest of Pooka, is an ancient old stone farmhouse at the front, which now has Brady Hughes standing beside it, waving to her excitedly. As usual, he has donned a plaid shirt, but this one is in a dressier oxford cloth and is tucked into khaki pants, not jeans. Her heart warms a little as she sees a person who is genuinely and uncomplicatedly happy to see her. Perhaps it doesn't hurt to have a friend. She pulls the car in front of the building, turns off the motor, and emerges to meet him. The air is so still that her footsteps crunching on gravel sound like gunshots.

"This is all yours?" she asks, eyeing the complex buildings behind him.

"All of it," he says. "This is how we are transforming farming for the future."

He smiles proudly as he turns to gaze at his buildings, and Megan realizes that this transformation absorbs all of Brady's attention. That the scruff of his face isn't there because of style, but because he doesn't think to shave in the morning. That his clothing and car are just afterthoughts. It's nothing like the men in Boston. Like Daniel. And yet, she finds herself oddly drawn to this man…as a friend, of course. He takes her hand to lead her to the first building, and she realizes what is so attractive. It's his eyes. It's the spark that lies in them. The spark that comes from having a calling. She's never felt that spark. Not in her whole career. She wonders if many people do.

"As retailers have merged," Brady says, "they have become behemoths that require mass supplies of product. Think of Walmart, Target, and the grocery chains. They don't want to deal with small farmers anymore. It's too complicated to handle all those contracts. They need produce and meat suppliers who can handle distribution nationally. That's where we come in."

Brady walks Megan into the first building. It looks more like an Amazon warehouse than a rural storage facility. Huge metal bins filled with produce are stacked all the way to the top of the two story building. Automated robots traverse the space, putting produce in some bins and taking others out.

"We take product from all the farmers in the area and consolidate here," Brady says. "That way, the small farms can still operate independently, but since distribution is consolidated, they are now at the scale needed by retailers. We have different buildings housing different product. This is the produce building, obviously."

Brady takes her hand once again and pulls her through the building and out the other end. He points to three other buildings. "Those house meat, grain, and dairy," he says as he points to each. They cross a dirt expanse and enter another long building that is the last on the property. This one has tracks conversing from every building to it. Inside are about twenty bays. Enormous trucks are parked in four of them.

Brady's face glows as he studies them and then turns to face her. "All our shipping is automated to keep costs down. Retailers place orders electronically. We sort these by geography, and then robots fill the orders. The trucks follow the assigned routes. It's an efficient model that leaves little waste as again we have the advantage of so much product going to one place."

"This is amazing." Megan forgets her problems for a moment as she watches the robots carry crates of product to the loading docks. Because of the automation, there are barely any people here other than herself, Brady, the driver, and a few loaders.

"It's helped save a lot of farms," Brady says.

She bets it has. She hasn't been on many farms in her life, but she can't imagine the inside of their barns looking like this. For just a moment…a very short second…she feels a twinge of guilt at the way she spoke to her mother and her friends. Perhaps Pooka is not as backwards as she'd implied.

"How do you get all the money for this?" Megan asks.

"That's where the waste treatment comes in at the old Aisling estate," Brady says. "This model works and in the long run, it makes farming more profitable. But it takes a lot of upfront cost to build it out. I've made deals to process manufacturing waste and use the funds from that to build this. It's kind of like making a deal with the devil, but sometimes that's the only way to achieve progress. And I tell myself that I'm doing a better job than they would. The Aisling Estate is ideal, as it isn't near any residents and was already deserted. We aren't harming anyone."

Megan follows him out of the building and turns in a circle to take in the full size of the complex and machinery running it. "How, on earth, did you get into this?"

Brady laughs. "Now that sounds like a story best told over dinner. Any interest?"

Megan hesitates, but then nods. Brady is just a friend. And

friends are allowed to dine together. Brady takes her hand and leads her back to her car.

19

Biddy

Biddy surveys her team as they stand before her in the prep kitchen of Ruby's pub. Ruby wears a tight black turtleneck and black pants just like she saw Audrey Hepburn wear in How to Steal a Million, the movie she announces she had watched in preparation. Sheila went more the Marilyn Monroe in How to Marry a Millionaire route. In a black bandage dress with black stilettos, her only concession to the night's project is to not wear red, which, she shares, is her signature color.

"Are you sure you're going to be comfortable in that?" Ruby asks.

Sheila shrugs. "I had to come straight from work, but I'll be fine. I wore my comfy stilettos."

"Well, that's good then," Ruby says, eyeing the four-inch platform heels like she doesn't believe her.

Amelia wears a faded black, peanut butter smeared t-shirt and a look of deep apprehension.

Biddy stands in front of them.

"Now," Biddy says, "all we are trying to do is find some evidence that Eileen worked at the company. It can be the formula for the glaze, a record of payment, paperwork with her signature, or more of the pottery we found with her initials on it. It could even be a picture. Anything to lend credence to the argument."

"Got it," Ruby says.

"And, no matter what happens," Amelia says, "we can't tell anyone that Lulu gave us the key. We can't be responsible for her losing her job."

"Agreed," Biddy says. "If we get caught, we say that we broke in."

Everyone nods in acquiescence.

"Ready?"

Only Amelia nods. Biddy looks at Ruby.

"Ready!" Ruby says. Her voice is filled with false bravado, but at least the bravado is there, false or not. "For Eileen."

The rest of the group perks up in response to the enthusiasm.

"For Eileen," they say.

The old factory looms large above them as they cross the street. Not wanting to draw attention, Biddy leads them around the far side of the building and heads down the narrow road that weaves to the back of the building. With the high stone wall of the building lining one side and a thick forest of trees on the other, it is dark, and Biddy walks slower to give her eyes time to adjust. Visibility becomes fainter and fainter as they make their way down the path. The building blocks more and more of the ambient light from the road. Now closer to the river, the rush of water over the dam, powering the great water wheel, also blocks out any surrounding noise. Biddy is both blind and deaf to her surroundings. Her world narrows to the massive building to her right and the river on her left. She comes to a stop in front of the loading docks and fights fear as she lets the factory have its way and become her sole focus.

Like most docks, there are three elevated concrete bays with steel garage doors pulled tight over them. To the left of the farthest one is a crumbling concrete staircase with a metal door in front of it. Biddy leads them there, ascends the four steps and tugs on the door. It's locked tight.

Now or never, she thinks.

She pulls out the key provided by Amelia, twists it in the lock, and the door swings open.

The inside is dark but lit in the eery glow of exit signs and other safety lights. The group moves past the loading docks and into a room on the far side, Sheila's heels clicking on the dirty concrete floor. Crates sealed with shipping labels are stacked high in the room.

"Someone here certainly likes a good smoke," Sheila says as she bends to pull a cigarette off her stiletto.

"How odd," Ruby says, taking it out of Sheila's hand. "This one hasn't even been used."

Biddy shrugs and notices that none of the cigarettes have been smoked. The place is a mess. Cigarettes and boxes are scattered everywhere. It looks more like a UPS shipping center than a manufacturing business.

At the far back of the shipping room is another metal door. Biddy opens this and leads them through. Thankfully, the cinderblock walls of this room are lit with evenly spaced square fluorescent casings that provide just enough light for people to find exits in an emergency. The room looks to be the manufacturing portion of the pottery. Pottery wheels take up most of the middle space while long tables holding jars of glazes, paints, and paintbrushes are on the far end. Tall metal shelves where pottery sits in various stages of production and painting line the entire rim of the room.

"Should we look around here?" Ruby's voice echoes in the large concrete space.

Biddy shakes her head. "This room is for new product. We need to find the space where they keep remnants of the past."

Ironically, Biddy feels more exposed walking through the large open space of the potting area than the loading docks, which are exposed to the outside. She reminds herself that no one is watching. There is no risk. When Lulu gave Amelia the key, she confirmed there are no guards nor security cameras that she's seen. Biddy pushes through another door.

Now they are in the massive main showroom. Unlike the other two rooms, this one is immaculate. Blonde wooden floors gleam in the hundreds of pinpoint lights above the displays. Pottery sits on various sized pedestals with sparkling glass domes covering the pieces. Designs range from intricately painted tea cups to modern feeling platters with only the slightest hint of a green stripe around the edge. All are dipped in the signature glaze, a creamy white with just the faintest tinge of green.

"Wow," Ruby says.

Wow, is right. For a moment, wonder replaces fear. Biddy wishes Megan had seen this. It is one of the most beautiful showrooms in the world, and Biddy would know, having visited most of them. It might've changed Megan's opinion of Pooka. Whoever created Aisling Pottery wasn't just a businessperson. They were an artist.

Biddy has to force her eyes away from the beauty to continue the search. She promises herself she will return to give the showroom the time and appreciation it deserves. But now, she wanders to a hallway off to their right. She peers down it.

"This looks like the way to the offices," she says.

With Biddy in the lead, the group follows down the dark hallway. Back here, there are no longer security lights, so Biddy fishes her cell phone out of her bag and switches on the flashlight. Directly ahead are steep old stone stairs leading to the second floor. To her right is a closed wooden door. It is fancier and smaller than the commercial metal doors they passed through previously, and Biddy wonders if this might not be Finn's office door. She twists the knob, and it opens.

Inside was once likely an elegant study. It has a fireplace against one wall, a deep red Oriental rug draping the floor, and a large antique desk in the center. Paneled walls surround the space in a dark mahogany. Biddy would say that it is beautiful. However, gaudy, bright modern art now covers the walls. A poorly painted portrait of Finn hangs above the desk. Staring at it, Biddy finds it hard to believe that people would think that someone so gauche as Finn could create something as beautiful as Aisling Pottery. Little could she know her niece had the same thought when she met the man. Biddy walks to the desk and tries a drawer. It is unlocked.

"Someone should stay here and see if they can find any financial and sales records while we search the other rooms."

"I know my way around a spreadsheet," Sheila says. "I was halfway through an accounting degree when I shifted my focus."

Nothing is surprising Biddy these days.

"Alright," Biddy says. "You stay and the rest of us will head upstairs."

Sheila sits behind the desk and opens a drawer to get started.

Biddy leaves her and Ruby and Amelia follow. The stairs are steep and slick as they climb, and Biddy slows her pace while clutching the bannister tightly. She notes Ruby do the same. Their agility is not what it once had been. Biddy's flashlight casts a narrow beam of light on each step as they wobble their way up. Finally, the staircase turns sharply to the right and they mount the last six steps. Biddy shines her light around the space. The room extends the entire length of the building and appears to be nothing more than a storage space for unneeded things. Pottery is stacked along the floor and covered in a thick layer of soot. Cobwebs extend from the pottery piles to the walls. The room has a thick haze of dust to it and smells of chalk and mold. It takes no time at all before Ruby is sneezing. It echoes loudly.

"Well," Biddy says. "This looks to be the right vintage. Let's spread out and see what we find. We are looking for anything with Eileen's name on it, or at least more pieces with the initials as the signature."

Ruby and Amelia pull out their phones, turn on the flashlight feature, and their three beams light a narrow space along the two sides and far back of the space. The pottery is so thickly coated with dust that it all appears brown. There is no way to see designs or artist signatures without rubbing the piece clean. Biddy moves to one end of the far wall and methodically wipes a piece. Seeing nothing of note, she sets it down and moves to the next piece to her right.

While she does this, she watches her best friend take a different approach. Ruby stands in the middle of the room, closes her eyes, spins slowly around, comes to a stop, opens her eyes and points her flashlight in the direction she is facing. Almost directly in the center of her beam of light, a pitcher gleams as if sparkling amid the dust.

"That's where I'm starting," she says.

Biddy shakes her head but says nothing. This approach is hardly the most thorough, but there is too much here to check, anyway. Why not let Ruby have her fun?

Ruby walks over to the pitcher in her beam of light, squats down and holds it up. There is a thin coat of dust over most of the piece, but somehow it has fared better, as Biddy can see the shine from where she is working. Ruby uses the sleeve of her sweater to wipe at it. Then she stands up and rubs at the rest of the stacks surrounding it.

"Uh, Biddy," she says, as she sets the last piece down. "You need to see this."

Biddy walks over. Amelia joins them as well. Biddy takes the pitcher Ruby holds out to her.

"I don't think those were initials on Maude's pottery chip," Ruby says. "They're just a piece of scrollwork. The pattern is on a bunch of these. It looks nothing like initials when you see the whole thing. It's just decorative loops."

Biddy stares at the pitcher. It has the traditional creamy glaze tinted with green and, around the edge, is scroll work just like the chip Maude had shown them. Biddy sets the pitcher down and looks at the rest of the pottery surrounding her. It all has the same scroll pattern. Maude had lied to them. That was why she couldn't meet her eyes at the meeting this afternoon when they discussed the chip of pottery.

"I haven't seen a signature on any of the pieces," Amelia says. "They are all just stamped with the Aisling Pottery insignia on the bottom."

"Same with mine," Biddy says. She wants to sit down and cry. She just convinced a bunch of women to break and enter for no reason.

"Maybe Sheila has had more luck," Ruby says, always the optimist.

Biddy is pretty sure that none of them believe that. However, she can feel both Ruby and Amelia's eyes on her. Poor Amelia, who had risked so much to be here.

"I think you're right," Biddy says. "Let's check with Sheila."

"Should we check the rest of the space first?" Ruby says. "There are crates stacked really high against the back wall."

Biddy looks over at them. They look cleaner and newer than the rest of the space's contents. What they are doing up here is a mystery. She thought all the shipping crates were down in the shipping room.

She shrugs. "I don't think so. Those look like they were packed recently. Eileen wouldn't have had any part in that."

"Um, Biddy."

Biddy turns to see Amelia looking at the door through which they entered. Directly above it is a blue light.

"What's that?" Amelia asks.

All three move closer. The blue light is high above the door, which explains why none had seen it when they entered. As they crane their necks up to see it, it looks to be attached to a black box. Something glints in their flashlight directly to the left of the light.

"That's a security camera." Amelia's eyes grow wide. "We need to go. Right now."

"I thought Lulu told you there weren't any security cameras," Biddy says.

"She did. And there weren't any in the shop portion of the building. But apparently there are up here."

Amelia flies through the door and down the stairs. Ruby

scrambles after her. Biddy stares up at the camera and then slowly brings up the rear.

Why would that be? Biddy wonders. Why have cameras in an old storeroom and not the store? Nevertheless, this is clearly a thought to be had later. From the safety of her own home.

By the time Ruby and Biddy make it to the bottom of the staircase, Amelia has already entered the office and Amelia and Shelia's voices echo towards them. Biddy and Ruby hurry down the hall and into the office. Sheila has turned on the desk lamp, some awful thing that looks like a leg with a lampshade on top. On top of the desk now are piles of papers boasting numbers neatly aligned between ruled edges. Sheila looks at them when they walk in.

"I found sales records. None of them match the names Amelia found tucked in Eileen's mattress."

This comes as no surprise to Biddy. The others look crestfallen and she feels a little bad for not telling them sooner. Perhaps Megan had been right. She has led a bunch of trusting people on a folly.

"I found another camera." Amelia points to the corner above a bookshelf.

Again, Biddy wonders, why? This room has nothing of value in it.

"I did find something weird though," Sheila says, still seated at the desk, pointing at a spreadsheet, and clearly dealing with the risk of arrest better than the others. "These numbers don't add up. Sales don't match the reported revenue."

"Sheila! Who cares? The police could be coming!" Amelia shouts.

"This is financial fraud," Sheila says. "But why inflate

revenue if you aren't a public company? You would have to pay more in taxes."

"Leave the papers and let's go," Biddy says grimly. She is not the IRS, and this is a problem for them. She needs to get her group safely out of here.

Sheila shrugs, but pauses long enough to take a few pictures of the pages with her camera. Then she stands up, flicks off the desk light, and all three crowd after Biddy in the hallway. They re-enter the large showroom and veer to the left to get to the door leading to the manufacturing and packaging side of the business. Biddy is just twisting the handle, with the others pushing behind her, when the large front door at the far end of the room flies open. In stream four officers with a flashlight. The beam scans the space and falls on them.

"Hands up!" shouts the officer in front.

20

Megan

Dinner is more lovely than Megan could have ever imagined. Brady found some remote farmhouse in the middle of the countryside that converted into a restaurant. Despite its distant location, cars flood into the large parking lot surrounding the old whitewashed home.

"Where are all these cars coming from?" Megan asks as Brady meets her at her car's door.

He smiles. "Just because farmland is spread out, doesn't mean quite a few people don't live here and enjoy nice things. Agriculture provides over 10% of US employment. Lots of people call this home."

Megan feels slightly chastised as they climb the steps to the porch and then enter through a screened door. Again, she's reminded of her mother's pride in her town. Maybe coming from a farm isn't the worst thing in the world.

The rooms inside flicker in candlelight and people murmur happily at each of the tables. While not dressed in Boston society clothes, the crowd is in their Sunday best and looks perfectly presentable, if not elegant. The owner has kept the layout of the original house. Diners sit in spaces that were clearly once the living room, dining room, and long enclosed porch. It is a cozy change from the open floorplan favored ad nauseum in cities.

Once they settle at their window table in the porch room and take a first sip of a red wine, which is startling good, Megan looks into Brady's eyes glowing in the candlelight. Maybe, just maybe, it is he, not she, who is a Pooka. The shape of her opinion of him has shifted more than she ever could have imagined. She relaxes back in her chair, admires the black and white tiled room with its window-lined walls and potted palms in the corners, and smiles at him.

"Now tell me how you decided to build a farming cooperative in Pooka."

"That requires a story," he says. "But you don't seem to like stories. You roll your eyes at them."

Nope, he is still strange. But interesting.

"I'm willing to try," she says.

"Alright then." He takes another sip and sets his glass down. "The reason, I know so much about pooka is that I was raised by one."

He is right. She is going to find this hard to believe.

"Once upon a time—I always say that. Don't you think all the best stories start that way?"

Again, no. But she nods anyway.

He beams at her. "There was a family living high in the hills of Dubois County."

Megan manages not to laugh when he pronounces it Du-Boy-Zee.

"It was a beautiful, remote place to raise a family. The father was a farmer who grew just enough crops to support his family.

But—and this may surprise you—he was also a great historian. He loved his Irish roots and thought of himself as a custodian of the land. He raised his son to see himself as the same."

Once she tunes out the obvious embellishments, Megan realizes that this isn't completely a fairytale. She feels herself drawn in as she sips in silence.

"Now, possessing a deep respect for Irish mythology, the father knew he needed to nurture a relationship with the other inhabitants. So, when he came across a scrawny ancient man sitting on a bench, his arm resting on his cane in front of him, he stopped and sat beside him, even though he was very busy. The two sat on that bench for over an hour, staring at the farmland, never once speaking. The father was struck by the amber color of the old man's eyes." Brady breaks from the story and smiles at Megan. "They were the same color as your own."

Megan smiles back and tries not to roll her amber eyes.

"Eventually, the old man stood up, thanked the father for his time, and wandered off into the woods. A few weeks later, while passing the same spot, the father came across the same old man. They sat on the bench and this time they spoke. Over time, a friendship developed. The father discovered that the old man was a playful man. Sometimes, instead of seeing the man, there was a huge pile of carrots that sent his horse into a frenzied run that nearly toppled him right off. Sometimes he thought he saw the old man, but when the father sat beside him, he found it to be a scarecrow. And sometimes it actually was the old man and they talked and talked. The old man gave him good advice about his crops and upcoming weather threats. Then one day, the old man looked at the father gravely.

'It is time for you to take your family and leave,' he said.

The father was shocked. He loved this land and believed the old man felt the same.

'I will not,' he said.

The old man shook his head. 'The land has been poisoned. It is not safe.'

'I will not leave my land,' the father said.

The old man stood up and looked down at him. 'I admire your commitment, but this is not a fight you will win.' Then he walked off.

A few weeks later, the farmer's wife fell ill. A few weeks after that, he did as well. As he lay dying in bed, he regretted not taking the old man's advice, not for himself but for the sake of his child. That night, a large wolfhound came into the child's room, picked him up and put him on his back. On his way out of the house, the wolfhound paused by the father's door. The father looked at him first in surprise and then in gratitude. He nodded to the wolfhound, who bowed in return. The wolfhound carried the little boy all the way to Evansville, where nuns cared for him. The boy never forgot the wolfhound since he was so struck by its amber eyes. Nor did he forget the animal carrying him past a large truck that had overturned and oozed sewage into the earth, near to their home."

Megan puts her drink down. She is sure her face has turned white. "Is that true?" she asks quietly. "Is that what happened to your family?"

Brady looks deep into her eyes. "Does it matter? It's true for far too many families living in rural towns, forgotten by the rest of America. It's always important not only to understand the history of one person but the context of the larger environment."

Brady takes a sip of his wine, sets it down and smiles, breaking the moment. "Now, tell me about you. You looked troubled when I met you earlier."

Megan thinks of Daniel's message. Of the man waiting for her in Boston. But it suddenly, somehow, feels smaller than this. That man is less impressive than this savior of farms before her. She has been foolish. Maybe fairytale love is achievable.

"Did you ever think you didn't deserve something? That you weren't worthy or capable of having the very best?"

Just then, Megan's cellphone rings.

It rings twice, and Megan ignores it, hoping it will stop.

"You should answer that," Brady says.

It rings a third time. Megan glances at it and then turns off the ringer. "It's just my mom. It can wait."

He raises his eyebrows. "Believe me, if I had a chance to answer a call from my mom, I'd take it without hesitation."

Megan doesn't want this moment to be interrupted by the real world. However, Daniel's words shame her. She's been dismissive of her mother. Pooka really isn't so bad, after all.

She accepts her mother's call, listens, and quickly realizes that no, in fact, she'd been absolutely right to doubt her mother's sanity. And the bad influence of her so-called new friends. And that happy endings were possible. She hangs up the phone and stands to leave.

"I'm sorry, Daniel, but I need to leave," she says. "Apparently, I need to go bail my mother out of jail."

"Megan." Brady grabs her arm before she turns to go. She looks back at him. "Sometimes we all do the wrong thing for the right reason. Try not to be too hard on your mother. Or yourself."

21

Biddy

Biddy waits alongside Amelia, Sheila, and Ruby on a long bench in a large holding cell at the back of the police station. The room is cold and stark with its blue cinderblock walls, but is thankfully devoid of other occupants. They sit in silence, engrossed in their own thoughts, listening to the murmur of voices in the station's front. Eventually, Megan walks through a door, looks at them through the bars, and leaves without saying a word, presumably to return to the front desk to fill out the paperwork to get them out. Once her daughter finishes whatever process is involved in this, a bored-looking officer unlocks the door and leads them to Megan, who is standing in the entryway waiting. They take plastic bags with their belongings from the desk clerk and then face Megan. Megan again says nothing, turns on her heel, and leads the way to the car. Biddy watches as Sheila saunters calmly after Megan. Ruby pauses to take a selfie with the officer in charge and then follows. Amelia meekly trails behind her. In the car, Biddy opens her mouth.

"Not a word," Megan says. "I don't want to make a scene in

the middle of town. I have some pride left."

Biddy wonders how her daughter's evening went. She worries Megan doesn't have much of a social life. But Biddy also knows it probably hadn't ended well since her daughter had to come get her and the others. They drive home in silence.

Biddy's house is dark. Only a lamp in the living room provides a faint glow through the window, lighting a few of the smooth stones of the wall. Megan switches off the ignition, but everyone stays seated in the car as if confused by what comes next. Even Megan appears a little flummoxed. What does one do after an arrest?

Biddy's cell phone notifies her she has a text. She pulls it out of the plastic bag she is holding and stares at it. It's from Muffy.

"My car is at the pub," Amelia finally says.

"So's mine," Sheila says.

"Why didn't you say anything?" Megan's voice is angry, and she makes no move to reverse the car and drive them back to town.

"You told us not to speak," Sheila says.

"Maybe we can call an Uber?" Ruby says. "Biddy, can we wait inside?"

Biddy nods, barely registering the conversation.

They all climb out and walk to the front door. Biddy opens it, still reeling from the text message she just received, flips on the lights, and leads them into the living room. In front of them is a blown-up photo of the pottery factory taped to the wall with rooms marked in bright red X's. They all stare at it.

"What were you thinking?" Megan shouts.

So much for silence.

"I'm defending a woman no one else cares about," Biddy shouts back.

"For good reason," Megan shouts in return.

Everyone flinches at how horrible this truth sounds.

"We should wait outside," Ruby says quietly.

"No." Biddy whips around to face Ruby. "No one is going anywhere. Sit down. My daughter owes you an apology for being rude."

Without another word, Ruby, Sheila, and Amelia sit, all three lined up like guilty children, on the couch, looking like they'd rather be anywhere but here.

"I'm not apologizing to them. You can't keep living like this," Megan says more calmly, not taking her eyes off her mother. "You need to return to Boston with me."

Biddy blows out a slow stream of air to calm herself. "You don't respect me at all, do you? When Charles got sued for bringing that ancient bowl back from the Middle East for the Smithsonian, I don't remember you getting this upset."

"That was different," Megan says. "That was an antiquity that should be shared with the world."

"What was different," Biddy says, "was that he took something worth millions of dollars against the will of the original owners. We took nothing and want to help the original owner. To share an achievement with the world."

Biddy has a bigger bone to pick with Megan than this, but can't find the words yet.

"Mom." Megan looks like she is fighting the urge to shake her. "Eileen was crazy. Even the doctors agree."

"Megan," Biddy looks at her through sad eyes. "You've lost all hope in the world. You aren't changing it. You are settling. You are acting like a snob. You are just like your father."

Megan's eyes widen. "Since when is it a bad thing to be like my father? And I'm not a snob!"

"Okay, then I'm not a prostitute," Sheila says.

"Of course, you're not a prostitute." Ruby says and pats her leg. "Why would anyone ever think that?"

Sheila looks at Ruby. "You really are the nicest person I've ever met."

Biddy keeps her eyes on her daughter. "Daniel cheated on you and you are considering staying with him?" This was what was in Muffy's text.

"No way!" Sheila gasps. "Even you can do better than that."

Biddy keeps her eyes on her daughter. She had hoped Muffy was wrong. That this was just some sort of cruel rumor. But she sees in her daughter's eyes she is right. Her heart sinks. She can barely find the energy to say her next words. "Your father cheated on me. I never want you to think this is okay or normal. That world isn't worth it."

"Biddy," Ruby says, her voice soft. "Maybe this isn't the time or the place—"

"This is exactly what I'm talking about," Megan says, not looking the least bit penitent.

Biddy can't believe it. Her daughter is defending her decision.

Megan's eyes are wide. "You're out of touch with reality. People cheat. It's unpleasant, but it happens. It isn't the end of the world."

"How can you say that?" Biddy's stomach tightens in a knot. "You deserve better." Biddy can't believe she has to give her daughter this lecture.

Megan averts her eyes. "I'm just being a realist."

With some hope, Biddy sees Megan doesn't really mean this.

The only problem is that her daughter wants to believe it.

"And this isn't about me or dad, right now," Megan continues, now meeting Biddy's eyes. "You were arrested. You had no business pursuing this investigation. Degrees and institutions mean something. You should have left this to the authorities."

"Life experiences also mean something. How many founders of tech companies don't have a college degree?"

Megan sputters. "That's different."

"How?"

Megan walks over to stand in front Amelia, Sheila, and Ruby. "Let's go over the evidence." She holds up a finger. "First, the initials."

"They were actually part of a scroll pattern," Ruby mumbles, "not initials."

"Second, the list of names," Megan says.

"Maybe those sales were so early, they weren't recorded in the pottery's records?" Amelia looks hopeful.

"They weren't sales," Biddy says quietly. "Eileen got caught blackmailing people in high school to make money. That's what the list was."

"That's weird," Sheila says. "Declan's name was on the list. Why would she blackmail her own brother?"

"Because that clearly is the type of person Eileen was," Megan says.

"Just stop this," Biddy walks between Megan and the group. "It's like you take joy in making them feel bad. I know how that feels and wouldn't wish it on anyone."

"How would you possibly know how that feels?" Megan asks. "You were beloved in Boston. People worshipped you."

"Both you and Charles made me feel small every minute

of my life. He cheated on me, made me the laughingstock of Boston. Neither of you considered me your equal. Is it so hard to understand why I would want to live someplace that valued me? And just so you know, when I was pregnant, I put my education on hold. I'd been accepted to Radcliffe. You came along, so I never went."

"You got into Radcliffe?" Megan says.

"Kids will do that to one's ambitions," Amelia says, nodding her head.

Biddy's eyes stay on Megan. "I didn't want you to think you were unwanted because that would be wrong. You are the best thing in my life. But I also want you to know that I'm not stupid. And I'm sad that knowing I was accepted into some ridiculously posh school is what will convince you."

"I know you're not stupid." Megan sighs. "But I don't think you know how this world works. You've been sheltered. I think you should come and live with me. You can take those classes at Harvard. You can join the historical society there. You can do anything you want. You've made your point. But this..." Megan gestures to the three women sitting on the couch. "...is stupid. Eileen Delancy did not found a multi-national company. Every piece of evidence you found backs me up. It's time to let this go."

This last bit, Megan mumbles. Biddy's heart sinks. No matter what her daughter says...no matter how wrong she is about Biddy being sheltered...Megan needs her. And a mother always puts her daughter first. Always. Even ahead of Eileen.

"Maybe we should let it go," Ruby whispers.

The others nod.

The ring of Megan's cellphone pierces the quiet. She quickly pulls it out to turn it off.

"Who is it?" Biddy asks.

"It's a Harvard number. I'll take it later."

Biddy shakes her head. "You need to take it now. If your career and old life is this important to you, then prioritize it."

Megan shakes her head and punches the accept button. She says hello and then listens intently.

Biddy looks around the room while Megan speaks. Amelia looks like she wants to seep into the fabric of the couch and never be noticed again. Ruby stares at Biddy with such concern it breaks her heart. Sheila tries to cheer them all up with talk about a lawyer who she knows who would be way more helpful than Megan.

"You're sure?" Megan asks, speaking into the phone.

She listens to the response, disconnects the call and turns to look back at the group. She looks shaken. Confused.

"That wasn't about my job." Megan says.

"Well, I'm sure it was still more important to you than all of this," Biddy says.

"It was important." Megan looks like she's still trying to wrap her head around the conversation. "Because it was about all of this. That was the specialist I know in the science department. Ruby had insisted he run Eileen's bloodwork, and he just did. He's been trying to call me for weeks, but I haven't kept up with my messages. It turns out Eileen had the blood markers for dementia. "

This again, Biddy thinks. "Yes, Megan. You've made your point. Eileen had dementia."

Megan takes a deep breath. She oddly can't even meet her mother's eyes now. "But he found something else. Eileen didn't die of natural causes. You were right to think something was wrong. She was murdered."

22

Maude

The Women's Club called a special meeting on Sunday so they could fill me in on their pottery investigation. As I walk up the path to Biddy's front door, I see the group sitting in the living room, talking animatedly. When I ring the doorbell, they immediately stop talking and all the heads turn to see me standing on the stoop. I give a smile and a friendly wave through the window, but they just stare back. That's the first sense I get that something's wrong. Unlike the rest of Pooka, they're usually friendly to me.

Biddy opens the door. She looks her proper self in a green navy trimmed sweater and navy knit slacks. However, she steps forward and hugs me. This, too, is out of the ordinary. Biddy is not the touchy feely type. It is then that I know she failed to find evidence supporting my mother's claims and is trying to be nice about it. When she lets me go, she says "come in" and gestures for me to have a seat in the living room. I apologize to everyone for being late. But no one says a word. They all just stare at me.

"Maude," Biddy says.

She says my name all drawn out. Like my mom once did when she had to tell me we were getting evicted. My heart drops in my stomach.

"As you know, we visited the pottery last night."

All their eyes look so sad staring at me. I just know they're going to tell me that there was no evidence and they are quitting. I've failed my mother.

"To make a long story short," Biddy continues, "I need to tell you something upsetting."

"She didn't found the pottery," I say. I couldn't even do this right for my mom. My mother devoted her entire life to me and I couldn't even get her the recognition she deserves.

"No, it's not that," Biddy says.

It isn't that?

"Maude."

I'm very confused.

Biddy reaches over and takes my hand. Her sleeve is touching the top of the turkey roll on the coffee table and I want to tell her she is going to ruin her pretty sweater.

"Your mother was murdered."

Biddy's grip tightens on my hand. I focus on that like it's an anchor. It is cool and firm. Protective. The words register.

Murdered? There has to be a mistake. I look into her eyes, but they hold no doubt. They do not waver. I fall back into my chair.

"She was poisoned." Biddy is still staring at me and speaking in her calm voice. Somehow it pierces the roiling storm in my head. "Megan and Ruby had a doctor look at her blood tests. They found markers for dementia, but they also found lethal levels of lead."

"Like from pencils?" I can barely follow Biddy's words. All

I can hear is Biddy's voice saying your mother was murdered. Over and over again.

"No." This time it's Megan who speaks. She, too, is looking at me kindly, which is so unusual, it's terrifying. "Graphite is in pencils, not lead. Lead was used in paint. However, the levels found in your mother's bloodstream are much higher than anything she would have gotten from normal product exposure. Someone gave it to her to kill her."

The whole thing about graphite, lead, pencils, and paint is lost on me, but one point drives its way home. My poor mother was being hurt, and I was so stupid I didn't know. I didn't save her.

"There wasn't anything you could have done." This comes from Amelia. It's like she can read my mind. "Dr. Enniskillin hadn't even caught it. It was only because of your persistence that we did. You did well by her."

I know she's trying to be nice, but this isn't true. I still feel guilt squeezing my heart.

"We're going to figure out who did this," Sheila says. "And we are going to prove she was telling the truth all along."

It's sweet of her to say, but I don't really care anymore. I wish I had never heard about the stupid pottery. I wish my mom never brought it up. Then she'd be alive and happy and we could be nobodies in peace. I just want my mom.

"What did the police say?" I ask. "Do they have any leads?"

Everyone looks at everyone else. No one looks at me. It doesn't take me long to piece together why. The police don't care. I should have known that.

"Since the police explained they have their hands full with some drug smuggling investigation, we thought we might give them a little help," Biddy says. "Of course, we'll share everything we learn with them."

She means that my mother isn't important enough for the police to make a priority. This is below even my lowest expectations. This is their job. These women mean well, but I highly doubt that they can solve a murder. No one is ever going to know who did this to her. And no one cares. Biddy's face goes foggy as tears form in my eyes.

Biddy frowns. "I know we don't look like much, but we will help you. You have my word. We've already done more than they have."

This is true. But sad. So very sad. I suddenly want to go home. Curl up in a ball and give up. I tried so hard, but the truth is there is no justice for people like me and my mom. People in power don't care about people like us.

"Maude, look at me."

I look into Biddy's eyes. They're still blurry, given my tears, but they are also confident and steady. They glint with a slight slash of gold.

"I will help you," she says.

The way she says it makes Biddy look like an actress in a movie. Then, I remember something important. There are movies about nobodies who win against the somebodies. My mother and I loved those. Like Erin Brockovich, a secretary who took on a power company for contaminating a town. Or that lady on QVC who invented a mop, made millions and then helped others to do the same. Biddy has that same look about her as Erin Brokovich and the QVC lady, but is even better dressed.

I suddenly believe Biddy is capable of what she promises. When God parted the Red Sea for Moses to cross, he then slammed it shut on the evil Egyptians and they all drowned in a painful, agonizing death. In my heart of hearts, I know Biddy could do something like that. So, maybe people like me don't get the police. But, the really lucky ones get a Biddy. My tears subside and I hiccup. I nod at her.

"Alright then," Biddy pats my knee and sits back in her chair. She wipes the turkey roll off her sleeve with a napkin, not the least bit upset. Like I'm more important to her than her expensive sweater. Then she looks at the rest of the group. "I think we need to put the pottery ownership project on hold and instead focus on Eileen's murder. The two problems are probably the same. It's likely that she was murdered because she was claiming ownership of the pottery. Find the murderer, find the truth about her pottery contributions. Does anyone disagree?"

Everyone shakes their heads and I notice no one is doing anything other than paying attention. Neither Sheila's timesheet nor Megan's cellphone are in sight. Instead, notebooks are in laps, pens poised above them, and all eyes glued on Biddy. My hope increases.

Biddy looks to Amelia. "Instead of taking meeting minutes today, why don't you put together a murder board for us? I checked out a book on detective procedures from the library. This is the recommended way forward."

Biddy gets up and walks over to the built-in cabinets next to the fireplace. Leaning against them is a large rectangular paper bag and what looks to be a folded easel. She sets it up in front of the fireplace. She then pulls out a large sheet of white cardboard and sets it on top of the easel. Finally, she turns the bag upside down and a black magic marker falls out. She hands this to Amelia before sitting back down on the couch.

"Subdivide the board into four columns. One is for suspects.

The next three are for motive, means, and opportunity."

Amelia stands up and does as Biddy says.

"Now," Biddy says. "We just have to fill in the columns. Does anyone have any suggestions?"

"I think it's Finn," Ruby says. "He had the most to gain by pushing Eileen out of the business."

The others nod their agreement. Personally, he'd be the one I'd pick too.

"Astute observation," Biddy says. "Amelia, let's write that down."

Once Amelia finishes writing, Biddy looks at the group again. "Who else?"

"Declan should be up there," Amelia says. "I know he's your brother, Biddy. But he resented his sister. She embarrassed him, and according to what Sheila found, she was blackmailing him. He strikes me as someone who could have a violent temper."

Biddy doesn't look happy about this. "I don't think he could kill anyone."

"Biddy," Ruby says quietly. "When Eileen begged him for money, he punched her in the face and said he'd already spent far more on her than he should have. That's why she never spoke to him again."

Biddy's face goes white. No one says anything. Amelia writes his name.

Biddy looks away from the board. "Who else?"

"What about Dr. Enniskillin?" Ruby asks. "As a doctor, he should have done more for Eileen."

"He's a doctor," Megan says. "He wouldn't hurt someone."

She says this like people with lots of degrees don't do bad things. Clearly, Megan hasn't been out and about in the world much.

"Well, I'd avoid him, if I were you, doctor or not," Sheila says. "I happen to know him professionally and he is one son of a—"

"Bad seed," Biddy supplies, jerking her head in my direction.

Sheila squints at Biddy, glances at me, and then shrugs. "Right. Son of a bad seed. Anyway, I won't work with him anymore. He's on my blue balled list."

"Isn't it supposed to be a black balled list?" Ruby asks.

"It's kind of a play on words—"

"Let's try to stay focused here," Biddy says quickly. "Amelia, write him down."

Sheila nods, happy with her win, and settles back in her chair.

"Anyone else?"

Everyone is silent. I can't think of anyone else either. Although, I'm sure it's Finn. It has to be Finn.

"Very well," Biddy says. "These are our three suspects. Should we pair up again and each take the one we know best?"

Everyone nods their agreement and gathers their things to leave. I sit and watch. I don't really have things to gather, but I can't even gather the energy necessary to move. What am I supposed to do now? Go make dinner after hearing my mother was murdered? Everyone seems to notice me sitting there. And they all freeze and fall silent.

"Maude, dear," Biddy says. She comes over and squats in front of me. Given the noise her knees make, this must be really painful to her. "Megan and I are just about to start a roast."

That must be nice for them. I wish I could have a roast with my mom. I wish I could have a hot dog with my mom.

"Why don't you stay for Sunday dinner?" Biddy says.

"With you?"

I didn't see that coming. I look at Megan, and she gives me a little smile. It looks like it might hurt her face, but it's there. And so I nod, very grateful for the thought. The two of them head to the kitchen to start on dinner and the others walk out the front door to their cars.

Alone, I stare at the board. I look at the suspects. There is no doubt in my mind. It has to be Finn who did this. Rage replaces shock and an emotion I never thought I'd feel as a good Christian takes hold. I want to kill Finn. If he killed my mother, he deserves the same to happen to him.

I quickly realize Biddy would be so disappointed in me if I did that. And she's been so kind. I take a breath and decide I'll give Biddy a chance to do her thing. But, if that doesn't work, I swear to my mother, right here and now, I'll get my revenge. I'd kill Finn. I'm just that mad.

23

Megan

After Maude leaves that evening, Megan forces herself to rejoin her mother in the kitchen and sits at the table. The time has come for her to be honest with her mother. And herself.

Her mother sets a cup of coffee in front of Megan and then slides into a chair across from her, taking a sip from her own cup. The kitchen is dim, lit only by the undermount cabinet lights and the candle dancing on the table's center. It feels like a cocoon, with the rich scent of the evening's roast still in the air. Megan rubs her fingers over the table's scarred wood surface as she studies its texture. She feels her mother's eyes on her.

"I'm sorry, Mom."

"It's not me you owe an apology." Biddy's voice is surprisingly calm.

"I know." Megan looks up at her. "I spent all my life doing what I thought was the right thing. I studied hard and worked hard. I was so disciplined and focused on success. I thought that was the goal. To be better than everyone else."

"To be good at something doesn't give you the right to make everyone else feel that they aren't special too. And it certainly shouldn't come at the cost of feeling like you should always settle in order to get ahead."

"I know." Megan feels her face redden. "I called Daniel and broke up with him. I'm also sorry Dad cheated on you, too."

Biddy shrugs. "Well, that, at least, is not yours to apologize for."

"Still."

Biddy sighs and relaxes back in her chair. "You aren't your father, Megan, and you never were supposed to be. You need to figure out what you want and who you want to be."

For the first time, Megan looks at her mother and sees a better role model in her. Dressed in her navy slacks and green sweater set, she is the picture of Boston society. Yet she somehow fits just as well here, in this cozy yellow kitchen and with the people who just filled her living room. In fact, she looks happier here. More relaxed.

"Do you really want to be president of the Boston Historical Society?"

Biddy smiles and her eyes flash yellow in the candlelight. "Maybe only to stick it to Muffy Gallagher."

"Mom." Megan smiles too.

"Hey, homemakers get a sweet reputation, but you haven't seen anything until you join a charity board."

Megan doesn't doubt this. After all, it is Mellie, the housewife, who proved to be the biggest threat to her life. Her smile slips. Her old life is over, at least the way she imagined it.

"I don't know what I want," Megan says.

Her mother looks at her the way she did when Megan was

a child. Eyes full of love and hope for her daughter. Megan realizes what a gift this is. To have someone who sticks by you, no matter how awful things are. "Then why don't you stay and take some time to figure it out?"

Megan wishes it were that simple. "I don't think that's going to help."

"Well, it can't hurt, can it?"

The thought is appealing. Megan has never taken the time to consider her life. Her father expected her to follow in his footsteps. He expected her to do well in every subject in school. And he expected her to shine in her career as a professor. But did she enjoy it? She isn't sure. The smallest hint of hope fills her heart. Maybe she can do something entirely different with her life if she wants. Something that makes her happy.

"No. It can't hurt."

"Good." Biddy reaches across the table and squeezes her hand. "Do you want another cup of coffee?"

Megan releases her mother's hand and shakes her head. "No, there is something I need to do. Something that is long overdue."

She texts Mellie that she is welcome to Daniel. That Megan deserves better.

* * *

The next day, feeling refreshed and lighter now that the truth has come out and she has done what she needed to do, Megan stands beside Ruby as they walk into the Pooka Community Health Clinic. Ruby is once again wearing her Murder She Wrote t-shirt and Megan reminds herself that this shouldn't matter. They join the long line snaking to the desk. People of all ages, sizes, and income levels shift from foot to foot while waiting ahead of them.

"We're here to see Dr. Enniskillin," Megan says to the nurse behind the desk once they make their way to the front.

The nurse's exhausted eyes quickly glance up. Her blue scrubs are so wrinkled, she looks like she is at the end of a twelve-hour shift despite it only being nine in the morning. "Any emergency medical condition?"

"No," Megan says.

Ruby groans. "Your mother would've said yes."

Megan shrugs. She is done with lying.

"I appreciate your honesty," the nurse says with a dirty look towards Ruby. "Have a seat. This'll take a few hours."

Megan looks at the crowded waiting area, packed with a smorgasbord of patients on dingy chairs. "Isn't there enough money to get you and the doctor more help?"

She shrugs. "Depends on who you ask. We just got acquired by some medical group, and Dr. Enniskillin is a partner. The group paid $15 million, so you'd think there was money. Plus, we fill pricey prescriptions at a rate most train stations sell tickets. But Dr. Enniskillin just laid off three more people last week. Budget cuts, he said."

"That makes no sense."

"That's how the world goes round. To maximize profit." The nurse nods her head at the long line behind them. "Now, if you don't mind…"

They find two seats together between a five-year-old with a bloody knee and an 80-year-old man who strikes Megan as more lonely than sick. She sighs and grabs an out-of-date magazine from the coffee table to stave off any attempts by the lonely man at conversation.

An hour and a half later, a different nurse in identical blue scrubs shows them back to an exam room. When Dr. Enniskillin walks in, he raises his eyebrows and then glances down at his stack of files, revealing the top of his head, which has a small bald spot surrounded by red hair.

"We don't have a file," Megan says. "We're here to speak about Eileen Delancy."

"Again?" Dr. Enniskillin hesitates and then shuts the door to the hallway, almost catching his white lab coat on the hinge. "I have many living patients who need my help. This is getting ridiculous."

"It certainly is, but I think you'll find what we've learned to be interesting." Megan turns to Ruby, who is trying so hard to contain herself, she is clenching her hands. "Ruby, this was your discovery. You should tell him."

Ruby unclenches her fists and points at the doctor like a cheerleader pointing the way to a touchdown. "We caught you. We did it. You are going down!"

Ruby's smile spreads ear to ear. Meanwhile, Dr. Enniskillin squints at Ruby as if a narrowed view might help him understand.

"Thank you, Ruby," Megan says. She turns to the doctor. "What Ruby has just summarized is that my colleague at Harvard University looked at Eileen's last blood tests. He found high levels of lead in her blood. So high, in fact, that it is likely she died of lead poisoning. We have shared these results with the police."

Dr. Enniskillin's eyes widen. He falls into the swivel chair in front of the desk and pulls out a pair of wire rimmed reading glasses to study the document Megan hands him. He looks back up at them. "I only had the blood work done to study her organ functioning and vitamin levels."

"Well, you may have wanted to spend a little longer on it to make sure that everything else was aligned too," Megan says. "Did you know lead poisoning can also create confusion and paranoia? Just like dementia."

"Where would she have been exposed to so much lead?" he asks.

"That is the question," Megan says. "It would have been really helpful if you had noticed this and asked her that yourself. When she was still alive."

Despite her words, Megan does have a guess about the location of Eileen's exposure. She thinks back to the waste pit at the old Aisling Estate. She hates to consider it, but wonders if Brady didn't get the soil as purified as he thought. Still, Eileen would have had to consume large quantities of the dirt for it to be that toxic. She doesn't think Eileen was so crazy as to eat it.

Dr. Enniskillin takes his glasses off and rubs his eyes before looking at her again. "Ms. Bramley…"

"Dr. Bramley."

He flinches. "Dr. Bramley. I realize that catching this seems obvious to you and your friend sitting in a well-endowed lab in Boston. But look around. I'm completely overrun with patients and have no help. I do the very best I can."

"Burnout is nature's way of telling you, you've been going through the motions your soul has departed," Ruby says.

Both Megan and the doctor glance at her.

"Sam Keen," Ruby says. "He went to Harvard too! I just love quote books."

Megan still can't quite believe that this is the woman who

discovered the scientific evidence proving Eileen's murder.

Megan looks back at Dr. Enniskillin. "If you're so under-funded, why don't you do something about it? I heard you're the owner. Why haven't you hired more people?"

"It's not so simple." The doctor spreads his hands on the desk. "I'm just one person on the board. I have to do as they say. They voted to merge clinics, so many patients drive here from outlying areas. Also, there has been a real emphasis on preventative medicine, so now we are running tests and writing prescriptions for mostly healthy people, in addition to treating the sick. That's where the profit is, but it has overstressed our system."

"And an otherwise healthy woman died as the result of it," Megan says.

"She had dementia," Dr. Enniskillin says.

"Which was not fatal when she died," Megan says.

Dr. Enniskillin looks up at the ceiling and then back at her. "I'm not sure what you want me to do. I can call our attorneys. I'm sure they can reach an acceptable settlement if you sue."

Megan takes the copy of the blood test from him and slips it back into her bag. "I'm not calling attorneys. In answer to your question, I guess I want you to care. And maybe do a better job so this doesn't happen to someone else."

Megan stands up and walks out without another glance back. She can hear Ruby's squeaky sneakers trailing right at her heels. When they get to the parking lot, Megan unlocks the car, but Ruby comes to her side of it and throws her arms around her in a hug.

"You were amazing," Ruby says. "Just like—"

"Please don't say Jessica Fletcher," Megan says.

"I was going to say your mother."

24

Biddy

Biddy is worried about Megan. She tried to put on a calm demeanor for last night's conversation with her daughter, but, in truth, she cannot fathom how unhappy and how much stress her daughter must have been under to even contemplate marrying a man capable of infidelity. She can only hope a little time away from Boston will help her daughter reset her bearings. No matter how old your child is, she is still your baby. But now Megan is in Ruby's safe hands at the medical clinic, and Biddy has other family members to worry about.

Biddy feels Amelia's eyes glued on her. They are sitting in the Broken Egg Cafe, a diner new to the town since Biddy lived here. Amelia is at the long marble breakfast counter, and Biddy sits at a table for two in the back corner with Declan. Both Amelia and Biddy have an untouched BLT with chips in front of them. She knows Amelia's is untouched because the timid woman with a strong moral compass is worried about Biddy…not that Declan would hurt her, but that Biddy might kill him. Biddy can't eat because she is furious at this brother of hers, sitting before her, who always put the farm above the family, leaving Eileen to suffer through life on her own. She had tried to defend her brother to the others…she had even felt sorry for him after her visit to the farm…only to learn that he had punched their sister when Eileen asked for help. Declan has turned out exactly the same as his father. Cold and uncaring.

Biddy would have preferred this conversation alone, so she could shout at him to her heart's content, but Amelia was insistent on accompanying her. This noisy restaurant and distant but visible seating arrangement is their compromise.

Declan apparently experiences no such emotional turbulence and digs into his ham on rye.

"Did you know?" he says, as he is chewing. Biddy sees the hints of yellow mustard and bread in his mouth. "This ham came from the McGuire's farm. The McGuire's almost went under, but that new farmer's cooperative processed the meat for him and now he has a pile of contracts for lunch meat. Who would have ever thought?"

Biddy doesn't care about the McGuires, their farm, or any of the farms of Pooka, for that matter. She cares about her deceased sister and Eileen's struggling daughter. She tries not to stare at his open mouth. "Declan, what really happened between you and Eileen? Did you hit her?"

Declan drops his sandwich and wipes his mouth with a napkin. "This again? I told you to let it go."

"You didn't tell me you hit her."

He has the decency to turn red.

"Well, it doesn't matter." Declan leans forward. "Things were different back then."

The comment, combined with the scent of bacon, further roils her stomach. Biddy cannot fathom all that is broken in this world. What has happened to manners and civility? To an immovable right and wrong. "I don't care how different they were. That doesn't justify such shameful behavior."

Declan gestures to the rest of the restaurant with its shiny yellow wood paneling, white marble tables and counters, and boisterous guests at the mostly packed tables around them. The echoes of conversations bounce off the marble and tile and overwhelm the room.

"I know it doesn't seem like it now, but things got really bad after you left. All the farms were failing, which meant all the shops were failing too. It was a ghost town."

"You've said that before."

"But I don't think you really understand it!" Declan takes a breath to calm himself. "Mr. McCartney shot himself. Families were starving and being turned out of their homes. I was barely hanging on. And in the middle of all that, there's Eileen asking for thousands of dollars. Yes, I got angry. Yes, I punched her. But you know Eileen. She never knew when to quit."

"You don't hit her!"

Declan doesn't even flinch. "Babs…Biddy.. don't judge me! You weren't even here. Look at you. You're all hoity toity and clearly don't know what desperate times are. I did my best for Eileen and the whole family. I tried to save the farm. And, contrary to popular opinion, I even tried to save her from herself. I stayed."

The words punch Biddy's gut worse than the scent of bacon. There is truth in them. Even though her father had banished her, she should have stayed in touch with her siblings.

"You didn't stay to help the family, Declan. You stayed for the farm. The only person you tried to save was yourself. I found her notebook, Declan. Eileen was blackmailing you. What did she have on you?"

Declan barks out a laugh, but his eyes swivel away from Biddy's. That was always his tell. "That was years ago. I don't even remember. Probably that a teenage version of Shanna and me did it under the bleachers at a Friday night game."

That was what Biddy originally thought, too. Just high school antics. Until she went back through the notebook. And saw that new names and dates had been added at the end, using a different pen, and a sharper, more hurried script that comes with age.

Biddy holds her eyes steady on him. "I think she restarted that blackmail line of income after you refused to give her money. New names appear at the end of the book. People who weren't in school with us. Some people I don't know. And your name reappears on the list. This was after high school. It was more recent."

Declan leans toward her and drops his voice so low, Biddy herself can barely hear. "Babs, trust me when I tell you I am not lying. I did everything I could to provide for our family and save our farm. I know what things look like, but I tried to save everyone. You lost any right to judge me the moment you took the easy lane and left. I did my very best for Eileen."

"Well, apparently, it wasn't good enough." Biddy sits back and eats a potato chip. "She was murdered."

"What?"

Declan's face goes white. So white, she's afraid he'll pass out. He falls back in his seat as if her words had physically hit him.

"Are you sure?" he asks.

He looks pleadingly at her, as if begging her to change her

statement.

Biddy takes in his reaction and is relieved to see the truth. Declan did care…and still cares…for Eileen. Whatever his faults, he didn't kill her.

Biddy relaxes a little. "We're sure. She was poisoned. A blood specialist at Harvard studied a sample and found lethal levels of lead."

"Like from pencils?"

Biddy is reminded of Maude. Family is such a strange thing. "No. Like someone gave it to her on purpose."

The two sit in silence staring at each other. It's such a mystery how blood forges bonds. How people who would never have cause to have a relationship otherwise feel such a tie to each other through shared parentage. How, even when you try to walk away, it pulls you back.

Declan puts his hands on the table and pushes himself up.

"I need to go."

He pats at his pocket as if desperately searching for his wallet.

"Declan, I can get it. I can pay."

"Fine."

He stops fussing and stares at her, as if debating what to say.

"You were right," he finally says.

"About what?"

"About how the Delancy name should mean something in this town."

"Declan, I didn't mean you should do anything stupid."

Declan doesn't heed her words and stalks out of the restaurant. Biddy lets him go. However, she notices Amelia slide off her stool at the counter and trail after him.

Around her, the cafe continues to bubble with life and noise.

Three old women sit at a window table playing gin, shouting cards at each other to be heard through age-clogged ears. A group of six…maybe eight…teenagers sit at two-round tables pushed together in the back, shouting at the same volume as the old ladies to be heard over each other's own excited voices. And, in between tables of laughing twosomes and hungry foursomes, sits a table of five middle-aged men, looking like farmers, in soil splattered jeans, flannel shirts and caps, talking quietly. All are strangers to her.

She had never meant to disappear from her family. This community. Declan had said he'd tried his best. But had she tried hers? Who was she to judge Declan and defend the Delancy name? She hadn't used it in years. Her own daughter looked at this as a strange land filled with strange people.

Amelia returns with a jingle through the front door. She swipes the plate with her BLT from her place at the counter and carries it over to Biddy's table. She sits down in Declan's chair and takes a bite. Mayonnaise drips onto her shirt and she brushes at it as an inconsequential annoyance.

"That couldn't have been easy," she says.

"It wasn't." Biddy takes a bite out of her own sandwich and then sets it down. "He didn't murder Eileen. I'm 100% confident this was the first he'd heard of her murder."

Amelia says nothing. She takes a bite out of her pickle while studying the sandwich on her plate. Then she takes a sip of iced tea, sets it down, and looks at Biddy. "I've been helping Liam…that's my oldest…with his science project on ants. Did you know that queen ants aren't actually queens in the definitional sense of the word?"

"How fascinating," Biddy says, even though it isn't.

"They don't have any power over the group. It's a total

misnomer. Their task is to reproduce. But there is no hierarchy. Some unknown consensus makes decisions like whether to fight or when to expand the colony. It's impossible to say who decides what. There is no queen. Or king. No clear leader."

Biddy doesn't understand what brought on this science lecture. She gives it her best guess. "So you're saying it's everyone's fault Eileen died and we all need to live with it?"

"No. I'm saying sometimes good ants get caught up in bad group decisions. Even strong powerful ones."

"Amelia," Biddy says, realizing that dealing with young people is exhausting. She is pretty sure that isn't what the teacher had intended the kids to learn, but catching on to what Amelia wants her to learn. "Tell me what you saw when you followed Declan outside."

Amelia turns her eyes away from her.

"Declan went to see Finn. But he wasn't shouting at him. They were conspiring. They are working together."

25

Megan

Megan is confident the Aisling waste purification site is not behind Eileen's lead poisoning. After listening to Brady's story, she knows he is diligent about waste containment and purification. It is his calling. And Eileen would have had to eat the dirt to get that level of contamination.

That said, Sheila is less convinced of his innocence. She wants the soil she took from the site to be tested for lead. Normally, Megan's network would make this task easy, but Megan is not excited to call her former co-workers for a favor. They already thought she won her professorship because her father ran the department. Now, she looks like a little wronged waif with no idea her own fiance was cheating on her.

But, as her mother told her, she needs to face her consequences. So, with great hesitation, she calls Danny Osterfeld, Harvard's specialist in environmental studies, and that's how she and Sheila come to stand in Biddy's garage, staring at the screen of a portable XRF analyzer. Danny had been kind and hadn't brought up her fiance's infidelity or the cancelation of her wedding. When Danny heard of her project, he sent the analyzer to borrow.

The device looks like a shiny radar gun used by police, but its purpose is to detect lead levels. It is now pointed at the sample of dirt Sheila collected from the Aisling waste management site. It is by far the fanciest thing in the garage. Dust fills the garage and dim lighting and a mildew scent speaks to filthy windows and wooden beams erected over one hundred years ago.

Sheila, as usual, has dressed for the occasion, which appears this time, to call for a hazmat suit. Although, Megan notes, Sheila's hazmat suit has an unusually deep V cut neckline that would seem to inhibit its protective powers. Megan has opted for jeans and a long-sleeve t-shirt.

"Why do you always dress like that?" Megan asks.

Sheila frowns. "You mean appropriate for the situation? A hazmat suit isn't such a bad idea. I've got to be careful around you. You were covered in this dirt."

"Sheila, I'm not radioactive!" Megan hopes this is true. She should ask Danny next time they speak.

"Let's see." Sheila points the gun at Megan and it beeps, sending a small jolt of concern through Megan.

Megan snatches it from her and points it back at the soil sample. The sample sits on a white dish Megan commandeered from the kitchen. This sits on a marred wooden worktable against a wall but under a window, which allows for some light. They both peer at the screen of the analyzer in Megan's hand. Squiggles and numbers fill it as if it is a Magic 8 ball trying to decide on a fortune. But then, they stabilize. Megan looks at the number and compares it to the chart Danny sent along with the loaned device.

"The lead levels are higher than they're supposed to be for decontaminated soil, but not high enough to kill Eileen."

Even though the news is good, this surprises her. Brady had said the soil was completely decontaminated. Megan thinks back to Brady and his story. The little boy orphaned because of pollution. He will be devastated to hear his method isn't working as well as he thinks.

"Well," Sheila says, now apparently feeling safe enough to pull down her paper-like hood, "at least your new boyfriend isn't a murderer. Just a cheat. Or inept."

"He's not my boyfriend, and he's not a cheat. I'm sure Brady doesn't know this soil is still contaminated. I'll tell him so he can fix it."

"I'm sure he'll get right on that," Sheila says with an arch of her well-defined brow.

Sheila is wrong about this. Megan is certain Brady will fix it. However, she also will not waste her time justifying this to Sheila.

"So, if it wasn't spending time at the Aisling site, what killed Eileen?" Megan asks.

"The answer to that, my radioactive friend," Sheila says, taking a finger full of dirt and dabbing it on Megan's nose, "is probably at her house."

Megan realizes she needs new friends.

*   *   *

Megan drives this time. Likely to annoy her, Sheila has scooted as far as she can away from Megan's body, as if Megan's supposed radioactivity is an enormous threat. Sheila rolls down the window, and makes a show of breathing only the fresh air from the window, which causes her fake hazmat suit to crinkle and flap in the wind.

"How is your cousin doing?" Sheila asks, sneaking a quick glance at Megan, but careful not to breathe in any of their shared air before looking back out the window.

"My what?" Megan can barely hear her over the wind.

"Your cousin. You know. Maude."

"Oh." Megan always forgets that Maude is related to her. She thinks of Maude sitting beside her at Sunday night dinner. Besides grace, she barely said a thing all night. "She's sad."

"Ha!" Sheila snorts the words, as she glances over at her again. "You don't know your cousin very well. I don't think Maude does sad. In fact, if I were Maude, I'd be spitting angry. Talk about drawing the short end of the stick. Hey, I just thought of something. Do you think she could have lead poisoning too? I mean, if she and her mom worked together and lived together, wouldn't she also be poisoned?"

Megan's eyes open wide at the thought. How has she not thought of this? She is severely off her game if a prostitute is exhibiting stronger reasoning skills than herself.

"Someone needs to tell her she should get tested," Megan says.

This time Sheila turns her head and her eyes stay on Megan. "Shouldn't that someone be you? You're her family."

"No," Megan says quickly.

Sheila raises her eyebrows.

Megan knows Sheila thinks the reason is that Megan doesn't like Maude. But that isn't it at all. The real reason Megan doesn't want to speak with Maude is because she is ashamed of herself. Maude probably can't stand Megan. And she has every right to feel that way. Megan doubted her all along.

Megan had looked down on her.

"It should be you," Megan says to Sheila. "I don't think she likes me too much."

"Well, avoiding her isn't doing much to change that, is it?" Sheila turns her head back to the window.

When they arrive, Megan and Sheila climb out of the car and survey the house in front of them. The house, although it has a foundation, is really more similar to a trailer—long and rectangular, but without the wheels. A multitude of other homes surround the house, identical in shape and size. Megan guesses that this was the housing used for farm help once upon a time. Grass has mostly given up its effort to carpet this space, with only a few, particularly ambitious tufts scattered between pine needles and empty beer cans.

"Cousin!" Maude shouts from her door. A grin spreads across her normally dour face. "You've come to visit."

Implied in this, is that the girl had never even considered it a possibility that Megan would visit. Megan doesn't know what to say. So she says nothing.

Sheila shoots Megan a dirty look and takes the lead. She bounds up to the door and throws her arms around Maude. Maude's head disappears in Sheila's very large bosom. Megan hopes Maude doesn't get a paper cut on her face from the surrounding fake hazmat fabric.

"We've both come to visit," Sheila says, emphasizing the word 'both.' "Do you mind if we come in?"

Maude holds the door open as Sheila leads the way into the house. She and Megan sit on a couch to their left, and Maude takes a seat across from them. At least the house is clean and tidy, Megan notes, completely unaware that this new found ambition had not been the case only a few short weeks ago.

"Maude," Sheila says, "Megan and I are looking for the source of your mom's lead poisoning. Megan borrowed some tool from Harvard. Could we use it and look around your home?"

"Of course." Maude nods vigorously.

"There's one more thing." Sheila hesitates and Megan feels bad for making her do this. She is sure that delivering bad news is not a well-practiced skill in Sheila's career. But, under all that make-up and the ridiculous costumes, Megan sees a genuine kindness. Faced with this, her shame deepens.

Sheila pats Maude's hand. "Since you spent so much time with your mom and she got sick…We think it might be smart for you to get tested just to make sure you weren't exposed to lead too."

Maude's eyes open wide.

"I'll pay for it," Megan says quickly. "It's just a blood test. You can get it at the clinic."

Megan means the words to be comforting. To allay any fears about the price or the procedure itself. However, she can see in Maude's wide eyes she has done nothing to ease her concerns. And her words earn her another dirty look from Sheila.

"Thank you," Maude whispers.

"But, I'm sure you are fine," Sheila says quickly. "You look healthy as can be. If there were something concerning, I'm sure we'd see it by now."

"Okay," Maude says, now looking a little better. How had Megan not thought to say that?

"On that note," Sheila says. "It's likely that the lead is someplace or in something your mom uses, but you don't. It could be really helpful if you can think about what this is."

Maude's eyes move upward, which Megan takes either as a sign of deep thought or prayer. The rest of her face pinches in on itself, as if whatever she is doing is very difficult. Then Maude looks back at them.

"Mom read books. I was never much of a reader. There are stacks in her room."

Maude stands up and Sheila and Megan take this as a sign to follow her into a tiny back room, about the size of a train sleeper compartment. Books are stacked floor to ceiling, all looking very well read. Megan picks one up from the top of a stack to her right. *The Chemistry of Color.* Shock floods through her veins.

"This is good, Maude. We'll check here," Sheila says. "Anything else?"

Maude thinks again. "Nooo…wait!"

Maude turns and they follow her once again, this time into the kitchen area. Maude opens a top cabinet, reaches in and pulls out a bottle. It's a liquor bottle of some sort, very fancy with intricately cut gold foil surrounding a deep red crested label.

"Where did she get that?" Megan hopes the question doesn't sound rude, but compared to everything else in the place, this is by far and away the most expensive item.

Maude shrugs. "A client. I don't like it. Tastes like cough syrup, if you ask me, but Mom loved it. Had a sip every night."

"Thanks Maude." Sheila puts an arm around the waifish girl and escorts her to the door. "We're going to do a thorough testing of the place, paying special attention to those two places. And while we do that, why don't you go to the clinic and get yourself checked?"

"What about you?" Maude asks her. "If there's something

in here, I don't want you to get sick, too."

Megan's self-worth sinks further as she sees Maude's concern for her.

"Don't you worry," Sheila says, tapping her hazmat costume. "I've got my suit and Megan's already been exposed. If she dies, she would've anyway."

Somehow, Megan feels like she deserves this.

"You don't want my help?" Maude looks at them hopefully.

"Nope," Sheila says. "We want you healthy." She puts her arm back around Maude's shoulders and gives her a little push out the door. "Off you go then."

Megan and Sheila watch her walk towards a covered carport and then head to the car to get the lead detector. No one should have to see their home, a place of safety, searched for threats.

"Poor thing," Sheila says. "The only consolation is that she probably doesn't much care if she is dying or not. That mother was her whole world."

Megan flinches at the thought. Where would she be without her mother? She picks up the XRF device and heads back into the house. She surveys the space. "Books or booze first?"

"Booze," Sheila says. "Given all those books and their subject, we might need the booze for ourselves to get through them."

Megan heads into the kitchen, retrieves the bottle from the cabinet, and twists off the top. She pours a little into a bowl she finds in another cabinet and then points the XRF analyzer at it. This time, it doesn't take long for the machine to settle on a number and it's a big one. Megan doesn't even need to consult her chart.

"Hot damn," Sheila says.

Hot damn is right. How would lead get into booze? And expensive booze at that?

Megan's phone rings. She fishes in her jeans pocket and retrieves it. After greeting the caller, she listens for a minute, and then hangs up. She looks at Sheila. "That was my friend in the chemistry department." After Megan's success with Danny, she made one more call to someone else she knew. "He compared the molecular components in some of the dirt you took from the old Aisling estate to the glaze on a piece of Aisling pottery. It's a match."

"Maude was right," Sheila whispers. "Eileen did invent Aisling Pottery."

Apparently, even Sheila hadn't been fully sure.

"And no one believed her." Sheila shakes her head.

Megan feels sick. Maude kept repeating it and repeating it and no one ever considered she might be right. However, even as a convert, Megan is realistic enough to realize the job isn't done.

"This still isn't enough to prove it beyond a reasonable doubt. Finn can claim he was the one who used dirt from the old Aisling estate to make the glaze. He could say that Eileen watched him and stole his idea."

"Unbelievable," Sheila says. "Eileen spent all her time at that disgusting place and held up handfuls of dirt, calling it gold. We all know Eileen created that glaze. And now she's dead. Boy, if I were her daughter, I'd want to kill that Finn Murphy."

Megan knows this is just a phrase. A common saying. Maude wouldn't actually do that. No one is ever driven to commit murder except murderers, right?

"Sheila," Megan says. "What did you mean before when you said Maude wasn't the type to get sad?"

Sheila shrugs. "She seems the type to get even. An eye for an eye, you know."

Megan frowns. "You don't think she'd try to hurt Finn, do you?"

A crash sounds outside.

"What's that?" Sheila asks.

26

Maude

I wheel my bike out of the carport, and it scrapes against the metal wall as I try to clear the stacks of stuff my mom and I store there. I hope Megan and Sheila don't hear it since I dawdled to listen in on their conversation. As Mama used to say, eavesdropping is the swiftest path to knowledge. And that certainly holds true now. For Megan and Sheila's conversation has changed my mind. I won't be going to the clinic for a blood test. I'm going to kill Finn Murphy, the man who clearly murdered my mother.

I hop on the bike and pedal with speed so Megan and Sheila won't see me. Not that Megan would care much about my destination, but Sheila just might. Evergreen needles poke at me as I brush by, leaving a sticky scented goo on my arms. I pedal as hard as I can through the forest, towards the pottery. I no longer care what time of day it is, or who's going to see me, or even that I'm going to miss cleaning Mrs. McCardle's house and she is one of the few clients who remains.

I reach the road and turn left on Main Street. The neighborhood changes from heavily wooded trailer parks to beautiful rolling farmland, but I keep my eyes straight ahead, glued to the now visible pottery. I shoot through town, cross the tip of the bridge and then swerve onto the little drive on the far side of the pottery that leads to the loading docks. I steer off the narrow drive and into the bordering forest, where I tip my bike over in the leaves. I creep up to the edge of the woods and stare at the building.

The moment I heard Megan say the pottery glaze used dirt from the Aisling estate to get its color, my heart soared. The Women's Club had actually done it. They'd proven my mother right. She is vindicated.

But then I heard Megan say it wasn't enough. And I knew then and there, nothing would ever be enough. It doesn't matter how many nice new friends I have. It doesn't matter that Biddy cares or Megan is someone important. It doesn't even matter how much evidence there is. People like me always lose. I gave Biddy a chance to prove me wrong, but I know what I have to do to get justice.

Now that I'm here, though, I realize I have no plan. I don't know how to kill Finn. Leviticus says "Anyone who injures their neighbor is to be injured in the same manner: fracture for fracture, eye for eye, tooth for tooth." This is pretty clear and, frankly, my mother would love the symmetry of his death for her death. But I don't know where I can get lead, little less how to use it. Is it a liquid? Do I pour it down his mouth? Apparently, forcing him to eat a pencil won't work, which still makes no sense to me. Anyway, it seems like it's just too much work.

I don't have a gun. I have to be honest, I'd probably lose in a knife fight. This is a dilemma. I think and I think. I finally decide on something simple. I'm just going to walk in, catch him unaware, and bash him in the head with something heavy. This I know I can do. I once dropped a soup can on my mom's head by mistake. I'm sure I could do it on purpose, too.

I take a deep breath and emerge on the tiny drive. I decide I should do this in style and enter through the front door, since I don't care if I'm caught. In fact, I have another great idea. I should use a piece of my mom's pottery as the weapon. That at least gets me closer to Leviticus' guidance. I hope Mom made the vases heavy.

I turn to the right to walk up the drive, when—of all the things I didn't expect—Megan comes walking down. It's rare that things surprise me anymore, but this does. She doesn't look angry. Or rushed. She just looks like she's taking a walk. Down a path that leads only to dumpsters.

"What are you doing here?" she asks, even though I'm the one with a reason to be here and she has none.

I hold my head high and use my best formal language. "I'm going to visit Mr. Finn Murphy. What are you doing here?"

"I'm going to stop you from killing Finn Murphy."

Well, that flummoxes me. How did she know?

"Can we talk?" she asks. "Cousin to cousin?"

Now, even in the sunset of my holy crusade, I realize this is probably the nicest thing Megan has ever said to me. Against my will, I feel my face crumple. It's so hard to be strong. I've been trying so very hard. For people like Megan or Joan of Arc, it comes easy. I mean, Megan doesn't even have any feelings—how strong that must make you be. But it shouldn't be this hard for the rest of us. I just want the world to be fair. Not even kind. Just fair. Tears roll down my face.

"I just want justice for my mom," I say. "I miss her."

"I know," she says. "I know."

She looks around as if trying to find a place to talk, but the options are slim. She sees my bike supposedly hidden in the woods and leads me there. In retrospect, it would have helped if my bike wasn't bright yellow. I'd picked it out because it reminded me of the sun. Now, it doesn't. It just looks yellow.

We both sit down on the fallen leaves next to it. The earthy scent of the soil and foliage calms me.

"How did you find me?" I ask her.

Megan smiles. "You were riding your bike, Maude. No matter how fast you pedal, a car is faster. I followed you the whole way. I just took a minute to drop Sheila off in town."

She is smart, like her mother.

She plays with the leaves beneath her hands. Her perfectly polished red nails are beautiful. I look at my red, callused, chafed ones.

"I know I was dismissive when I first met you," she says, keeping her eyes on the leaves.

I'm not exactly sure what she means by this, but if she means rude, cruel, and belittling, I agree.

She lifts her eyes to meet mine. "And I want to say I'm sorry."

This would've been sufficient for me, but she doesn't stop there. She launches into some spiel about the plight of women. Something about gender disparity and patriarchy. I get confused and find my mind drifting back to how to kill Finn Murphy. But I get the idea she's trying to be nice. This can't be easy for her. Maybe that's why she's so bad at it.

"Maude."

I look up at her.

"We are going to get justice for your mom. I promise."

This is laughable. "You can't. Finn's too powerful."

"Finn's too powerful here. But honestly, Maude, no one

outside of Pooka, knows who he is or cares about him at all."

"Yeah, but people outside of Pooka don't know or care about me, either."

Megan smiles, and when she does this, she looks just like Biddy. Their smiles are rather unique. They're not normal, happy smiles. They're actually rather scary. Like when coyotes turn their lips up.

"Then that needs to change," Megan says. "I'll make the world care. I can do that."

I bet she could. Megan is tough. She's like my mother that way. There's only one problem.

"Why would you help me? You hate me."

Megan frowns. "Hate's a rather strong word."

At least she didn't lie and say she likes me. I can respect that. Still, she doesn't leave it at that. "I'd do it, because we are family."

Well. This day is just full of surprises.

She puts her hand on top of mine and wraps her fingers around my palm. I drop the leaves so I can do the same and she squeezes. Her hand feels like butter. I wonder if she thinks mine feels like sandpaper.

"Plus," she continues, "if you kill Finn, you'll make him the victim. You and your mom will be seen as the bad guys. She'll be even more hated."

My heart sinks. This sadly makes sense.

I pull my hand out from under hers, wipe my dripping nose with it, and then stick it back inside her hand. It feels so nice and warm there.

With a sinking feeling, I realize she's right. Killing Finn will not solve my problem. Nothing I can do will put this right.

"The world isn't a very fair place, is it?" I ask.

Megan inclines her head. "No." She says quietly. "It isn't."

And, for the first time, I wonder if Megan might know what loneliness feels like, too.

27

Biddy

Biddy surveys the Pooka Women's Club from the doorway to her living room. The last to arrive, Maude, is making her way to her seat. Megan stands up, hugs Maude, and they sit down next to each other. Hope, for both girls, springs into Biddy's heart.

The murder board is back on its easel next to the fireplace and everyone scrutinizes it, as they talk amongst themselves, sharing information. This, unlike prior gatherings, includes her daughter, who sits on the edge of the couch, leaning forward to be closer to the others in conversation. And also Sheila, who has somehow forgotten to produce her timesheet to account for her hours.

Despite this enthusiasm, Biddy is nervous. She is about to ask them to do something risky and she wonders if the rest of them will think the risk is worth it. At her age, Biddy realizes she has less to lose than the others in this room. She doesn't have to worry about keeping a job, or affording a house, the welfare of dependents, or even public opinion. This isn't true of the others. They have long lives ahead of them and the many responsibilities that come with that.

Biddy walks in and sits on the chair next to the murder board. She calls the meeting to order and everyone pulls out notebooks and pens.

"Let's start with updates on each of our assignments."

Megan looks up from her notebook. "Ruby and I can go first. We went back to the clinic to meet Dr. Enniskillin again. I don't think he's directly involved in the murder or the coverup. It feels like he just didn't care all that much about her. He believes his job is to focus on the profitability of the clinic for his shareholders, not maximizing care for his patients. In a way, that seems a crime in itself, but I don't think it applies to Eileen's murder."

"I agree," Ruby says, nodding. "As Jessica Fletcher says, I may be wrong, but frankly, I doubt it."

Biddy looks around the group. "Any questions or disagreement?"

Each person shakes her head. Amelia draws a line through Dr. Enniskillin's name and writes 'too overworked to notice poison' beneath it.

The next name on the board is Declan. Biddy tries not to cringe. This moment is going to be particularly painful.

Amelia points her marker at Declan's name. "I was assigned to watch Declan's reaction when he received news of Eileen's murder. He genuinely looked surprised and angry. But then I followed him out of the cafe. He went straight over to the Pottery. He seemed friendly with Finn Murphy and the two were discussing some delivery that is supposed to be made tomorrow night. They looked secretive, like they're in cahoots."

Everyone looks at Biddy. As a leader, she knows what she

needs to do.

"Therefore, Amelia and I conclude he should remain a suspect," Biddy says. Her heart feels like it is being wrenched in a fist.

The others say nothing, but their eyes speak volumes. Pity is there, which Biddy hates. So is support, which is better. And one more thing. She sees respect.

"Finn should also remain a suspect," Megan says, looking back at the board. "He has to be involved. Sheila and I discovered Aisling soil is used to make the pottery glaze. All roads seem to lead back to the Pottery."

Amelia underlines Finn's and Declan's names on the murder board and writes the comments beneath the names.

"So that summarizes our progress on suspects and motives," Biddy says. "I believe we also have information on the means."

Sheila looks up from her notebook. "Megan and I borrowed a device from Harvard to check lead levels. We found that there is lead in the Aisling estate soil but not enough to kill Eileen. However, there are extremely high levels of lead in a bottle of expensive booze that Eileen received from a client."

"Which client?" Biddy asks.

"I don't know," Maude says. "She never said."

"Well." Biddy watches as Amelia writes these facts on the board. "It seems to me we need to consider that more than one person committed this crime. Finn has the clearest motive in that he stood to lose the pottery and all its revenue if Eileen's claims proved true. But others might have been involved. We need to know why Declan and Finn are friendly and meeting each other. One is a farmer and the other is a potter, so there are no obvious business connections. Plus, I know my brother, and Finn is not a person he'd be friendly with."

The group nods.

"Then there is whoever gave Eileen the bottle of alcohol. It's not like Eileen had many friends to give her such an expensive gift. And that person likely isn't Finn. She would've never accepted it from him."

The group nods again.

"And, therein, lies our problem," Biddy says. "We still have too many suspects and not enough evidence." She takes a deep breath. "I think we need to investigate further. Based on what Amelia heard, we know there is a meeting tomorrow night and it sounds like they are trying to keep it a secret. I think we need to be there to see who shows up and what goes on."

Biddy clenches her folded hands, waiting to see if the others are game. If they are willing to take this risk.

"I agree," Amelia says.

Biddy flinches in surprise and sees the rest of the group widen their eyes as they look at Amelia. Of all the people in the room, Amelia seemed to be the least likely to lead the charge towards danger.

"This is incredibly risky," Biddy warns. "These people have a willingness to murder. And a capability to cover it up. "

"I'm still in," Amelia says. "When the victim is a mother, it's even more important that other mothers stand beside her."

"I'm not a mother but count me in," Ruby says.

"Me three," Sheila says.

"Me four," Megan says. "I'll be there."

"Then who's going to bail us out?" Sheila mumbles.

Maude smiles through her tears. "I'll bail you out."

The words are so touching, no one questions where she'd possibly come up with the money.

"Alright then," Biddy says. "Amelia, did you hear what time

they are meeting tomorrow night?"

Amelia shakes her head. "They didn't say. Just that it was at night."

"Fine. Let's reconvene at the pub tomorrow at nine, when it closes. I can't imagine anything will happen until after the pub has cleared out, as it's right across the street and they won't want witnesses."

"Seconded," Sheila says.

Ruby smiles. "All in favor, say aye."

The 'ayes' are jubilant and Biddy realizes something important. No matter how this ends, she has already achieved something good.

28

Biddy

Biddy is nervous as she pulls her car into a spot behind the pub, Megan sitting beside her. Now that she's here, Biddy doubts herself. What has she gotten everyone into? If Megan were to get caught, her career would be ruined. Sheila would likely serve time, given her previous infractions. Amelia could end up with some public defender and a judge who'd worry she is incompetent to raise her own children. And Ruby could receive community service that would prevent her from running her business, her sole income. And that assumes they don't get hurt, which would be so much worse.

They get out of the car and walk through the darkness towards the back door of the pub. Biddy knocks, causing the metal door to clang loudly as it vibrates in its frame. Two minutes later, it swings open and Ruby stands there in her white blouse and apron, the vacant kitchen in the background. She lets them pass and pulls the door closed behind her.

"I'm going to go upstairs and change," she says. "Can you let the others in?"

Biddy agrees and Ruby leaves Biddy and Megan standing

there, surveying the large empty kitchen. Biddy glances at Megan. Should she be putting her daughter and the others at risk? Is she doing it for Eileen or is this just because she needs some purpose in her own life? Megan has always been so very like her father. But tonight, in black cigarette pants and a black turtleneck with her hair in a ponytail, Biddy realizes that Megan doesn't look like Charles at all. She looks like Biddy. Charles would've never broken into a building with her, Biddy realizes. She wants to laugh. Megan and she finally have an activity that is all for themselves. It just happens to be breaking and entering.

A loud knock sounds from the alley door, and Biddy's wait ends. Megan goes to open the door. When her daughter returns, Amelia and Sheila are on her heels. Ruby thuds down the stairs and joins them, now dressed in black. Everyone's faces are pale and serious.

"Should we take a group photo?" Biddy asks suddenly.

"What?" Amelia says.

"Oh we should," Ruby says.

"So we can provide our own mugshots this time?" asks Sheila.

Biddy shakes her head. "For posterity. It just dawned on me we don't have a photo of the founding members of the Women's Club. And I don't think there is a better moment to represent what brought us together and what we stand for."

Sheila shrugs. "I haven't been in a group photo since class pictures in grade school."

"Well, that's just sad," Ruby says. "I'll hang this picture in the pub so everyone can see you."

Megan nudges her with her shoulder. "I'll even tape your business card next to it."

Laughter fills the room and Sheila, without realizing it, relaxes and moves closer to the others. Biddy's heart calms as she realizes not everything is about her. This group of women is here because they want to be here. They believe in the cause and find membership rewarding, even if each woman has her own reasons for joining.

"I can set my camera on a timer," Megan says. She pulls out her cellphone, pushes some buttons and then sets it on the metal work island, leaning it against a bowl filled with oranges. Everyone else lines up across from it, metal shelving in the background with bottles of booze stacked on top. They will look like a bunch of waitresses, Biddy realizes, all dressed in black in a kitchen. And then she thinks that it doesn't matter. Megan races over and pushes in close to her. They all smile. The camera flashes and then clicks.

"Well, now that we have an official picture, what do we do?" Sheila asks.

Biddy's mind clears as she focuses on the task at hand. All they need to do is get close enough to the pottery to see who attends this meeting with Finn and Declan and what they talk about. They need to hide in the back of the pottery and wait.

Biddy leads the group out the back door and pauses while Ruby locks it. Then they creep down the alley, behind the shops lining Main Street, and around the corner of the last building in the row. This puts them directly across the street from the pottery. It stands, towering before them. There are no sounds other than distant goats. Also, no lit windows. Whatever is going to happen tonight hasn't started.

She crosses the street and heads down the now familiar drive around the side of the factory. The night is cool and crisp, with hints of the upcoming seasonal turn to fall. The cool air enlivens Biddy's senses.

As they make their way down the road, the roar of the watermill overcomes all other sounds. Biddy stops as the road curves towards the receiving docks. She surveys the scene. She needs to find a hiding place.

Behind her is the forest, which would provide great cover but would be too far away from the parking area to overhear any conversation. In front of her is the loading dock, an obvious choice but too well lit and exposed. She sees bushes lining the foundation of the building directly next to her. These aren't ideal, being only waist height in size and a little skimpy in the foliage, but they will have to do. She leads the group into them, wedging herself between the building and the shrubs. She slides across the smooth stone wall as the bushes in front of her prick at her. She stops about five feet from where the side of the building meets the loading docks.

In front of her is some grass, the driveway and Bent Elbow Creek beyond that. To her right is the wide paved space for delivery trucks to back into the loading docks. From this position, they can see everything, and the sound of the water provides extra protection covering any noise they might make.

Biddy slides her back down the wall and comes to a seated position behind the bushes, her knees bent into her chest and her arms hugging her legs. Down the row, the others follow suit. Now, they wait.

Perhaps, not so surprisingly, Amelia turns out to be the best at waiting. Sitting right next to Biddy, she leans her head back against the wall and appears to doze off. Biddy is reminded of those early days of motherhood where any minute you can sleep, you do. Mothers can sleep anywhere. Even if it is while hidden behind bushes on damp soil, apparently.

The worst at waiting is Megan, who sits beside Amelia, fidgeting with her hands. Biddy can practically see her fighting the urge to reach for her cellphone. She looks a little like a drug addict, reaching for her pocket and then pulling her hand back when she remembers they are not supposed to use them.

Ruby and Sheila are whispering to each other at the end of the row. Biddy knows she should stop them but, if she can't hear what they are saying with the rushing water in the background, she highly doubts anyone else can either.

After forty-five minutes, the air becomes cooler and so does their initiative. The river increases the dampness in the air and the hard ground presses against Biddy like an ice cube. Amelia lifts her head and stares straight ahead of her at the creek. Biddy looks at her and wonders if Amelia got this right. Perhaps Amelia misheard Declan and Finn. Or maybe they'd somehow done whatever they were doing earlier and the group missed it.

Megan sits stoically in silence. Biddy appreciates that. Ruby is looking at Biddy, always ready to follow her lead. And Sheila looks ready to call it a night. In fact, she leans over Ruby and says so.

Suddenly, the roar of a truck fills the night air and headlights bounce down the driveway, curving around the building and heading toward the loading docks. The driver blinks his headlights twice and the metal garage door to one of the loading docks clangs and slowly rises. The truck does a U-turn and backs into the now exposed dock.

The truck is black and much larger than Biddy had expected. It is more the size of a delivery truck than a personal vehicle. In fact, the words 'Produce World' are emblazoned on the side with a picture of a tomato and lettuce below. The driver cuts the engine and climbs out.

Amelia whispers in her ear. "That's Declan."

Biddy can't believe it, but she's right. It's her brother. Although the location is out of character, the rest of Declan is recognizable. He is rather sloppily dressed in dirty jeans and a dark plaid flannel shirt, with the faded Delancy shock of red hair shining in the headlights of the truck. He stretches his arms over his head as if he were cramped after driving a distance and then walks to the loading dock. He hops up and thumps the backs of two of the three men standing there in greeting. Biddy realizes how lucky they had been to stay hiding. The other men must have been in the building the whole time they were here.

Two of the men wear jeans, ragged dark sweaters, and skull caps. They unload boxes from the truck and stack them against the back wall of the loading docks. This makes no sense. What would a produce truck be doing making a delivery at a pottery? In the middle of the night, no less?

Declan steps to the side with the third man, and they gesticulate angrily. Biddy can now see this third man well enough to know it's Finn. Even from a distance, he strikes Biddy as someone who's never done manual labor a day in his life. He sports dressy wide leg jeans, a green and white striped Oxford shirt and a fitted navy sweater. Thick black glasses frame his eyes, and Gucci loafers finished the look.

Try as she might, Biddy can't hear what they are saying. Only the roar of the watermill fills the air. They are curious partners. One not that well-educated and working class. The other with a continental, if crass, flair. Biddy wonders how they came to develop a working relationship. Biddy also wonders what on earth Declan could unload, that the pottery would need so badly it couldn't wait until morning?

By the time the men finish, the crates are stacked on the loading dock, five high and ten across. Then the men emerge from the truck carrying large heavy looking plastic bags. They are rectangular shaped and sag in the middle. They look like soil bags.

"Not those, you fools," Finn shouts at them. "Get those back in his truck and make sure none of that dirt has spilled out on our floors. If it has, clean it up."

Biddy watches as the men shrug and put the bags back on the truck. Then Declan walks away from Finn, not even saying goodbye, slaps the other two men on the backs and hops down from the loading dock. The men slam shut the rear doors to his truck as Declan climbs in the cab. He starts the truck, and it bounces back up the drive and disappears around the side of the building.

The men on the loading dock walk back to Finn, who is studying the stack of crates. He gestures first to these and then to two other stacks that line the walls. Then all three men disappear through a side door back into the building.

The five members of the Pooka Women's Club remain completely still, staring at the loading dock. Finally, Biddy motions for them to come closer and they all scoot together and huddle their heads, still well below the bush line and unable to be seen.

"I couldn't hear anything," Biddy whispers. "Could any of you?"

They all shake their heads.

"What do you think is in those boxes?" Ruby asks. "It can't be produce."

"I don't know," Biddy says, keeping her voice low. "But we need to find out. Is it possible that Eileen stumbled onto something illegal and that is why she was killed?"

"It sure is looking that way," Sheila says. "I think one of those men was Liam Lafferty."

"Liam?" Ruby's eyes grow wide. "But he has three kids and is active both in the Church and the town council."

"Well, I can attest from personal experience that he's active in other things as well," Sheila says. "He's a bad egg."

"I'm going to see what's in the boxes," Megan says. She begins to stand up, but Biddy grabs her wrist and pulls her back down.

"You are doing no such thing," she whispers angrily. "That's dangerous."

"This whole thing's dangerous, but someone has to do it." Megan looks at Biddy and Biddy can't help but see a younger version of herself reflected back. "I'll just sneak up on the dock, open one crate, take a picture of the contents with my phone, and come back. I've done field research before. I'm trained for this."

Biddy knows this is an exaggeration. Megan has not been trained for this. Megan's been trained to do research in books. In a library. Biddy wants to go herself, but she knows there is no way her knees and hips are going to get her up on that dock. Ruby would be in the same boat. And Megan is by far the most level-headed of the remaining three.

"Five minutes," Biddy says. "Only five minutes. Then we are leaving."

Megan nods. She rises into a crouched standing position, careful to keep her body below the bush line. She brushes off her bottom and then looks toward the docks. Biddy's eyes mirror Megan's focus. Nothing moves. Megan takes a breath and then slowly takes a few steps out of the bushes, hugging the wall to keep shielded in the darkness. She creeps forward.

"I wonder why they didn't close the loading dock door," Amelia whispers.

Biddy looks at her in alarm.

"It was closed when we arrived," Amelia says. "You would think they'd want it sealed up tight, especially now if there is something valuable sitting on it."

Biddy processes this point quickly. Why would they leave the loading dock open? The only reason Biddy can think of is that they aren't done receiving deliveries for the night. They are going to come back out.

Biddy gestures wildly towards Megan to have her come back, but Megan is looking towards the docks. Biddy can only watch and pray as her daughter reaches the corner of the building.

At this point, Megan has no choice but to fully expose herself. She needs to run to the middle dock and jump up on top of it. The area is dimly lit by a security light, but in the surrounding darkness, it looks like a bright stage waiting for its star. Megan will be easily visible.

Megan dashes from the corner to the dock and lithely lifts herself up onto the platform. She hurries to the crates and lifts the top one down. Although it is the size of an extra large packing box, it doesn't appear to be too heavy from the way she is carrying it.

Hurry up, thinks Biddy. Hurry up.

Megan sets it on the ground, finds a hammer against the wall and uses the back to pry open the top. She freezes for a minute, staring at what is inside, pulls her camera out of her pocket, and takes three photos. Then she pushes the lid back down and gently taps the nails into place. She lifts the crate up and puts it back on the top of the stack. She then takes photos of the shipping labels attached to that stack of crates and the two others lining the walls of the dock.

Enough, thinks Biddy. Come back!

"You must be so proud of her," Amelia says.

Biddy is. But she's also worried.

Suddenly, another large motor sounds on the road snaking around the building. Everyone else turns towards it, but Biddy keeps her eyes glued to Megan, willing her to have heard it. She did. Her daughter's head swings towards where Biddy is hiding and then to the far side of the dock bordering the river.

She'll never make it back, Biddy thinks.

Megan apparently draws the same conclusion. She throws herself off the platform and into a cluster of weedy vegetation on the far side of the docks, near the river, just before the headlights of a truck round the building.

If the last truck was larger than Biddy expected, this one is a behemoth, rarely seen in a little town like Pooka. It is a very large semi-trailer, white with orange swirls on the side. It takes three swings for it to turn itself around and reverse into the dock. The truck is so long that the cab is practically even with where the group is hidden.

Biddy can't see around it to where her daughter is hiding. She prays for the first time since she was a child. The only thing she cares about at the moment is her daughter.

Two men climb out of the cab and walk back to the loading dock. By now, Finn and his two men have re-emerged from the building. This time, there are no handshakes and small talk. Finn simply nods to the men, and they open the back doors of the truck. Finn's two men plus the new arrivals carry all the boxes from the loading dock into the truck, including those just delivered by Declan. It looks like over two hundred boxes are loaded. Biddy wonders if there is pottery in any of them.

"I gotta wiz," one man says when they finished the loading.

"Well, you're not doing it in here," Finn says sharply. "Use the bushes."

Biddy's breath catches in her throat as the man jumps down the far side of the dock near where Megan had dove into the bushes. She can't see anything now. Her heart beats hard against her rib cage. Amelia looks over at her and clutches her hand. Biddy grips it as if it were a lifeline. They all sit still as mice. Three minutes pass. Then four. Then the man reappears, heaving himself up on the dock and sauntering back over to where the others wait. Biddy exhales and gives Amelia's hand a gentle squeeze of gratitude. Somehow, Megan must've moved away from where the man had landed.

"That everything?" The driver says to Finn. He is a big man with an accent that suggests he grew up in a working class environment.

Finn nods. "That's it. You should get going."

"I get the feeling you don't want us here," the man says with a laugh. "Funny thing, seeing how many years we've been at this."

"Just go," Finn says.

The man spits on the ground next to Finn and turns around. His partner follows him to the edge of the dock. They are just about to jump down when, suddenly, a rabbit flies out from the shore of the creek, across the parking area and leaps into their bushes. Sheila gives a small scream of surprise.

"What was that?" The driver stops in his tracks on the edge of the dock.

"It was a rabbit," Finn says. "I saw it."

"That didn't sound like no rabbit," the other guy says.

Both men jump down and head in their direction.

29

Megan

Megan lands in the bushes seconds before the headlights appear on the driveway. She hits the ground hands first, and the gravel imprints itself into her skin. Her right wrist takes the brunt of her weight and a shooting pain goes up it, into her arm. She quickly pulls her legs under her and scoots around the corner of the building for a little more protection. The bushes are not as thick here as where the others are hiding. In fact, these aren't so much bushes as just scrub that hasn't been mowed. She is very exposed.

She rubs her wrist, and the act leaves a smear of blood. Before starting this surveillance, she'd feared getting arrested for trespassing. However, after seeing the contents of that crate, she now knows the consequences could be much more dire. A broken wrist and a few scrapes are nothing. Those men catching her is not an option.

The men, thankfully, must not have seen her dive, because they climb out of the truck's cab and stretch for a minute before sauntering to the loading dock. Above her, a metal door opens. She assumes that Finn and his crew have re-emerged. Then she hears boxes being loaded onto the truck. She uses her good hand to pat the surrounding ground. Just as she's getting desperate, her hand falls on the sleek metal back of her iPhone case. It had slipped from her hand when she landed. Now she grips it tightly. It contains the proof of illegal activities.

She wants to shout at the others to run away. That this is so much worse than they thought. She'd give anything to warn her mother, but of course she can't. She can't even see them on the other side of the large semi.

Right next to her, the water of Bent Elbow Creek roars, but Megan stays hyper-focused on the sound of the footsteps moving on and off the truck and the bang of the boxes deposited inside it. She should leave now. The men are all focused on the boxes. She'd be able to scoot along the wall of the building facing the creek, emerge on the far side of the building bordering the bridge, and call the police. But doing this means leaving her mother and the others on their own. She isn't sure what she thinks she could do to help them if something did happen, but that doesn't make leaving your mother in danger any easier. The group is hiding right in front of where all the men are facing.

"One more stack," a man mumbles.

Megan takes a deep breath and holds it. Should she leave or should she stay? Most likely, this truck will depart just like the last one and then they can all reconnect. But what if that doesn't happen? What if they get caught? The responsible thing to do is to go get the police. Her mother will be fine, she tells herself. Her mother will be more than fine. After all, it was her mother who had gotten them to see the truth. Megan needs to get the police.

She scoots along the wall towards the bridge, clutching her phone. When she is halfway down the building, she breaks into a run, her wrist throbbing with every jolt as her feet meet the ground. She reaches the far corner, and that's when she hears it. A scream from where the others are hiding. She turns to run back. To help them. She flies back down the wall and toward the trouble. But she forces herself to stop when she reaches the midway point. It wouldn't help them. They need real help and she is the only person who can get it.

Fighting every familial instinct to protect, she turns back towards the bridge, runs back up the embankment and towards Main Street. Main Street is pitch black, not even security lights are on in the vacant buildings' windows. Is the police station in this small a town even open twenty-four hours? She peers through the dark towards the far end of the street. There are no lights in the station's windows, nor police cars in front.

Suddenly, she sees a distant pair of headlights on the road winding towards the bridge from the highway. Someone is coming and coming fast. Her heart leaps with joy. But then it sinks with dread. The only people out and about at this hour so far have been bad guys. This is most likely more.

She looks around for a place to hide, knowing that every minute she focuses on her own safety is one minute less spent getting help for her mother. Still, she stares at the quickly nearing headlights and knows she can't be caught. There are no buildings behind her except the pottery, so she must reach town to hide. She darts across the street and towards the Broken Egg Cafe. However, the headlights flash across her like a spotlight as the car comes flying over the bridge. She's been seen.

She runs without looking back. Her breath is raspy, and her lungs burn, but she flies up Main Street.

The car makes a sharp left off the bridge so that it is parallel to where she is running. It screeches to a stop, and she dives once again behind small bushes, this time ones that border the patio of the cafe. She knows she is caught. There is no way she wasn't seen. However, the survival instinct makes her try to hide so she cowers behind a planter.

She hears footsteps approach like hammers in the quiet night.

"Megan, is that you?" a voice shouts.

Megan stays crouched and her heart thumps against her chest. It sounds like Brady, but that couldn't be possible. What would he be doing here?

"Megan?" the voice shouts again, nearer this time.

It's Brady, she thinks again. It IS Brady. She collapses in relief. Then, she suddenly realizes that he needs to stop shouting. The men at the pottery could hear him. She jumps to her feet.

She runs towards him. Safety, she thinks. Help. She throws herself into his arms.

At first, his body is rigid in surprise, but then he cradles her.

"I was just coming back from a business trip to Evansville," he says into her hair. "Are you okay?"

Megan pulls away from him. Brady's face is white. His large eyes are studying her, reflecting her fear. Megan can't imagine what she looks like to him. Her hair is falling out of her ponytail in a frizz and blood is oozing from her wounded hands, one of which is bent at an unnatural angle.

"Who did this to you?" He grabs her arms as if to support her and, in that moment, Megan just wants to fall back against him. To feel his warmth against her body.

Instead, she shakes his grip off. "It's the pottery. They're moving drugs. And my mom…" Megan fights to say the words out loud. "My mom is stuck outside, hiding from them with her friends."

Brady stares at her for a long moment, likely processing this unusual story.

"We need the police," Megan says, hoping this is a better summary.

Brady nods. "Get in the car."

The light that dances in Brady's eyes is gone now. His face is so serious, it is like he is a different man. Megan hurries around to the other side of the old truck and climbs in. Brady gets back in the driver's seat and shuts the door.

"We need to go to Evansville," he says. "The police station in Pooka is long closed."

He shifts the car into drive as he speaks, does a U-turn, and flies back across the bridge.

"I know it's closed, but we can't leave her," Megan says. "Can't we just call 911 and go back to help Mom?"

"Evansville is only twenty minutes away," Brady says calmly. "And we need the police. You and I can't do anything for your mom alone. Start calling now and we'll head over to Evansville to make sure they are coming."

Megan feels tears forming. This makes sense. It all makes sense. But she wants to run to her mom. Not away from her. "Please hurry."

The car flies up the road that winds through the cornfields.

"Nothing will happen to your mother," Brady says quietly. "Hang in there."

Megan dials 911. She can't find a signal and she remembers

her mother saying that it was impossible to get one in the cornfields. "We need to go back to town. I can't get a signal."

"This will be faster, I promise."

Megan keeps dialing. A small part of her can't help but question if this is true. But then, as they speed past the rock pooka, Megan remembers the story Brady told her, presumably about his own parents. He understands what it is to have parents at risk. He will hurry. Looking at those pooka now, she no longer finds them stupid. Instead, she wishes with all her heart, a golden eyed being is now racing to her mother's rescue.

The old Ford makes a sharp left onto the highway and they fly up the wider road, winding beside large rocky hills. She can hear the wind rushing against the little truck as it travels at a speed higher than intended. Megan continues to dial the emergency number, but it feels like she is relentlessly pushing numbers to get to a human and only gets a connection failure. But, true to Brady's word, they reach the turnoff for Evansville in no time at all. Brady shoots down the exit ramp, around a roundabout, and comes to a halt in front of a brightly lit police station. Megan disconnects from the endless stream of call failures and her heart flutters with relief. Still, she can't help but wonder if it would have been faster to call the police from town, when she had a signal.

Before Megan has unbuckled her seat belt, Brady is already at her side, opening the car door for her. She leaps out, and he leads her into the police station. The moment they enter, they draw looks. The woman standing behind the counter is glaring at her as if she is a new criminal arrival, while two drunk men sitting on a bench, likely waiting to be processed, appear amused. Megan self-consciously puts a hand to her hair and tries to smooth it. The station is small and quiet. The town of Evansville is not much larger than Pooka. Outside of these three humans, the only hints at other occupants to the building are two voices chatting and laughing in a back room.

Brady steps up to the lady at the counter.

"We have an ongoing crime to report. Drugs are being moved at Aisling Pottery in Pooka and there are a few women trapped in a hiding place nearby."

The women's eyes grow wide, and she takes another look at Megan before looking back at Brady. Megan is so grateful he is there. His calm demeanor gives credence to an otherwise hard to believe story.

"Sean," the lady calls, looking towards the back room. "You need to come out here now."

Megan wants to jump across the desk, grab this person named Sean by the arm, and throw him into his car. However, she fights the urge. She knows screams and demands are not helpful. Still, she shifts her weight to control her energy.

The police officer, presumably named Sean, saunters out.

Run, Megan wants to shout at him. Hurry.

But Sean has a young innocent face, without a note of urgency. Megan's heart falls just a little bit. Who else would work the night shift?

Brady gives no reaction and calmly repeats his story.

Megan wants to throttle them both. They are wasting time. She stares at this young police officer, her only hope at this point.

To his credit, Sean's body tenses as he listens to the story. He picks up a phone and places a call to someone Megan assumes is his superior. He briefly describes the situation to this person, calling him 'sir'.

This is good. This is progress. But it's slow.

He hangs up the phone and then calls for the other man in the backroom.

"Ryan," he says. "We've got a drug bust with citizens in danger. Let's go."

He turns to Brady and Megan. "We've called in reinforcements, both from our town and from others. Stay here and we'll take your statements when we return."

Sean and Ryan rush out the front of the building and quickly disappear in the direction of the parking lot.

"Brady," Megan says. "I can't wait here—"

"Of course you can't." He takes her hand and squeezes it. It hurts like hell as it is likely broken, yet it's a comfort. "Let's go."

He leads her out of the building, not releasing her hand until he's opened the passenger door and helped her inside. Every scratch on her body burns, but she can easily ignore them all. She only hopes that a few scratches are all the others suffer too. Brady races to his side and starts the car.

As the truck whips into a U-turn, Megan looks at him. "I can't thank you enough for everything you're doing."

He keeps his eyes glued to the road in front of him. "You don't have to thank me. I care for you."

30

Biddy

Biddy's heart sinks as the men head through the darkness towards their hiding spot in the bushes. Amelia clutches her hand so hard it hurts. Ruby looks at her with such trust that it hurts more than Amelia's vise grip. But perhaps the saddest face is Sheila's who, as experience has likely taught her, is resigned to the fact that evil is about to befall them. Sheila also likely feels it is her fault as she screamed. She is wrong. This is all Biddy's fault.

It is Biddy who has demanded to change history. It is Biddy who doubled down on looking into Eileen's murder instead of leaving it to the police. And it is Biddy who asked these women to risk themselves tonight.

The men come closer, their strides firm and quick. Both have their fists clutched at their sides, ready for use. Biddy wonders what the men will do. They don't appear to have guns. Will they kidnap them? Kill them? Kidnap them first and then kill them?

"I think I see something white," the first guy shouts.

"I'm telling you, that's a rabbit," Finn says, thoroughly

annoyed.

Biddy didn't think it was possible to like Finn, but she finds herself warming to him.

"It's hair. Blond hair." Both men move toward them a little faster. All the women look at Sheila's hiding spot. She shrinks back as if that would somehow make her hair less visible.

A beefy fist reaches through the bushes and grabs not Sheila, but Amelia. As the man tries to yank her out, the bushes scratch against Amelia's face. She fights back, swinging her arms against the fist.

"Run," Biddy says to the others. "Run."

And they do. Ruby and Sheila take off through the bushes, racing towards the road. However, Biddy is directly next to Amelia, and cannot run as Amelia blocks her way.

One of the men runs after Ruby and Sheila.

"Over here," Biddy shouts.

It's enough to break his stride, and he stops his chase to grab Biddy. He yanks her out of the bushes and Biddy stops struggling to watch Ruby and Sheila's progress. She wills them on. Run, ladies, run.

Sheila and Ruby make it to the end of the bushes and huff up the incline of the road. They race to the corner of the building and then round it, disappearing from sight. Biddy breathes a sigh of relief. Unless there are other men Biddy doesn't know about, they are free. That, Biddy tells herself, is something.

Biddy then turns to Amelia, who is standing beside her, tears in her eyes and two large fists attached to her shoulders.

"I'm so very sorry," Biddy says to her.

Amelia looks too frightened to speak but nods. Biddy only feels worse.

Their best hope is that the others find help. However, Biddy knows that isn't as easy as it sounds. The police station is closed. There are no neighbors nearby. Empty commercial buildings surround them. Therefore, Amelia and she are going to be on their own, at least for a long while.

"Jesus," Biddy's captor says. "It's two ladies. What are we supposed to do now?"

That is exactly what Biddy is wondering. She studies her captor. He is huge. Bigger than anyone she's ever seen around town. He strikes her as more urban in his roots. Because he's Italian, she realizes. He has a faint Italian accent like they have on the North End of Boston. He, like his comrade, is in a white t-shirt and jeans. However, their necks shine with chains.

"I don't know," says the guy gripping Amelia, "but we gotta figure it out quick and get out of here. A few got away."

"Shit."

Biddy's captor turns her around and shoves her towards the loading dock. She walks in the intended direction. Putting up a fight now isn't going to help anything. She will never win against these men. She can hear Amelia stumbling behind her. As she draws closer, she can better see Finn. He watches their approach with fear in his eyes. If Biddy had thought he might intervene on their behalf, she knows better now. Finn is not the one with the power in this relationship.

"Who are they?" Biddy's captor asks and shoves both Biddy and Amelia at him.

"I don't know," Finn says. "Just some women from town. They aren't important."

"Well, they are now," says Biddy's captor. "They saw everything."

"They don't know what they saw," Finn says weakly.

Biddy is surprised. This is more support than Biddy expected from him.

"That's true," Amelia says. "All we saw are trucks making a pickup. It's probably pottery."

Biddy flinches at the desperation in Amelia's voice. She says nothing. Despite Amelia's hopes, she is sure her words will not change anything.

"What do we do with them?" the second guy asks the first again. "We've got to go right now."

The first guy sighs. "We kill them and dump the bodies on the way."

Amelia screams and tears roll down her face. Her captor quickly clamps his huge hand over her mouth to mute the noise. This time Biddy struggles in her captor's arms as she listens to Amelia fighting to inhale through her nostrils, now buried beneath his hand. If she could take back this whole quest, she would. Now, not only Eileen has given her life to this mess. Amelia and she would, too. God, Amelia's children. Biddy suddenly thinks of the four car seats in Amelia's minivan. Those poor, poor children.

The second guy shrugs and nods at this announcement. Finn and his crew remain frozen where they are standing.

Biddy's captor spins her around to face him. "I'm going to my truck to get my gun. If you move…if you scream… my friend shoots your friend ten times before I kill her. It will be a long and painful death."

Biddy has no choice but to nod. Amelia is still struggling to breathe. Biddy watches her captor walk back to the cab of the semi. She racks her brain for a way out of this. Amelia is in a vise-like grip, tight against the other man's body. No matter what Biddy could try, Amelia would never be able to get away.

Biddy cannot leave her to her death, even if it means Biddy might save herself.

She closes her eyes and tells herself to accept her fate. It was a good life. And she can be with Charles. Boy, she'd like to give him a piece of her mind. That cheater.

Surprisingly, this thought gives her strength. Without a captive hand on her body, she stays standing stoically beside Amelia. She reaches over and takes her hand, just as Amelia has done so many times for her.

Biddy's thug returns.

"Get down on your knees."

Biddy does so and notes that Finn and his men move far away from her, out of the line of fire. So much for their help. Amelia emits a muffled scream and is shoved to the ground beside her. She lies there for a second, but then she pushes herself to her knees beside Biddy. Biddy retakes her hand.

"He's going to shoot you next," Biddy says to Finn. "I've seen it in the movies. When a drug operation is burned, they kill everyone."

Finn's eyes widen. He's thinking about this. Then he leaps off the dock into the bushes below and his two compatriots follow. Bushes rustle as they presumably run away.

"Shit," mumbles the man with the gun. He looks at his partner. "Go get them."

The man jumps down after them.

The sole remaining captor stares into the darkness after the others and the gun falls to his side while he waits. Biddy exhales. This stunt bought them a reprieve. Biddy squeezes Amelia's hand and cheers Finn on in her head. Five minutes pass. Then ten. Then fifteen. They can no longer hear anything other than the roar of the creek travelling over the water wheel. After another ten minutes, they hear rustling in the bushes again. Five minutes after that, the thug who gave chase reappears, shoving a bloodied Finn and his friends ahead of him. Biddy's heart sinks.

The men climb up the steps to the loading dock and the thug shoves them down onto their knees beside Biddy and Amelia. He then returns to stand next to the guy with gun, which is pointed right back at them.

It is over.

Biddy looks at Amelia.

"Close your eyes," she whispers.

Biddy watches Amelia do this and then closes her own. She thinks of Megan and warmth spreads through her body. It has been a rewarding life, despite the painful moments. Despite even Charles' cheating.

She waits to hear the click of a trigger. She tries to enjoy the last natural sounds she'll ever hear. The water rushing. An owl hooting. Instead, she hears sirens. The sirens, faint at first, sound as if they are drawing nearer and nearer.

Could it be? Could it really be? Could Sheila and Ruby have gotten help that fast? The sirens grow louder, piercing the quiet night. Biddy opens her eyes and looks at Amelia. Amelia stares back hopefully.

"What the hell is that?" Biddy's captor says to the other.

"It's the police," the other one says.

"There's no way out of this," Biddy says. She tries to keep hope out of her voice. "The only way into and out of Pooka is that bridge, and the police are now on it. They are going to catch you. The only decision you have to make is whether you are arrested for shipping whatever you are shipping or for murder."

Neither says anything. But they don't shoot either. This is good. Biddy feels hope spread inside her chest.

Now, the sirens are louder than the water mill. Biddy watches as flashing blue lights speed across the bridge in front of her and then disappear as they turn right onto Main Street. Soon, the siren sound is accompanied but the crunch of wheels heading down the Pottery's driveway towards them. Biddy twists to watch. The cars completely block the driveway, fencing in the truck. Doors open and male voices shout the command to drop their weapons.

Biddy prays for acquiescence.

The men stay frozen in silence. It would make no sense to shoot the women with the full police force as witnesses, but then again, these men are not the most logical. Another minute passes.

Finally, Biddy sees the arm with the gun waver. Then it drops.

"Let's go," the man says.

She feels a shove as he takes off past her, running towards the river and the backside of the building. Amelia's captor does the same.

Biddy pushes herself up off the cement. "Megan," she shouts. "Megan."

Her heart is bursting. For they are racing right towards where her daughter is hiding.

"Mom," her daughter's voice screams.

But it isn't coming from the direction of the thugs. It is coming from the direction of the police cars.

Biddy whips around and desperately tries to make out Megan's figure. The spinning blue lights allow for only flashes of the rescue crew below to be seen, like some sort of terrible

Halloween display. Most are bulky and racing towards the pottery. But there, blessedly there, right at the very top of the drive crowded with cars, running towards her, is her daughter. Biddy would recognize the shape of the body anywhere. She takes off in her direction. They meet behind the first line of cars surrounding the pottery and throw their arms around each other.

"Mom," she says, her voice muffled in Biddy's sweater.

"Megan" Biddy says. "Thank you, god," she whispers.

Amelia runs up to them and Biddy releases Megan to hug the other young woman as well. All three turn to watch as the police put handcuffs on Finn and his two employees, still kneeling on the dock. Shortly after that, four police officers, breathing heavily from exertion, appear from the back side of the building, gripping the two drivers of the semi, also in handcuffs. Sheila, Ruby, and Brady emerge from the top of the road and come to stand beside them. The five members of the Women's Club join hands to watch the criminals loaded into police cars.

31

Megan

The photo of the Women's Club makes its debut on the front page of the Dubois County News and World Report, which Megan thinks is a rather ambitious name for a county paper, but she now possesses enough good sense to keep this thought to herself. The title under the photo proclaims *Local Waitstaff Foil Rotten Produce Delivery*. And, although pretty much entirely wrong, Megan has to give them points for creativity.

"I can't believe they didn't even bother to verify that we are most certainly not waitstaff," Biddy huffs. She throws the paper down on the kitchen table and takes a sip of orange juice. "Just because one photo makes us look like waitstaff doesn't mean we ARE waitstaff."

"Well, at least you got the front page," Megan says encouragingly. She takes a bite of her croissant. She doesn't care what the newspaper writes as long as her mother is safe.

Biddy pushes her plate away, the croissant almost untouched. "Yes, I got the front page. With nary a mention of Eileen or our mission. It's all about the drugs. This makes us look like we just happened onto the drug bust. That isn't

236

at all true. We were the ones who planned the entire sting!"

This is a bit of a stretch as none of them had expected to be in on a drug bust, but again Megan lets it go. She is learning that silence is sometimes a very appropriate course of action. Instead, she nudges the plate back toward her mother. "You really should try to eat something. We have a long day ahead."

The doorbell chimes. Biddy looks questioningly at Megan, over her raised cup of coffee.

Megan sighs. The moment has come.

"Mom," Megan says hesitantly. She knows she should have cleared this decision with her mother. But things were so chaotic last night, she hadn't had the chance. Sitting in an ambulance while paramedics bandaged her wrist, surrounded by hordes of police and dozens of flashing lit vehicles, didn't seem like the right time to point out that this was only the beginning of what was likely to be a long legal battle. That they were all witnesses in a serious criminal case and would likely be called on again and again by police and prosecutors to sort the mess out. They would need someone to look out for their own safety and interests. "I called Richard."

Biddy frowns. "Richard who?"

"Davenport. Our lawyer."

The doorbell chimes again, but Megan remains seated, watching her mother and waiting for her reaction. "I would've discussed it with you, but things were crazy last night and I knew Richard would have to leave immediately to get here from Boston for our appointment with the police this morning."

Megan tries to remain stoic before the impending tirade. Of how Megan doesn't trust her mother to take care of herself. Of how Megan tries to make decisions for her.

But none of that happens. Biddy shrugs and sips her coffee. "That is probably a good idea."

* * *

Richard drives Megan and her mother to the police station in his rental Cadillac Escalade. They pass the pottery, now surrounded with garish yellow police tape and teeming with people garbed in t-shirts sporting an array of acronyms, including PD, FBI, and DEA. Megan reaches over and puts her hand on top of her mom's. Her mother wraps her fingers around Megan's and squeezes. The car continues past the pottery and up Main Street.

The police station is also crawling with people. This group, however, is wielding microphones, notepads, and massive badges, declaring them to be members of the press. The well-sealed car windows mute their din.

"Let me know if you see the Dubois County News and World Report," Biddy says to Megan as a police man flags Richard into a parking spot. "I need to have words with them."

Megan laughs. "You can start by teaching them the correct pronunciation of their own county name. It's supposed to be a French word. Du-bwaa not du-boyzee—contrary to popular opinion."

"The people at that rag would be more likely to tell France they got it wrong," Biddy mutters.

Richard flips around in his seat. "You will do no such thing. Haven't you been listening to a word I've been saying this whole time? You will say nothing. Especially to the press. Understand?"

Biddy and Megan nod, looking a lot like chastised children.

Then her mother winks at her. Megan smiles.

They climb out of the car to flashing light bulbs and screamed requests. As Richard advised, the two women ignore the fuss and follow him wordlessly into the building, a different police officer holding the crowd of press away from them.

Sheila, Amelia, and Ruby jump off a bench lining the wall and rush over to hug them. Over Amelia's shoulder, Megan sees Amelia's husband watching protectively from a chair in the corner. Amelia and Ruby are both in jeans and t-shirts, but Sheila—as she informs them—didn't want to waste good press coverage and has worn a hot pink spandex dress that closely resembles a wide rubber band.

Biddy looks at the group assembled and then at the well-suited man standing beside her. "I want to introduce you to Richard Davenport, our longtime family lawyer. He is going to represent us in our conversations with the police."

"A lawyer?" Amelia's eyes widen. "We need a lawyer?"

Sheila takes this announcement more in stride. "Of course, we need a lawyer. You always want a lawyer when talking with the police. Just having a little chat, they'll say…and then BAM." Sheila claps her hands together. "Next thing you know, you're in jail."

Amelia's eyes widen further.

"But you'll be fine," Sheila says quickly. "Money talks, and clearly, by the looks of this lawyer and the speed with which he got here, Biddy has it." She sticks her hand out to Richard. "Welcome to our team."

To Richard's credit, he simply shakes Sheila's extended hand.

"Do you want my business card?" Sheila asks.

Richard's eyes grow as wide as Amelia's.

After a quick conversation between Richard and the desk clerk, they are led toward an office in the far back of the building, marked 'Chief of Police'. As they walk through the large pit to get there, Megan sees Finn Murphy in the holding cell in the back corner. They enter the Chief's office and find a large desk with a leather swivel chair on one side and five folding chairs on the other. The Chief, a large flaccid balding man, stands up from his chair as they enter. He is the same man Megan spoke with after Biddy had been arrested for breaking and entering the pottery. He is also the man who announced that he was too busy to investigate Eileen's murder when Megan reported that. While Megan is eternally grateful to the police who came to her aid last night, this officer is not a man she respects and is also the reason she thought to call Richard. He is inept and ambitious, a dangerous marriage.

"I'll need a chair as well," Richard says, wedging himself in front of the women. He walks over to shake the chief's hand. "I'm Richard Davenport, a member of the Boston bar, and I'll be representing the women at the bequest of Megan and Biddy Bramley."

The chief looks flummoxed. "There's no need for that. They aren't under arrest. We're just collecting their statements as cooperating witnesses."

"Well," Richard says with a smile as their police escort drags in another chair for him, "I'm here to ensure just that. That it's a cooperative environment. On both sides."

He sits down on the middle chair, directly in front of the Chief, and the others squeeze their way around him to take seats on either side.

The chief clears his throat as his eyes travel over each of the women's faces. "Let's start with what led you to believe that

Finn Murphy was involved in trafficking drugs."

"Nothing," Biddy says. "We were investigating Eileen Delancy's murder."

"And since Eileen was involved with drugs, you staged a stakeout?" he asks, sounding hopeful.

"Absolutely not," Ruby says. "I've known Eileen my whole life. She never did drugs. We believe she is the true founder of the pottery."

The chief's forehead creases. "So, when did you become aware of the drugs?"

"Mr. Halloran," Biddy says, reading his name off the name plaque on his desk.

"Chief Halloran," he corrects.

"Chief Halloran," she says. "I'm glad that we could assist you in such a significant drug arrest. But our interest isn't in the drugs. It's in determining if Finn Murphy murdered my sister. We want him held accountable for that. Have you interrogated him on this? Has he confessed?"

"Let's focus on the drugs first, and then we'll get to that."

"No." Biddy sits back and crosses her arms. After her last conversation with Chief Halloran, where he showed no interest in Eileen, she clearly expected this response.

Ruby, Sheila, and Amelia all do the same. The only ones remaining with uncrossed arms are Megan, Richard, and the Chief, himself.

Chief Halloran raises his eyebrows at Richard.

"Biddy," Richard says, "As your lawyer, I advise you that the question is legitimate. Just answer it and then we can get out of here."

"No. Not until I hear about my sister."

Richard shrugs and looks back at the Chief. "You heard my

client."

The chief's face reddens. "There are sixty-eight officers from various agencies crawling around this town. We have the eyes of multiple federal agencies on us, not to mention those of state and government officials. I understand you are concerned for your sister, but this is bigger than her."

Megan thinks of Maude, who they called late last night to tell of Finn's arrest. She broke down in sobs. In Maude's eyes, Megan realizes, there is nothing bigger than her mother. Megan knows how she feels.

"No," Megan says. "Nothing is more important than the life of a woman."

Halloran's eyes bulge. "Fine," Halloran says, looking more annoyed than chastised. "He says he didn't do it. Finn denies murdering Eileen."

"And that's it?" Biddy asks. "Just because he says so, you're going to drop it?"

"It doesn't matter. We have him iron-clad on so many drug charges, he isn't going to see the light of day! We don't need him on a murder charge."

"I do," Biddy says. "I want a confession. For Maude's sake. Let me talk to him."

"No."

Biddy turns to Richard. "Isn't there some sort of law that gives victims the right to confront their attacker? Finn attacked me last night."

Richard exhales. "There is, but it usually takes effect after their trial. It takes months, if not years, in a case like this."

Biddy looks back at the Chief. "Then I'm not testifying until I can speak with Finn."

"This is outrageous," the Chief sputters.

Megan almost feels bad for him, knowing first-hand how irritating it can be to tussle with her mother.

Chief Halloran leans forward so his face is inches from Biddy's. "The prosecutor will call you as a hostile witness. You will testify or you will go to jail."

"She's a hooker," Sheila says.

Chief Halloran flinches and looks over at her. In fact, everyone looks over at her.

"What did you just say?" he asks.

Sheila, who has gone mostly unnoticed sitting in the seat closest to the door, smiles back at him. "I said she is a hooker."

Ruby gasps. "Is this true?"

Sheila pats her friend's hand sympathetically. "Just look at her. What man could resist?"

Everyone looks at Biddy in her navy Chanel jacket.

"Anyway, it takes one to know one, and Biddy is a hooker, so you should take her away and put her in the holding cell. With ALL the other prisoners." Sheila emphasizes the word 'all', and Megan sees her mother's eyes light up. A flash of gold streaks across her pupils.

"I'm not taking this lady to holding," the chief says.

Sheila shrugs. "You and I have discussed this thousands of times. According to you, it's out of your hands. There is a statute which requires—"

"I know the statutes." Chief Halloran's voice rises a few decibels. "But I'm not going to just take your ridiculous claim that she's a hooker. Look at her. She's not a hooker. This is asinine."

"I'm a hooker," Biddy says.

"I can't believe it," Ruby cries, "I barely know any of you."

"Biddy..." Richard says.

"Take me to holding," she says, extending her wrists. "I should be with the rest of the prisoners."

"Okay, that's enough," Richard says. "This is getting out of hand. My client, Biddy Bramley, is not a hooker and does not need to be incarcerated. She is just trying to achieve a legitimate outcome in a very inappropriate way. Her daughter can verify this."

All eyes turn to Megan. It is, Megan reflects, one of those moments in life where you wonder how things came to this. Sometimes, she is realizing, it is very hard to be a good daughter. However, she knows what she has to do.

"How could you?" she says to her mother.

32

Biddy

Sheila is promising all sorts of salacious details to the Chief as an officer leads Biddy out of the room. Biddy knows Sheila will keep the Chief busy with her complaint against Biddy, long enough for Biddy to interview Finn. She just hopes Megan, Amelia, and Ruby cover their ears or they are likely in for quite an education.

The police officer grips Biddy's arm and leads her towards the holding cells. He is one of the officers from the scene last night, and Biddy notices that his grasp is weak. It is clear no one actually considers her a threat, which is good since, at some point, she'll have to talk her way out of this. But first things first. They stop in front of the cell and the officer fishes in his pocket for his key.

Inside the cell sits Finn and his two associates. The larger men who had tried to shoot Biddy and Amelia last night are noticeably missing. Biddy thinks that the huge black eye and bruised legs of Finn may have had something to do with that. They must have been separated out of the general population. A dividing wall of bars, which Biddy assumes segregates genders, splits the cell in half. Confirming this belief, when the officer unlocks the door, he puts her in the other half of the cell. Thankfully, no other female prisoners are present. The officer slams the door shut behind her and walks away.

Biddy wanders over and sits on the bench bordering the divider. Finn sits on the other side. She and Finn stare at each other through the bars. He wears an orange jumpsuit, and this, combined with his black eye and swollen face, as well as his thinning hair and sagging jowls, makes him look mundane and ugly. Biddy suddenly realizes how much of his artistic persona was achieved simply through his garish clothes. She wonders what people would have thought of Eileen if she'd ever been given the opportunity to dress differently. Biddy wishes with all her heart that she thought to send her sister some of her used things from Boston. Maybe it would've made a difference in how people viewed her. Just maybe.

"If you think I'm going to shed some tears, spill my heart, and say I'm sorry, you're sorely mistaken," Finn says.

"You've ruined my family's life," Biddy says. She's surprised at how calm her voice sounds. "I just want to know why. It can be off the record. The police have no interest in Eileen's case and I'm fine leaving it to God to judge you. I just want to give her daughter closure."

Finn laughs. "I'm not that naive."

Biddy thought this would be his answer, but it was worth a try.

"How about I guess, and you just nod?" Biddy slides closer to the bars and grips them, her eyes glued to his face.

He doesn't say a word.

"I think you and Eileen needed each other," Biddy says. "You believed you were something special when we were in high school, homecoming king and all that. But you weren't. You were just an empty salesman. Eileen, however, was something special, but not a salesman. She was smart, but an outcast. You were dumb, but likable. You needed each other."

Finn doesn't nod, but he doesn't disagree either. Biddy realizes this is as much confirmation as she is going to get.

"So you go to her..."

Finn blinks, almost imperceptibly.

"No, she comes to you," Biddy corrects. This makes more sense. Her sister would be the one with more initiative. "She spent her days hiding out in various places, and the deserted pottery was one of those. She'd looked at the remnants of the old pottery pieces and thought there was a market for something that beautiful. So, always loving chemistry, she figured out how to recreate the glaze and paints. All she needed was someone to market this. And who better than a man who has no known athletic or academic skills and yet became the most popular kid in the school?"

Finn just stares back, one eye fully focused on her, the other almost swollen shut. Again, Biddy is struck at how anyone could have found this man trustworthy, little less a pillar of the community.

"Together, the two of you make it big...you in charge of marketing and she in charge of product. This makes you the face of the business, but Eileen doesn't mind since she hates the spotlight. However, you get greedy."

Now Finn breaks eye contact. He looks down and to the left. At the cement block wall next to him. It's just as well. Biddy is growing more and more confident that her story is the correct one. And with that growing confidence comes a growing sickness, causing bile to rise in her throat. She can barely look at this man. This man whose greed destroyed her sister with no compunction.

"Someone notices that you have a sizable distribution chain that crosses the globe. And that someone wants to use it to move illegal and counterfeit products. You start small..." Biddy thinks back to the unsmoked cigarettes they'd found strewn around the floor of the pottery. "...and then get bigger. Drugs."

Finn flinches. Biddy is definitely on the right track.

"Eileen finds out. She is furious. No matter what it looks like to the world, this is her business. Her pride and joy. Also, her income. Her ticket to a better life. This becomes even more important when she realizes she is pregnant. She is not going to let you risk her livelihood to make a few more bucks doing something illegal. She tells you to stop. More than that...she threatens to report you to the police."

Biddy thinks back to her sister. Her greatest strength was also her greatest flaw. Eileen never cared what people thought of her. In some ways, this made her invincible. In others, unsuspecting. That great brain of hers was so logical in every way. It saw black and white. Problems and solutions. Right and wrong. But, she believed everyone else acted logically too. In the end, Biddy realizes, this is what got her killed. She devised a way to gain wealth. Others wanted more and were willing to take illogical risks to get it.

Biddy looks right in Finn's eyes. "You threatened her back. Her and her baby. Told her you'd destroy her if she ever came near the pottery again. And, having seen your new partners, she believed you. She would've taken that risk for herself. But never for her child. So she walks away."

Biddy thinks back to the Eileen she knew, filled with so many hopes and dreams, that stayed home to raise her siblings after her mother dies and her older sister leaves. While not the warmest of individuals, she always put children first. She wouldn't have risked Maude's life, not even for the glory of her pottery.

"Then, time passes and that child grows up and now she wants to right an old wrong."

Those stupid, stupid, shortsighted police. They wanted to make this drug bust so badly, and there was Eileen shouting at their door. But they wouldn't listen to her. They dismissed her. The one person who could have testified and taken the whole thing down.

"So you killed her."

Finn's eyes snap back to meet hers. They are slits filled with anger and hatred.

"I didn't kill your sister," Finn growls. "I didn't kill anyone."

"Right."

"It's true." Finn grabs the bars and shoves his face against them. "Think about last night. I even tried to save you! You're so high and mighty. You think you and your family walk on water. Pillars of this community. Upholding right and wrong. Well, you're wrong." He shakes the bars between his fists and then releases them, leaning back against the wall behind the bench. "If you really want to know what happened to your precious sister—the one you walked away from and forgot all about until now—you should speak with your brother. Ask Declan what happened to her. Cause I didn't kill her."

Biddy feels as if she's been slapped. She stares at him through wide eyes, searching…searching hard…for a tell that he is lying.

Finn smiles. "You're also wrong about me going down for these drugs. I cut a deal. That's why I'm here and those other two thugs aren't. People like me always land on my feet. But I'm afraid Declan won't be so lucky. I might've been forced to mention his name to the police." He leans forward again and looks right at her, eye to eye. "You don't want to mess with me."

"Oh, but I really do." Biddy's heart breaks for Declan, but she is going to sort this out.

"Biddy Bramley?"

Biddy looks to her left and sees the young police officer standing by the cell door, keys dangling from his hands. His coloring looks a little green.

"Apparently, after much reflection…a great deal of reflection…Sheila Ryan has recanted her statement." He shifts his weight from one foot to his other. "She thinks it's a different old, pompous, stuck-up woman who is a prostitute…not you. Her words, not mine." The last part is spoken quickly.

"Well," Biddy says, standing up and straightening her jacket. "Mistakes happen. I recant my statement as well."

He unlocks the cell door. "You're free to go."

Biddy walks out and turns back to face Finn. "This isn't over."

Finn shrugs.

Biddy follows the officer to the front of the station. Shelia is standing there, waiting for her, looking like she just enjoyed every ride in an amusement park, which, Biddy thinks, surely is what happened in her absence. Amelia, Megan, and Ruby stand beside her, looking a little pale and shell-shocked. But it is Richard Davenport who looks the worst-off. His face is white, and he's gripping the handles of his briefcase so tightly,

Biddy worries he may have a heart attack. Megan had been wrong that they needed Richard Davenport to navigate the justice system. It turns out all they needed on their side was Sheila Ryan.

"I told them every single act I thought you had ever performed," Sheila says with glee, "and it wasn't until I got to the grand finale that I realized it wasn't you. This other woman had a totally different shaped butt. I can't believe I didn't realize it sooner."

"It's hard to believe," Biddy says.

"Did you at least learn some things while you were in holding?" she asks, this time more serious.

Biddy had. But like Richard Davenport, she didn't like everything she learned, either. Finn told many many lies in his tirade. Of that, Biddy is sure. Eileen had founded the pottery. Finn had used it for illegal means. And Eileen had been forced out when she threatened to report Finn's activities to the police. But when Finn denied murdering Eileen, Biddy thinks he was telling the truth.

33

Biddy

The Pooka Women's Club meets at the pub that evening. To celebrate, claims Ruby, always reaching for the sunshine. But everyone here knows that isn't what they are doing. They are settling. Yes, Finn will probably serve prison time for the drug bust, but he won't be tried for murder. Nor will anyone else, if his innocence claim is true. Maude is so mad, she refuses to join them.

Biddy takes a sip of beer and sets the glass back down on the bar top. She long ago traded this beverage in for wine, but the bitterness of beer is just what she needs tonight. It's been a day.

"I should've done more," Biddy says.

She still doesn't know who murdered her sister. If it wasn't Finn, then who? She tries to push one name out of her head, but it keeps popping back. Declan. Declan was at the drop last night. If he could be involved in the drug ring, was he also capable of murdering his own sister?

"What more could you possibly do?" Ruby smiles sympathetically from the other side of the bar, where she stands

252

drying bar glasses. Amelia squeezes her arm.

"Believe it or not, you can be wrong," Ruby says. "And you are this time. Your gut is wrong. Finn is the murderer. He's the only one with a motive. He stood to lose a lot of money if Eileen took back ownership of the company. He also had the means. Lead is used in pottery making. And the opportunity. Maude and Eileen worked all day. Anyone could get in their house and add lead to a bottle of alcohol. You need to let this go. Finn will get jail time."

She knows what Ruby says is logical, but Biddy can't let it go. Biddy's gut is not wrong. Finn did not murder Eileen. He doesn't have it in him. He'd even tried to save their lives last night.

The pub is crowded and the room is warm, both from the heat of the bodies and the fire in the hearth. Fall has arrived and, thanks to the peat that Ruby always adds to the tinder, the room has an earthy, comforting smell that is the perfect accent for the soft din of voices. None of this is making Biddy feel better, though. In fact, it feels like most of the bar's inhabitants are shooting the group angry looks. This, at least, Biddy knows she is imagining. What could the town possibly have against her?

"You know what," Megan says. "Ruby is right. We are being stupid. We single-handedly broke up a drug ring, proved that a woman was murdered, and the most likely suspect is in prison. We should be happy." Megan picks up her beer and holds it aloft. Amelia, Ruby, and Sheila follow suit. "To the Pooka Women's Club and my mom, who led the charge."

"Here, here," the other women shout and take a sip.

Biddy forces a smile on her face as she clinks their glasses. This so-called celebration can't end soon enough.

"Megan, there you are." All three women turn to see an attractive man wearing flannel, jeans, and a navy vest striding towards them. Although drawing long looks from quite a few other women as he wedges his way between the crowded tables, his eyes are only on Megan.

"Hubba, hubba," Ruby says, elbowing Megan.

"Oh look." Sheila rolls her eyes. "It's Doctor Dirt."

"How are you?" he asks Megan. He looks like he is about to hug Megan, but then notices the staring faces of her friends, changes his mind, and awkwardly squeezes her arm.

"I'm fine." Megan says, blushing at his touch. "It was quite a day. We spent most of it at the police station."

Brady leans against the bar. "What did they have to say?"

"Well, they arrested Finn, so the cops are pretty confident they broke up the drug ring."

Brady nods. "And Eileen's murder?"

Megan shakes her head. "They don't have any evidence to look into it. They said they had enough to bust Finn on the drug charges and told us to be happy he's in jail no matter what the reason."

"I see."

Brady runs a hand through his hair and looks appropriately sad for her. Biddy's heart warms as she watches their interaction. This man is a vast improvement over the cheating professor. And he seems genuinely interested in her daughter and even in their quest.

"So, this is all over for you now?" he asks.

Megan nods. "Yes, the police are taking over. Our brush with law enforcement is done."

He relaxes ever so slightly, and Biddy is once again happy to see the genuine concern for her daughter.

"Then how about a celebratory dinner tonight?"

"Oh…" Megan looks at her mother and the others, then back at Brady. "I think I'm going to stay here with the others."

"Oh Megan, go," Biddy says, thinking of the loneliness that must've driven her daughter into the arms of a cheating man. "It's fine. We're going to call it a night soon, anyway."

"How about I cook for you?" Brady says. "I promise, I'll keep it very low key. One glass of wine and dinner and I'll drive you home. You can just wear what you have on."

Megan looks tempted.

"Go on," Biddy says. "You should enjoy a night with someone your own age. And we owe him for his help last night."

Megan smiles at her mother and then at Brady. "I'd love to."

The group bids them goodbye and watches them walk to the door.

"He's handsome," Amelia says.

"He is," Biddy says.

"I don't like him," Sheila says. "And before you all ask, no, I don't know him professionally. It's just a feeling…Oh no."

Sheila's eyes had remained on the pub's door and now the other three women look in that direction to see the Chief of Police enter the pub and wedge himself through the crowd in their direction. He is still clad in his formal white collared shirt and dress blues. Camera ready, Biddy thinks.

"Beer?" Ruby says to him hopefully.

"No." He turns his attention to Biddy. "I need to talk to you."

Biddy was afraid of this. She shakes her head. She is simply exhausted. "I agreed to testify against Finn. Can't whatever this is wait until tomorrow?"

"Apparently, it can't," he says. "We've arrested Declan

Delancy."

Biddy's heart breaks a little. She knew it was coming…Finn had told her so. And Declan probably deserves it. Even so, he's her brother. She runs her hand over the cool beer glass. "I want nothing to do with that."

"He doesn't feel the same way," the Chief says. "He said he'd be willing to turn on everyone else involved, but only if he gets to talk to you."

"No."

Biddy doesn't even need to think about it. It's time she leaves the devastation of her family behind. She tried her best, but she can't save the world and she's not turning on her brother. She takes a sip of her beer, throws some money on the counter, and stands up. It is time to go home.

"He says it's about Eileen," the Chief raises his voice at her retreating back. "He says only you can fix this. Plus, I need you to find out who else was involved in this drug thing."

"I'm not interrogating my brother for you." Biddy says. However, she pauses, only two steps from the bar. Declan is willing to talk to her about Eileen? Was her brother really involved in her sister's death? Does she want to know the answer to that question?

"You don't have to do it," Amelia says, also to her back. "You've done enough."

This is true. And Biddy isn't sure she wants to hear the answers. But, that said, she's devoted her entire summer to Eileen's cause. Maybe it is finally time to learn the truth. Whether or not she likes it. She turns around to face the Chief.

"I'll talk to him."

* * *

The police station is mostly dark when Biddy enters, being that it is after hours.

She looks at the empty cells where she and Finn had spoken earlier and turns to Chief Halloran. "Where are the prisoners?"

He glances over at the cage. "They're transferred to Evansville every evening."

"Then why would Declan still be here?"

"He was just picked up, and multiple other agencies strongly suggested I meet his demand to see you. Finn helped us…but he doesn't know the biggest players up the food chain. Declan might. A lot is riding on your conversation."

Biddy sighs and follows him down the hallway past the Chief's office and comes to a stop at a door on the left with a slit of light shining from beneath. The door next to this one opens up and a young cop walks out.

"The DEA guy you left me with is pacing. Says the clock is ticking."

"Right." The Chief exhales. His hooded eyes turn to Biddy. "Look, I get this is uncomfortable for you, making your brother talk, but let's not forget he is the bad guy here. Be a good citizen and then you can go home and we can go home and all of us can put this behind ourselves."

Biddy is pretty sure she'll never be able to put this behind her. But she is going to be a good something. Not a good citizen, but a good sister. She just has to figure out to whom. Eileen or Declan.

The Chief opens the door for her, and she walks past his girth into the room. Declan is sitting at a metal table with his hands cuffed to a bar in front of him. To her left is a large plate of glass, behind which she is sure is the Chief, the young cop, and the nameless DEA agent. She takes a seat at the table with her back to the glass, facing Declan. He looks up from his hands and relief floods his eyes when they focus on her.

Clad in a dirty white t-shirt, with a faded flannel shirt over it, Declan looks as if he'd been in the fields just hours ago. His hands, crossed in front of him on the table, are embedded with dirt.

"You're a sight for sore eyes," he says. "Last time I had to call someone from the police station, it was dad and he didn't look half as sorry for me."

Biddy remembers this. Teenage Declan had gotten drunk and smashed the truck into a light pole. Dad had picked him up, driven him home, and beat him. Their father drove the damaged truck for two more years before he could afford to fix it. She suddenly realizes neither father nor son had an easy time running that farm. It seems to bring out the worst in people.

"The police want me to get you to talk, Declan," Biddy says. "They're sitting on the other side of that wall listening."

Declan smiles. The smile reminds her again of the teenage boy. Of the time he'd come to see her in the high school play. He'd sat in the back row and given her just that smile when she walked on stage. Half apologetic that it was he who was there and not her father. Half encouraging.

"Don't worry Babs. It's fine. I'll talk to them after I talk to you." He reaches across the table as far as his cuffs will allow and grips her hands. "I want you to know what happened to Eileen. And I want you to give the farm to her daughter. Can you do that?"

Biddy nods. The thought of Maude running a farm is laughable, but she'll deal with that later. She takes a breath and asks the only question that matters to her. The one she doesn't know if she actually wants answered.

"Did you kill Eileen?"

"What?" Declan jerks upright in his chair, dropping her hands. "No. God. No. How could you think that?"

Relief floods through her. She hadn't thought that. She'd never thought that. But she had to ask.

"So, it was Finn?" This is an answer she can live with. She must've been wrong, just like the others said.

Declan shakes his head. "No, it wasn't him, either. That man is incapable of doing anything other than talking."

Biddy smiles at the perfect description. "Remember the year you challenged him to an arm wrestling competition in the cafeteria when he said he lifted weights every morning?"

Declan laughs. "He lasted one second. Little Katie put up a better fight than that and she was only seven."

They both laugh.

"He was always full of shit," Declan says.

"Always," Biddy agrees. She lets the light moment linger and then both their faces grow serious again. "So what happened?"

Declan leans back in his chair.

"It all started a few years after you left. Dad had died, and I was on my own, trying to provide for all the kids. The whole town was struggling. Farming became less about growing quality products and more about price, volume, and distribution. Farming moved to Mexico and South America, where it could be done cheaper and at greater scale. No one wanted our product. We were all going out of business. I was maybe a month away from having the farm repossessed.

That's when the cooperative came in."

Biddy nods. "Everyone keeps saying that."

"Because it saved us," Declan says. "Suddenly, we were able to combine our product to get the volume we needed and ship it anywhere. We could compete against the foreign farms. We had money in our pockets again. We fixed the houses, shopped at the stores, ate at the restaurants, and paid at the clinic. Everything came bouncing back. It was a miracle. Apparently, Eileen rose with the tide, too. I knew she was sneaking around that pottery. And, suddenly, she was contributing more to our household budget than me. I didn't ask questions. I was grateful. Dad had died, and I was just trying to keep everyone afloat."

"Why didn't you call?" Biddy leans forward. "I would've helped you!"

Declan frowns. "I didn't need your charity, Babs. I needed to make my farm work."

She sits back and sighs. "Then how did you end up a drug dealer?"

Declan flinches at the words, but doesn't deny them. Biddy knows it is not a grocery delivery he was making last night.

"Like all good things in this world, there was a catch. The cooperative was expensive to run. Especially in the start-up phase. We had to pay for all the fancy equipment and machines to get the shipping right. And that had to happen upfront."

"And this fell on your shoulders?"

"It fell on the town's shoulders."

Oh, dear God. Biddy suddenly understands where this is going. She understands what Declan has been trying to tell her all along. The repeated mentions of the suffering of the town. Of it being bigger than Eileen. Bigger than him.

"The only way we could get the cooperative started was if all the farmers in the town agreed to do what was necessary to fund it."

"And that was the illegal activity?"

He looks pleadingly at her. "Enniskillin sells prescription drugs. All the farms devote a section of their fields to growing illegal drugs. And we sell soil from the toxic waste site at the old Aisling estate. None of it hurts the community, though. All the illegal stuff goes to cities. "

"It's drugs and toxic waste!" Biddy's voice rises.

"I know," Declan says. "But don't you see? We are just sending it back to the places that produced the toxic waste in the first place. These businesses have no problem dumping their waste here. They have no problem buying drugs with all their excess money. This was all going on before we got involved. We just decided to take a cut of it. And use the profit for good. We're growing America's food. America needs farms."

Biddy can't believe he is justifying this. No wonder the Pooka Women's Club is getting dirty looks everywhere they go. The whole town is in on this. The whole town is guilty.

"Where does Eileen fit into this?"

Declan has the grace to look apologetic at this point. "Finn had screwed her out of the factory by threatening her when she had the baby. When she got dementia, she started talking again. She kept going to the Aisling Estate, picking up soil, and walking around town screaming the truth needs to come out. I tried to shut her up. I really did."

"That's when you punched her."

"I was trying to save her," he whispers. "She needed to stop talking. But she wouldn't stop. She was risking everything…

She was drawing attention to the dump and the pottery where all the shipping took place."

He looks at Biddy, likely searching for forgiveness. He finds none. Still, he takes a breath and reaches his hands over Biddy's.

"So, who killed her?" Biddy asks. "Who?"

"None of the townspeople did it. We wouldn't. Not even Finn Murphy. It was Brady Hughes, the owner of the cooperative. Brady killed her."

34

Megan

Megan walks up to Brady's house, curious to see the home behind the man. He is a study in contradiction, and maybe that is what she finds so enticing. The successful startup, the belief he can change the world, the hands on attention he gives his investments—all speak to a driven business entrepreneur. But then there is his quieter side. The side of a boy who lost his parents at a young age, who is well versed in Irish history and lore, and who genuinely loves living in a small town.

His house is a simple cottage, a good fifteen minutes outside of town and surrounded by never ending farmland. It's smaller than her mother's and more remote, which she didn't think possible, but it is beautiful. The white clapboard house jets in and out, creating the promise of numerous nooks and crannies, so different from the cold open floor plans of today. The roof line mirrors this, with shingled peaks rising high in the air. Window boxes holding mums and ivy spill into the garden that surrounds the house.

As Megan passes through the cheerfully painted yellow door, she enters a long living room with a wood-beamed ceiling and a huge stone fireplace centered on one wall. Although not lit, it still carries the scent of peat. The furnishings are cozy and would have a museum director drooling. A deep green and navy plaid rug covers wide planked, pegged floors. Brown leather furniture surrounds the fireplace. Lamps and beloved trinkets sit on intricately carved antique tables, while early century landscapes cover the walls.

"Oh Brady, it's beautiful." Megan turns in a slow circle, hardly knowing where to look first.

"Thank you." He blushes a bit. "I spent years collecting everything you see. I never really had a home of my own before this, and I still travel a lot for business, so this place is important to me."

"I can tell."

He smiles awkwardly and Megan wonders if he's not had many other women over. Maybe not even other friends.

"Can I get you a drink?"

"I'll take a beer since I've already started with that at the pub."

"A beer it is." He heads through a doorway to the kitchen, and Megan hears the refrigerator open. "You don't strike me as a beer drinker."

His voice is slightly muffled as it carries through to the living room. Megan only half hears it as she looks around and notices a lack of photos of friends. How odd. He's done so much good for the town, you'd think he'd have tons of pictures. She picks up a porcelain figurine of a lone boy holding a lamb and studies it.

"I'm more of a wine person, but as Ruby says, when in Rome..."

God, is she really quoting Ruby now? Megan sets the figuring down and moves to admire the artwork on the walls. She turns when Brady comes back into the room carrying two glasses. He hands her one, and they clink them together.

"Well, you're looking more Roman now than the first day I saw you."

Megan cringes remembering the snobbish, ambitious professor she'd been just a few short weeks ago. "I'm feeling more Roman now."

"Good," Brady says. "Because I bought a true Roman meal. Refrigerated lasagna. It'll only take a half hour to warm and I'll make a salad as well."

"Perfect." Megan realizes she is starving. Chips and candy bars from the police station vending machine did not constitute a lunch. Plus, her stomach has been in a knot since yesterday, and, try as she might, she can't get it to untwist itself. She reminds herself constantly that the crisis is over. Her mother is safe. Nevertheless, the knot stubbornly remains. Maybe food will help.

Brady reaches a hand forward and gently brushes a wayward curl back behind her ear. Then he leans in and his lips gently brush hers. Warmth spreads throughout her body. The knot is still there, but she wants nothing more than for him to do it again.

He steps back. "I think I've wanted to do that since the first moment I met you."

She feels her face flush. She knows it's too soon. She just got out of one bad relationship and shouldn't dive into another. But this seems so good. Has she finally found a healthy relationship?

"Stay here," he says, "and I'll make the salad and get dinner ready."

Brady turns and goes back into the kitchen. A few moments later, Megan hears a saxophone swell over the banging of pots and pans from a speaker in the kitchen. She is glad she came. A little time away from everything is just what she needs.

Her phone rings in her bag. She pulls it out to see it's her mother. Her heart races just as it does every time she sees her mother's name. Megan moves her finger to tap the accept button. But she needs to stop this. Her mother is fine. Whatever it is, can wait. She hits the button to send the call to voicemail. Brady is right. She needs a few hours away from all of that.

Megan puts the phone on silent and drops it back into her bag, which she places next to the coffee table. She then wanders over to a writing desk under a window. The view out the window is pitch black now, as there are no other houses nearby. However, during daylight hours, it must be tremendous. Nothing other than rolling hills surrounds the little house.

Megan glances down at the desk and sees a tiny framed black-and-white photograph. Finally. A sign that Brady has a life. She picks it up. Two faces stare back at her. They look a little grim, long and thin. She thinks back to the story Brady had told her about the man and wife who died. Were these people his parents? She sets the photo down.

Next to the desk are bookshelves overflowing with books. They contain everything from literature and folklore to science and ecology. All appear well read. She smiles when she sees a black cloth bound one with gold foil, declaring it to be *The Legend of the Pooka*. Maybe this is where he got the story. She pulls it out and, sure enough, it opens naturally to a short story, where a tightly folded slip of paper marks its place. The short story is called 'The Prince of the Furies'. She flips quickly ahead and sees that it is only five pages long. She looks back through the doorway to the kitchen where Brady stands by the sink, washing lettuce. She should have time to read this. She curls up on the couch, tucking her legs under her. Then she starts the story.

It begins just as the story he'd told her, only this time, the father is a benevolent king and the boy a prince. The king honors and serves the gods well by being a good steward of their land. Over time, he develops a close friendship with a pooka and the two's pranks bring laughs to the kingdom. But then one day, the king grows ill. He gets sicker and sicker until he isn't able to rise from his bed. Eventually, the king dies. The pooka senses his son is in jeopardy as well and whisks him away to safety. Although the boy is gone, the pooka never gives up his search for what had killed the king. He finally finds the answer as other creatures in the land become ill and die. The land has been poisoned.

Megan pauses. This bit is exactly the tale Brady told her. However, she sees the story now continues. Why would Brady have left the second part out? She reads on.

Not knowing what to do, the pooka seeks the help of the Fury, three goddesses who bring revenge to all who cross their path. The Fury advises the pooka that the young boy is now grown and the true heir to his father's kingdom. He needs to be brought back to defend what is his. The pooka brings the boy back and leaves him with the Fury. The pooka can't stay, as it is not in his blood to be cruel. The boy is a good student. He learns to be just, fair, and kind to all who protect his land, but cruel and ruthless to anyone who damages it.

Over time, the Prince collects all the poison from his land and sends it back to the land of his trespassers, killing them all and bringing peace to his father's spirit. He summarily executes anyone who gets in his way.

Despite the cozy room, Megan feels a chill wash through her. She flips back to the first page of the short story and studies the black and white drawing at the top of the old man with yellow eyes and the king. The story certainly took a dark turn with the murderous acts of revenge. But, of course, this isn't the story of Brady's life. He just draws from the first part for inspiration. And that part is bright and cheery.

Curious now about how Brady's parents had actually died, she closes the book and walks back to the photograph on the desk. She opens the back and, as she expected, their names and date are written there. She pulls out her phone, ignores the alerts for the two texts and voicemail from her mother, and googles the names. What she sees makes her hold her breath.

Brady's parents had been part of a lawsuit against a large corporation for illegal dumping. His parents' fate is just like the story. Only there is a later story that the CEO of the company died mysteriously in a hit and run. Megan puts the photo back on the desk and opens the book again. This time she looks at the slip of paper marking the page of the story. It is a copy of the articles of incorporation for Brady's business. For business description, it says farming cooperative involved in the sale of meat, vegetables, fruits, dairy, and soil. And soil? Is he selling the poisoned soil back to people in large cities? Was the still-contaminated soil not a mistake? Had he done it on purpose?

"Megan, do you want a vinegarette or something creamy

on the salad?" Brady comes to a stop just inside the doorway to the living room and stares at the book she is holding.

"What exactly is your business model?" she asks.

His skin pales, but Megan has to give him credit for his voice remaining calm. "I told you, we sell farm products. Isn't that what the paper in your hand says?"

She looks back down at it. "And soil."

"Of course, farms need to make any money they can these days. Why not sell the soil?"

"How are you able to undercut all your competitors in price and still make money?"

She'd always wondered about this, but figured that she just wasn't smart enough to understand the business model. That had been silly. Things that went against logic and were inordinately complex were usually because someone was trying to hide a truth.

Brady looks uncomfortable. "We just figured out a way to do it more efficiently and move the merchandise more cheaply."

"Wow, you must really be smarter than everyone else."

Brady stares at her wide-eyed. He must've thought she'd just accept that non-answer and move on. In fairness, every part of her being wants to. She wants to just accept anything that is mildly reasonable and go back to a lasagna and salad dinner with a man who excites and intrigues her. But she can't. She's done that once before and it didn't end well.

She watches his face closely. It is tense and furrowed, as if he is trying to figure out a way to double down on the lie. But then it relaxes and his eyes turned pleading. She is going to get the truth. She is grateful. She is so tired of lies.

"My parents could barely make ends meet as farmers. People never think about where their food comes from. They treat farming like some easy thing that just happens. It's not. And I genuinely want to help farmers."

"But…" Megan encourages him when he stops speaking.

"But it isn't easy to do. The weather is unpredictable, and it's only getting worse. And then you add on top of it outsourcing to third world countries and corporations using rural areas as dumping grounds for toxic waste and it's almost impossible."

"So you decided to take the toxic waste, profit from it, and then send it back to the cities."

"Yes." His eyes plead with her. "The revenue has saved the farms. And that is exactly what they are doing to us. Why should we care about them?"

"But that isn't even the end of your story. When that income stream wasn't enough to build your distribution center, you decided to sell drugs, too."

Megan remembers Brady insisting on driving to the police station rather than calling 911 last night. He'd been trying to give his drug shippers a chance to get away. To delay the arrival of the police. And he'd risked her mother's life in the process.

"Megan, I know it sounds awful, but you have to understand. We didn't create the waste, and we didn't create the demand for drugs. The country is even legalizing drugs. We just decided to use the profits for good. Millions more would suffer if we don't protect our food supply. Look at this town. It's booming. The benefit outweighs the harm. People who buy drugs would buy them from someone else if they didn't use us. And our drugs are cleanly cut. They are the safest on the market."

"And Eileen?"

His shoulders slump.

"It was before I knew you." His voice is soft. "If I knew she was important to you, I would have never done it."

"Oh god." Megan slumps onto the couch. He was the one who killed Eileen. "She was important to her daughter, Maude. She was important as a human being!"

He takes a step towards her but stops when she cringes away on the couch. His eyes plead with her. "She was drawing attention to the pottery and to the Aisling Estate. I couldn't risk someone fishing around the building and finding the drugs. She was just one person. Our profits don't just benefit the farmers in our cooperative. We donate to churches and schools and are funding an addition and staffing to the Medical Clinic. All that would've stopped if she blew the whistle. I am on the right side of history here."

How could he believe that?

"The thing about history," Megan says quietly. "Is that it isn't just about institutions. It's also about individuals. And I'm coming to believe that history would be better served teaching the value of individual lives over so-called economic progress at any cost. My mother taught me that."

Ever so faintly, distant sirens sound. They stare at each other as they become louder and louder. Megan wonders what Brady will do. There is nowhere to run, so she sits on the couch and awaits her fate. However, Brady doesn't move. He just stands across the room, staring at her. A car screeches to a stop. This one without sirens. Then, there is pounding on the door.

"Megan," her mother's voice carries through the thick wood in a muffle. "Open this door this instant. Brady, if you have harmed a hair on her head, so help me.."

Megan glances at the door and the empty gut-wrenching

ache she feels inside, is mildly soothed. Her mother has come. She looks back at Brady.

"So what now?"

Tears form in his eyes. "I would never hurt you. Don't you get it? I'm in love with you."

He walks to the door and opens it. "Come on in, Biddy," he says. "She's fine. I'll go in peace."

<h1 style="text-align:center">35</h1>

<h1 style="text-align:center">Biddy</h1>

The problem with winning, with being right really, is that it is never as rewarding as you think it will be. By definition, winning implies that there are losers. And often, you have no real control over who those losers are. This time it is Megan.

The Pooka Women's Club reassembles for a brunch meeting at Biddy's house. Megan is on the couch looking dazed, holding a plate of little quiches Ruby has prepared, but she hasn't touched them. She hasn't touched any sort of food. Biddy is so desperate for Megan to return to her old self, she even disappears upstairs to find Megan's phone and carries it down for her. Megan doesn't even look at it.

Ruby sits in a folding chair next to Biddy, her large body spilling over the edges. She is doing her part to lighten the mood. She tells joke after joke while waiting for Maude to arrive. She must have spent her whole morning researching them in preparation because she's written them down on a sheet of paper and reads them off. What did the shark say when he ate a clownfish? This tastes a little funny. I told my friend that she paints her eyebrows in a little too high. She

273

looked surprised. What kind of tea is hard to swallow? Reality. Biddy gets mad at this one and Ruby finally stops. Now Biddy feels bad about hurting her feelings, too.

Amelia and Sheila keep stealing glances at each other as if this is a party they want to leave. They are sitting across from the others in two folding chairs, eating the little quiches in bulk so that they have an excuse for not speaking.

Finally, Maude arrives.

Amelia jumps up. "I'll get it." She runs for the door.

She's quick. Biddy notices Sheila had been about to do the same.

Maude strides in, with Amelia trailing slowly after her. Biddy reminds herself to feel love for her niece. It's not her fault Megan is so sad. It's Brady's fault. But Maude can be quite intense, and they are quite tired. Maude sits on a folding chair between Ruby and Amelia and looks at the group expectantly. "So what's next?"

Biddy exhales. "Maude, we proved that your mother was murdered, and we found her killer. We are here to celebrate that and begin healing. There is nothing next."

Maude's eyes open wide. "But you still didn't prove that she founded the pottery."

"Maude." This comes from Amelia. She looks at the rather distraught Megan, still sitting in a stupor beside Biddy, and then back to Maude. "I know that has to be a little disappointing, but I think the circumstances changed and what we proved is much more important. Does the pottery really matter in the face of the rest of what we discovered?"

"Of course it matters! My mom created it."

"I'm sorry Maude. We just weren't able to prove it," Biddy says.

Maude looks from one face to the other. They are all firmly set. Except Megan's. Megan's is blank. And, although Biddy is good at reading people, Maude is not.

"Cousin?" she says. "Aren't you going to do something? You promised."

Megan looks up, and her eyes focus on Maude. It's the first sign Biddy has seen that her daughter isn't catatonic since driving her home from Brady's house last night.

"I did, didn't I?"

The words leave Megan's lips so slowly; they are almost slurred. Even Maude looks a little taken aback by her lethargy.

Megan smiles and stands up from the couch. "Come on, let's go. It's time to look through all those books in your mother's bedroom."

The rest of the group jumps up.

"Are you sure?" Biddy asks. "You really don't need to do this."

"I'll do it for you," Ruby says. "You can stay here."

"I'll do it," Sheila says. "I practically have an advanced degree in biology. I'll figure it out."

"No," Megan says. "I'll do it." She speaks firmly. "It'll give me something to keep occupied. And maybe something good can come from all this. There are tons of chemistry books. There must be a formula for the glaze in there somewhere."

"We can all go," Biddy says.

Megan smiles, a sad little smile. "I think I'd rather do it myself. I need to be by myself for a bit. Besides, I'll have my cousin with me to cheer me up."

Everyone winces as Megan and Maude leave.

"Dear God," Sheila says, "if Maude is her pick me up, she'll be suicidal."

"We should go after them," Ruby says.

"I could get my kids to help leaf through the books," Amelia says.

Biddy considers their offers.

"No. I think we should let Megan do this alone." Biddy thinks back to the time right after Charles had died. When she decided to come here to Pooka and take on Eileen's project. It had been healing. It had given her purpose. "Megan needs to feel good about something. I think we should let her do this."

The celebratory brunch disbands soon after Megan's departure. No matter how many interests Biddy has, her primary job, now and always, is to be a mother. And, it's no secret, mothers will do anything to stop their children from hurting. So, if Megan thinks that proving Eileen founded the pottery might ease her pain, then, by golly, Biddy is going to just that.

Biddy has one more idea of where she might find evidence. She leaves the mess of food and chairs in the living room, heads to the kitchen to retrieve her bag and car keys, and heads out the door.

It doesn't take long to get from her house to the Delancy farm, although the difference in ambience would make you believe they are worlds apart. Biddy slams her car door shut and surveys the old house. Echoes of footsteps of six children and two adults seem to still play in the air. It is a house that, although not always perfect, was filled with life and even some laughter. Now, a little beat up and a little worn, the house still doesn't seem dead. It seems like a well loved sweater just waiting to wrap itself around its next owner. Soon Biddy will introduce Maude to it, as Declan had requested. The two slightly eccentric old souls will fit like a glove, she thinks. But that's not why she is here now.

She walks around the side of the house and heads into the back fields. Thankfully, she has worn a shiny green pair of wellies over her wool slacks. She'd found the wellies next to a bench in the rental house. They'd never been worn and Biddy is pretty sure that Linc, the homeowner, had put them there as a prop, to add to the country feel of the home. Now, they'll be a much more convincing prop, she thinks, as they sink into the freshly tilled soil and re-emerge from each step coated in dirt and shards of husk. Declan must have just cut the cornstalks before his arrest. He had been readying the farm for Maude.

The walk is longer than she remembers, but it is a beautiful crisp seventy degree day. The farm is about 250 acres in total and split into various fields by crop. Biddy reaches the end of the cornfield and makes her way around a cluster of scrub-brush to enter the soybean field. This is easier to traverse as Declan hasn't tilled it yet and the ground is firm. She walks the five acres, not being too careful about avoiding the plants with her footsteps, as she knows this crop will not receive the attention it needs with Declan gone. She comes to a stop when she once again reaches the straggly bushes that demarcate one field from the next. Only, this time, it's not another field on the far side of the bushes.

The view takes her breath away. Too big to be called a retaining pond, too small to be a lake, they had grown up calling it the swimming hole. It's about 3000 square feet in area and surrounded by towering trees. It is like a little lush hidden Eden buried amid rolling open land.

Biddy walks towards it through the tall grasses, picking her knees up high. The trees get thicker here, right around the bank of the swimming hole. She reaches a maple, just hinting at turning red. She puts her hand against its rough trunk and searches, surprised she can't find what she's looking for. But then she remembers over fifty years have passed and the tree has grown. She looks up and there it is. If she stands on her tiptoes, she can reach the carving. BD + CB 4Ever. Well, at least until death did them part. Biddy Delancy and Charles Bramley had kept their promise.

She remembers the day they made this carving, over fifty years ago. An eighteen-year-old farm girl with flaming red hair and a twenty-something TV star, handsome as the day was young. Well, he wasn't exactly a TV star in the permanent sense of the word, but he was for that day. He was filming a special about a town called Pooka and its heritage. He was the host, a budding historian. And she was the subject matter.

The moment she'd heard her town was going to be on TV and needed people to interview, she'd started prepping. Hair curled, blouse pressed, and navy cardigan buttoned, she'd even pinned green ribbons in her hair before heading to the town hall for the audition.

'Hello,' he'd said as she settled onto the stool across from him. 'What's your name?'

'Babs…Barbara…Biddy,' she'd said, quickly thinking of all the posh nicknames she'd heard when she snuck to Boston for her interview at Radcliffe just a month before. And so a new identity was born.

'That's quite a mouthful of a name,' he'd joked.

'Well, it's a big job finding a name to describe all of me,' she'd said.

And then they'd talked. Her knowledge of the town's history was unsurpassed. She'd helped him take the show from a silly little fluff piece that made the town look folksy, to an in-depth study of Irish immigration and the changing landscape of America. She'd impressed him with her opinions on how society should advance, and he impressed her with his ambitions to get the most influential people in America to hear the lessons of the past. The last scene they filmed was in front of two rocks on the edge of town which, Biddy explained, were pooka, each sporting the telltale sign: a splash of yellow for eyes. Charles had laughed at the tale with delight. Neither mentioned that the yellow slashes looked freshly painted. Nor that Biddy's fingers born an odd yellow tint. And so a new myth was born.

Although this was their last scene on camera, it wasn't their last scene off. That had happened right here, beneath this tree, beneath the light of the moon and with the musical accompaniment of the cicadas. When they had finished, they wrapped their bodies around each other's and turned to see the moonlight dance on top of the water.

'Come with me,' he'd said.

Biddy had laughed. She'd had fun and even let herself pretend she was his equal for the day, but in her heart of hearts she always knew that a guy like him wouldn't tie himself to a girl like her.

'I'm serious,' he'd rolled onto one elbow and looked in her eyes. 'You're too smart for here. Too funny. Come with me. I'll show you the world.'

And she let herself imagine. Living in a brownstone in Boston. Trips to New York and Paris and China. Dinners with presidents and kings and Hollywood producers. Books, music, museums, culture.

And then she said no. Just like she had to Radcliffe when

they accepted her. The reason was the same.

'I can't. My family needs me here.'

For in her heart, she knew she could never leave them. Her older brother Declan, her just a year younger sister Eileen, and the three other kids, too young to survive a cruel, authoritarian father on their own. Biddy was still young and didn't know much. But she knew that family came first. So she said goodbye to her Boston dreams. Goodbye to Charles.

Until she found out that she was pregnant. And that made the family first equation an entirely different one to solve. It meant she was a mother. And it was her child, not her siblings, who must now come first. This child's life would be so much better in Boston. The others would be okay, she told herself. They would have to be.

And they were. All thanks to Eileen. For when a pregnant Eileen had been confronted with the exact same decision to stay or go, she'd stayed. As a result, their brother, Tommy, who'd been ten at the time, is now a tax attorney in Pennsylvania. Siobahn, then eight, is happily married and living in Maryland with three of her own. And little Katie, then five, is a banker in New York. That is Eileen's real legacy, in Biddy's eyes. It's not founding a multi-million dollar pottery. It's something much rarer. It is selflessness.

Biddy wipes a tear that slips from her eye and stares out at the pond, now dancing in the sunlight. Despite his failings, Charles had been a good husband and a good father. He'd given her everything he'd promised. It had almost assuaged her guilt for leaving Pooka. Just almost. But now, Biddy realizes, it's not too late to keep her promise to the rest of the family. For just because so much time has passed since she became a mother, doesn't mean she can't also go back to being a good sister. She gives the tree trunk one last stroke.

And then she turns around and walks back into the scrub-brush. Because now it's time to give Maude her legacy. This is no longer about Eileen. It's about her child.

Of all the people Biddy has spoken with, it is Arthur who unintentionally cracked the case that day, so long ago, at the Town Hall. When he mentioned Eileen, grabbing fistfuls of dirt and calling it gold. It had made Biddy remember passing Eileen on her way to meet Charles at the pond. Eileen had been standing in a shed and lighting dirt on fire.

Biddy turns in the direction of the shed, saying a small prayer that it is still standing. She walks through the field used for squashes, with vines coiling like snakes across the brown soil, and a multitude of orange pumpkins popping from its furls. Some are big, some are small. Just like so much else in life, there is no rhyme or reason.

Edging the field are the sunflowers, now taller than Biddy. She grips their thick, hairy stalks and gently pushes them aside to make her way through. And there is the shed. Right on the border of their property and the Callahans, although if the Callahans still own their farm, is anyone's guess.

No one knows how the shed got there. Any farmer worth their grain would tell you that you don't put an equipment shed on the edge of the property. You put it in the center so it is convenient for all the fields. Besides, this shed is too small. It looks more akin to a toolshed you'd find in a backyard—a simple small box with a peaked roof for drainage. Old wood forms the walls and paint peels in long white strips. Little holes pocket the surface where mice and rats chewed through it. Biddy's father had never used the shack, so it had quickly become a haven for the kids to play. It also sat on the hidden route to the swimming hole so that late night rendezvous with boyfriends or girlfriends wouldn't be seen.

Biddy hadn't thought that Eileen would have continued to use it since she had the beautiful factory to use in town. But Biddy had forgotten one thing. After Biddy left, Eileen had needed to stay close to home. She needed to keep an eye on the children. So she might've kept the shed as her headquarters.

Biddy winds her way through the knee high grasses and bends down to move the brick propped against the door, holding it closed. The door swings open and Biddy steps in. Cobwebs so thick they look like gaudy Halloween decorations coat the space. Biddy goes outside again and grabs a stick. She waves it in front of herself like a wand to clear a path. Sunlight streams through the pockmarked walls, beaming enough shards of light to see her way. The space smells dank of rotting wood. Shelves and cabinets line three of the walls opposite the door, and, in the middle, sits an old work table. Biddy goes to this. On top is filthy glassware of all shapes and sizes. Chemistry equipment.

Biddy clears the way to the back wall of shelving. And there it is. The evidence. Like a perfectly preserved museum, the history of the founding of Aisling Pottery spreads before her. On the left are pieces of pottery covered in ugly clumpy, miscolored glaze. Hints of the trademark green tint can be seen, but the execution is so terrible, it's a science experiment with little promise. That is, to anyone but Eileen.

Because Eileen keeps at it. As Biddy makes her way to the right, the pottery gets better. First, a smoother coating. And then, the most beautiful shimmering green color. Biddy picks a few of the pieces up. Stuck to the back of each is the formula for that sample's glaze. It must've taken Eileen years to perfect the formula. There were so many test pieces.

Biddy turns to her right. Here are the first designs, once the glaze had been perfected. Shelving holds stack upon stack of beautiful pottery. And, at the end of the row, is a magnificent hand-painted platter, likely the last piece Eileen ever made, given its location. It doesn't look anything like the other elegant, quietly sophisticated pieces. For this one is splashy. It is covered with baby ducks and little dolls and tiny pink bows. 'I love you to the moon and back' is printed across the middle. And on the back are Eileen's initials and Maude's birthday date right below.

The evidence is irrefutable. Eileen founded Aisling Pottery.

Biddy's cellphone rings, and she fishes it out of her handbag to answer it.

"I found the formula for the glaze," Megan says. "Wouldn't you know it wasn't in any of the chemistry books? It was tucked in the bible on her nightstand."

Biddy stares at the beautiful works of art before her, shining through even the thickest layer of dust as a beam of light falls upon it. "And I found her pottery. Signed and dated."

36

Maude

I told you so! I. Told. You. So. Didn't I tell you so all along? My mother founded the pottery. And today the entire town has shown up to celebrate her. Finally.

We are standing in front of the town hall and a huge green satin ribbon drapes across the railings to block the entry way. That TV show Megan is always talking about—One Hour or something like that—wanted a red ribbon and red carpet, but I insisted on green. It was Mom's favorite color. The factory is similarly festooned with green ribbons draped between every window. That I didn't have to insist on. Since I am now the owner and can do whatever I want.

I am wearing my Sunday best for the occasion. Biddy had said she'd take me shopping in Evansville since this was going to be on TV, but I wanted to wear the dress that my mother made me. It's a floral print she rescued from curtains that one of her employers was tossing. It's so pretty, and it tucks in at the waist just right and then flows in pleats to just below my knees. She was very proud that she reused some of the drapes' pleats. Biddy agreed this was very special. Almost too good to wear for this, she said. I told her I'd wear it anyway.

The whole town is dressed up for my mom's special day. They all stop to shake my hand like I'm famous and say the nicest things about my mom while we wait to get into the town hall. Behind them are TV cameras and trucks and newspaper reporters. Frankly, it's a lot to take in. I'd suggested just having a mass said in my mother's honor, but Biddy thought this would be a nicer tribute. She was right. And boy, does Biddy know how to do a tribute!

Biddy's standing next to the stage in front of the town hall, arguing with Arthur about who gets to speak first. The stage isn't really a stage. It's the landing at the top of the steps in front of the door to the town hall. But now it has a podium like you see at church and folding chairs behind it. They remind me of all the Women's Club meetings at Biddy's house. In fact, it is the members of the club who take their seats on them now. I never saw them look so proud. Amelia keeps waving to her kids, who are lined up in the front row. Their dad is taking pictures of her up there as if she is graduating from university. Ruby giggles in her chair as if the whole thing is quite funny. All of her patrons had shown up at the pub very early to surprise her. They'd made posters and sang 'She's a Jolly Good Fellow' and toasted her. Many times. I think she is a little tipsy. Corinthians says you cannot drink from the cup of the Lord and from the cup of demons, too. But I think the Lord is willing to overlook this one. Sheila looks the most uncomfortable of the group, which is odd, since she seems to know almost everyone here. At least, the men. They all turn red with joy when they see her. Megan sits at the end closest to the microphone, talking to the TV lady, Leslie, something or other. For a rather spoiled child, she's learned a lot of lessons the hard way this summer, but I think she's going to be just fine. Who wouldn't be with Biddy as a mother?

Finally, Biddy and Arthur stop arguing, and Biddy angrily marches to the chair next to Megan and sits down. Arthur, the winner of their argument, strolls up to a microphone.

Father Doyle turns to look at me. "It's time for you to join them up there," he whispers.

I nod and climb the side steps to the landing. My heart is thumping since I hate being the center of attention. But Father Doyle smiles encouragingly at me and Biddy takes my hand when I sit down next to her and gives it a squeeze.

"Welcome ladies and gentlemen." Arthur's voice booms through the speakers, accompanied by the most grating of screeching noises. He should've let Biddy speak first. That would've never happened on her watch.

He taps the microphone as if that might help, then a man in front of something that looks like a keyboard adjusts a bunch of levers and nods to Arthur.

"Today we are here for the grand opening and ribbon cutting ceremony to our newest town hall exhibit, honoring Eileen Delancy." Arthur pauses and everyone claps and cheers. "Eileen was a treasured member of our community and we are proud to give her the tribute she deserves."

This is a lie. They hated her. I move to get up to say something, but Biddy pulls me back down.

"That said," Arthur continues quickly, "this tribute would not have come to fruition without the efforts of our newest group, the Pooka Women's Club."

Ruby's patrons cheer their support.

"Now I have a surprise for these ladies," Arthur says.

We all turn to look at him, and I see everyone's face crease.

Apparently, Biddy doesn't even know what is coming, and Biddy knows everything.

"The President of Harvard University contacted me about a new award the university is endowing. This award recognizes and funds outstanding community achievements that uncover and preserve local history. And the award is dedicated to a beloved, recently deceased professor. The exciting news is that the President decided that the Pooka Women's Club is the perfect first recipient of this award. So here to present the first Charles Bramley Community History award to our club is Dr. Daniel Sturbridge, a treasured student of Charles Bramley and graduate of Harvard."

Out of nowhere, some man appears, wearing a big black robe and funny cap like you'd see in Harry Potter. He steps up to the microphone and holds up the hugest plaque you've ever seen. Biddy, Ruby, Amelia, Sheila, and Megan's names are on it. Everyone is clapping and cheering, but the Harry Potter man is grimacing. I think he is jealous he didn't win the award himself. I tell Biddy this, and she laughs and says she thinks I am right. Oddly, Megan looks pleased to see his discomfort.

Arthur gestures to the women's society to go up and receive the award. As they stand to the cheering crowd, I notice that their chests puff just the slightest. They look proud. There are tears in everyone's eyes, except Ruby's. Hers are running down her cheeks. They all stand together and walk to the center of the stage. Biddy steps up to the microphone vacated by Arthur and accepts the award to more cheers.

"On behalf of the Pooka Women's Club, this is the greatest honor we could have hoped to receive, and we are grateful." More clapping ensues. "However, I think I speak for all the women, that the true prize was righting a wrong. Our job in studying history is to see it through a clearer, less biased lens. And our work to recognize women's achievements in Pooka has only begun. Our club is constantly honoring new applications for members and we encourage you to join."

This time it is Arthur who is looking a little distraught as the clapping starts all over again.

"Now, it is time to cut the ribbon." Biddy says. "And it is our greatest pleasure to introduce Maude Delancy, daughter of Eileen, to do this honor."

I stand up to more clapping. Arthur hands me the most ridiculously big pair of scissors you've ever seen, and I step up to the ribbon. I have to use both my hands to get the scissors open and then snap them over the ribbon, which breaks and flutters to the ground. Everyone claps again, as if this were a gymnastic feat. It's like they've never used scissors before.

"Now let's go see the life and achievements of Eileen Delancy." Biddy steps to one side and gestures to the door. People funnel up the stairs and into the exhibit. The women's club and I follow the last of them. We've already seen the exhibit, which features blown up photos of the farm where my mom had grown up, her first pottery designs, and, of course, my baby platter. I'm going to hang this up in my new kitchen at the farm.

So yes, the Pooka Women's Club has won a prize, but they were right that the real winner was my mom, who would've been pleased as punch to have an entire exhibit right up front in the town hall devoted to her. Biddy even called my other aunts and uncle and they all came to see mom's exhibit. They had the nicest things to say about her and were so sorry to have fallen out of touch.

Mom's story is even going to be on TV. I'm speaking to that Leslie Stahl woman later. Sheila told me I need to mention the pottery, its address, phone number, and website as many times as I can on camera.

Which brings me to a funny realization. Today should have been the greatest day of my life. It is everything I hoped for. But, as I stand just inside the doorway listening to all the excited voices studying my mom's things, I'm the saddest I've been since the day my mom died. No one had ever been near this nice to my mom when she was alive and she isn't here to see this.

That is, everyone except the Pooka Women's Club. They'd championed me and my mom, flaws and all. And they didn't quit, no matter what. I can see them now across the room from me, smiling and laughing with each other. It isn't the exhibit that gives me joy and hope. It is the five unlikeliest of people coming together that made me see that the future can be entirely different if you stick together. Of all of them, I think Biddy understands this the most.

Biddy turns to look at me and winks.

37

Biddy

Biddy walks through the old Pooka church graveyard with Megan at her side. In the distance, she can hear the remnants of the day's festivities finishing up. Chairs and tables are being collapsed and loaded into waiting trucks to be driven onto the next event somewhere else. But, here, it is quiet.

They head over to the far corner of the cemetery, under the old oak tree. Biddy bends down to rub her fingers across her mother's grave. She needs to visit more. She needs to tell Megan more about her family.

Megan, however, is not looking at the gravestone of her grandmother. She is mesmerized by Eileen's, sitting just beside Biddy's mother's. Biddy can't blame her. When Maude found out just how much money she was entitled to from the pottery, the very first thing she did was to give her mother's headstone an upgrade.

"You don't think it's too much?" Megan says, eyeing the monument.

Above Megan's head marble angels soar, trumpets point at the gods and on a banner between two cherubs, read the words 'She walked in beauty.'

Biddy looks over at it. She has to take a few steps back and tilt her chin upward to see the whole thing. Maude had wanted it to be taller than any other in the graveyard. She'd achieved that goal. "Not at all. It's a monument of a daughter's love."

Megan raises her eyebrows. "I'll be sure to keep that in mind for your grave marker, when the time comes." She spreads her hands. "Picture this. A lifesized you, carved into the marble, rising into the air, with an army of angels waving goodbye from below. And the words: loving wife, devoted mother, and caring sister inscribed. And, above that, the title: 'She's a hooker.'

Biddy laughs. She no longer worries about how many people will attend her funeral. She knows that the people who will come are the ones who matter. And she has a whole new life ahead of her to create more of a legacy. One that she's excited about.

Megan looks at her, her face growing more serious. "You aren't coming home to Boston, are you?"

Even though she knows she's doing the right thing for both of them, her heart breaks a little. Biddy will miss her daughter.

"No," Biddy says. "I'm needed here. I've talked to that Linc boy and he's agreed to sell me the house."

Tears form in Megan's eyes and Biddy is reminded of the little girl she'd once been who she loved with all her heart.

"You don't think I need you in Boston?" Megan asks.

Biddy is sure of this answer. "No. I think you've got that all on your own. In fact, I think you could use less of your parents' presence."

Megan smiles through her tears.

"You'll figure it out," Biddy says. "Besides, do you seriously think that Maude Delancy can run both a multi-million dollar pottery business and a farm without a little guidance?"

Megan laughs. "Probably not, but can you?"

Biddy shrugs. "Probably not, but I can find people who can. And then I can make sure they don't quit when they become acquainted with their new boss."

Megan smiles. "I don't know that anyone can do that."

Her daughter turns away from the marble cherubs and looks at Biddy. "President Elliott says I still have my job at Harvard if I want it. I think he feels bad that his wife cheated with my fiance."

Biddy raises her eyebrows. "And what did you say?"

"I said no." Megan shrugs as if this were nothing, but Biddy is sure it was the hardest decision of her life. "I think I need to start fresh. To create my own path without dad or anyone else's legacy hanging over my head."

Her daughter chose well. It'll be hard for Megan to find a new role as the higher education community is fiercely competitive, but Megan needs a fresh start. And she needs to do it all on her own two feet this time.

"I'm going to miss you," Megan says.

"And I'm going to miss you." Biddy squeezes her hand. "But I have a feeling we'll still see a lot of each other."

"True. What about my seat on the Pooka Women's Club?"

Biddy inclines her head. "Well, I heard that Mellie Watson is gunning for it, but the club voted to keep you on. We're just going to conference you in. Please be on time and no cellphones."

"Got it." Megan turns back to the monument and then looks at her mother again.

"Do you regret not going to Radcliffe? Not having the opportunities I have?"

Biddy hugs her daughter into her. "Of course not. There is nothing I enjoyed more than being your mother. Nothing." She gives Megan one last squeeze and lets her go. "And I'm proud of my volunteerism. All those events I chaired during my years in Boston gave people a chance to unite, acquaint themselves with others, exchange ideas, and fund important causes. I consider you and my charity work my greatest contributions to society."

Megan looks at peace with that answer, and Biddy is glad. Her daughter should feel no guilt for her decisions. Plus, it's mostly true. But Biddy doesn't say the part that isn't. That it hurts that society doesn't return the appreciation. That the world couldn't function without the roles she and others play, but that not going to college and having a certain type of job makes her less in the world's eyes.

Biddy now knows the answer to this problem isn't that every woman should strive to be CEOs or community leaders. The roles of women should be as diverse as the women themselves. And Megan will be their megaphone.

Biddy looks at her daughter and smiles. Megan is one of society's elite, a pedigreed contributing member with a respected global platform. But she is also one of the Pooka Women's Club. A Delancy of Dubois... pronounced Duboyzee...County. She has a foot in both worlds. She is the changeling that can bridge two universes into one, if she just remembers the dignity of both.

Suddenly, a stream of sunlight bounces off the church window into Biddy's eyes, which flash a hint of gold. Of course, Biddy couldn't know this. But what she does know, is that her daughter's eyes do the same. This is no surprise to Biddy. She'd recognize the tinge of yellow anywhere. After all, Megan is her daughter and Biddy had always been the one who gave the town its pooka.

The End

THE ADVENTURE CONTINUES IN BOOK 2: A CRYPTIC DEATH

🏆 IPPY Gold Medal Winner — Best Mystery
She doesn't know her own name. Someone does—and they want her dead.

A woman turns up at the convent with a fortune in her pockets but can't remember her name. She is about to take her vows when her unknown past comes hunting her. The only thing standing in its way? The most unlikely of friends for a soon-to-be nun—Sheila.

Turn the page to read the sample chapter and make your purchase here.
https://www.amazon.com/dp/B0GKCTCXFB/

Enjoy a sneak preview of Book 2 in The Pooka Women's Club Mysteries: A Cryptic Death

Confidence, Sheila tells herself, looking in her bedroom mirror. Have confidence. You are ready for this.

At least she knows she nailed the outfit. She spent hours picking it out. She's learned a few things from her time with Biddy Bramley, and one is how to power dress… with a few age-appropriate tweaks, of course. So today, she dons her new Shanel tweed skirt suit bought at Hookyourman.com, one of her favorite shopping sites for her gentlemen's companion business. They have everything you could ever need for a bargain. For example, this outfit looks just like a real Chanel but is literally a tenth the price and better fitted. For makeup, she goes all in on the red lip and is certain she's done Coco… and Biddy… proud. As Sheila always says, if you dress the part, you can play the part. She stares at her reflection. She has dressed the part.

"Now, you can play the part," she whispers. Then she grabs her keys and heads out the door.

Biddy's house looks like a fairy tale home as she drives up. Nestled in a blanket of fallen multi-colored leaves, the stone house stands proud beside a little stream, where it has been rooted for centuries. When Sheila first saw it, she thought its owner would be one of those perfectly manicured old-money people who are born, live, and die, all in the same beautiful place. The ones who spend more time lifting their eyebrows than their fingers. But over the last year, she's come to know Biddy better, and Biddy is not one of those people. It turns out she is a self-made woman. In fact, the two of them are a lot alike in that way, even if Biddy refuses to admit to it.

Sheila strides up the walkway toward the door, trying to settle the butterflies in her stomach. She hasn't wanted something this badly in years. And she's surprised how much she cares about these women's approval.

Through the picture window to her left, she can see the rest of the Women's Club has already arrived and sits around the massive stone fireplace. They are an unusual group. Amelia is in a folding chair with her eyes closed and wearing her trademark baby-food-stained sweater with carrot puree in her hair. Ruby bustles about with trays and trays of little cakes and cookies as if this were a party of twenty and those twenty hadn't eaten a meal in a decade. And Megan, Biddy's spoiled daughter, stares out at this vignette through the computer screen set on the coffee table. Sheila isn't really sure why she is still part of this club, since she doesn't live in Pooka. But somehow these women who Sheila never would have met without her mandatory service hours (the result of a ridiculous law and conviction, of course) have become family. In fact, they are the first female friends she's ever had.

She rings the doorbell, and within seconds, hears Biddy's confident footsteps tapping on the other side. Sheila breathes in. Biddy swings the door open and her eyes grow wide.

"Look," Sheila says. "We're twins!" She knew she nailed the outfit.

Biddy's forehead creases. "We most certainly are not."

"Yes, we are." Sheila holds her blue and green tweed-clad arm against Biddy's. "It's the same suit."

"You need to go home and change." Biddy makes to close the door, which is rather shocking to Sheila. If it were her, she'd be flattered that a younger, more beautiful woman selected the same clothing.

But Ruby's hand shoots out to stop the door from completely closing. "What's going on here?"

Ruby appears at Biddy's side as the door reopens, still holding one of her trays. "Oh look," she giggles. "You're twins!"

Ruby opens the door wider and Sheila heads past a glaring Biddy into the living room. This isn't exactly the way Sheila hoped to start today. She'd hoped to impress Biddy. However, it's also not the first time Biddy has tried to close a door in her face either.

"Hello," Sheila says to Amelia and Megan.

Megan squints through the computer screen at her and laughs. "You have the same—"

"That's enough!" Biddy picks up her gavel, bends down, and taps it on the coffee table. "Welcome to our first annual year-end board meeting. A year ago, I officially filed all our necessary paperwork to become a 501(c). Under this designation, we are required to hold annual board meetings to elect directors and approve budgets. This meeting today will fulfill that obligation. Let's start with club updates. Amelia, do you want to review the minutes from the last meeting?"

Amelia, the club's secretary, pulls a stack of papers out of her handbag, wipes a smear of banana off the top one, and looks down at her notes. "At our last meeting, we discussed doing a project to help the free food pantry."

"Yes, that was a great idea!" Biddy says.

"Biddy," Ruby tugs at her sleeve until her best friend looks at her. Ruby is the Vice President. "I called the pantry, and they refused our help."

"Oh." Biddy looks momentarily flummoxed.

In truth, the club has pitched many charity projects and no one in the town wants anything to do with them, even when they are donating money. The townspeople are still a little bitter that the club shut down Pooka's major revenue stream on their last project. That the revenue stream was illegal doesn't seem to matter to them. Sheila has learned that people only seem to care about the legality of revenue streams when it applies to single women, minding their own business, and doing what they need to do to support themselves, like herself.

Biddy shakes her head. "Well, let's move on to our finance report from the Treasurer."

This is Sheila. She clears her throat. "We agreed to annual dues of $20, so everyone hand it over."

Biddy rolls her eyes as everyone reaches into her wallet and passes Sheila the money. Megan Venmo's it. Amelia's face turns red as she passes Sheila $8 and then opens up her change purse and begins counting quarters. Sheila hands her back the $8.

"I've got you," she whispers.

This is the perk of owning a successful business. Sheila's job is surprisingly recession—and anger—resistant. Amelia's blush deepens, but she takes back the money and nods gratefully.

Sheila takes the rest of the money, adds hers and enough to

cover Amelia, puts it in an envelope, and passes it to Biddy. "We have $100."

"Wonderful," Biddy says, but she doesn't look like she means it. "In the future, perhaps it might be better if you mail out a statement and then people can mail you back the dues."

This doesn't seem like a better method at all. Sheila can tell you that rule number one in business is that a customer doesn't leave your workplace without paying in cash on the spot. On the front-end of delivery, in fact. But she keeps this thought to herself.

"Next up, is membership. Ruby—any updates?"

Besides being Vice President, Ruby is also in charge of new member recruitment. Now, she shakes her head.

"No new members."

Biddy's forehead creases. "What about the ones who signed up at the launch of Eileen's exhibit in the museum?"

"They all quit when the co-op failed and their farms went under. I'm barely staying afloat myself," Ruby says.

Ruby runs the local pub and if that is hurting, the town has truly hit rock bottom.

"Well." Biddy gathers herself together and appears taller. "That's okay. Moving into our second year, as the President, it's my mission to make sure the club stays relevant and healthy—"

"Wait a minute," Sheila says. "Aren't we supposed to have an election?"

Biddy looks shocked.

"Well, yes," Biddy says. "But do we really need one?"

Shelia frowns. "According to Roger's Rules of Order, I thought we were supposed to have one."

"It's Robert's Rules of Order and no, that doesn't dictate

leadership terms. Our bylaws do."

"Well, whatever. I thought there was supposed to be an election."

"She's right," Megan says helpfully, although she looks like she's fighting back laughter.

"You are right." Biddy always looks to be in pain when she utters these words. "I'm jumping the gun a little, but I thought we'd all just keep our current positions since we don't have new members vying for leadership roles."

"Oh goody," Ruby claps her hands. "I love being Vice President. I'm number two again."

Sheila's heart is racing. She takes a deep breath. "I'm running for President."

Everyone freezes. Four pairs of wide eyes stare at her. Sheila reminds herself that she is ready for this. She needs to project confidence.

"YOU want to run for President?" Biddy says. "That's ridiculous. I'm the one who created this club and bring years of experience serving on boards. You aren't qualified to be president. This is your first club. And you have a criminal record."

"That hasn't stopped other politicians," Ruby points out. "In fact, it's quite the trendy thing these days."

"I think it's a great idea." This unexpected announcement comes from Megan, of all people. "That'll free up some of your time, Mom, and you can come back to Boston to help me with Dad's memorial."

"I'm not going to Boston and I'm certainly not attending a memorial for your father."

Apparently, Biddy still hasn't gotten over learning that the man cheated on her. Sheila doesn't want to say anything to anger her further, but in her experience, it happens more often than one would imagine.

"I think it's a good idea," Amelia says quietly. "I'm always telling my children that they should take turns and try new things. I think that should apply to us adults, too."

"Thank you, Amelia," Sheila says.

She doesn't like to brag, but she's pretty good at math, and thus far, if you include her own vote, along with Amelia's, and Megan's, it looks like she's got three in her camp and only two for Biddy. Ruby, of course, would never vote against her best friend. She was hoping for unanimity and Biddy's blessing, but she's got to take what she can get.

"Then it's settled," she says. "All for me being president?"

"Aye." Megan's, Amelia's, and her own hands shoot up.

"Nay," says Biddy.

Ruby says nothing and looks at her hands folded in her lap.

"I'll just mark you as abstaining," Amelia whispers to her.

Ruby looks back gratefully.

Sheila looks around the group and can hardly believe it. She did it. These women trust her enough to be president. She blushes as they all clap. Biddy rolls her eyes, but Sheila knows she can win her over. She will spend the year proving she learned so much from Biddy.

"As my first act as president, I'd like to propose that we reinstate Ruby as Vice President since she's done the job so competently."

"Really?" Ruby's eyes light up.

"I second the motion," Amelia says. Even Biddy agrees to this. And in no time at all, Ruby is Vice President once again.

"I'd actually like to try my hand at Treasurer," Amelia says. "I'd love to learn more about finance."

"Good for you," Sheila says. "I'll give you all the help you need." They vote and she is in.

Sheila looks at Biddy. "With Amelia taking my place as treasurer, that makes you Secretary."

"You've got to be kidding," she mutters. "I should at least be President Emeritus."

"If Emeritus is Latin for Chief Note-Taker, then you're good to go!" Sheila says cheerfully.

Biddy frowns and is about to speak but Megan interrupts.

"I'll do it," she says. "I'll be Secretary and Mom can be President Emeritus."

Sheila shrugs. At least Megan finally has a job, and Biddy is looking slightly mollified.

The room falls silent, and everyone looks at Sheila. She looks back at them and realizes something upsetting. Sheila hasn't really thought much about what she should do after winning. What will be their mission this year? Sheila suddenly misses the drama and near death incidents of last year. It's going to be hard to live up to Biddy's year without something to do. The doorbell chimes cut off her dilemma. She looks out the bay window.

"Is that a bloody nun?" Ruby asks.

Sheila's lips pull up in a smile. This, she thinks, will do just fine.

Buy A Cryptic Death: A Pooka Women's Club Mystery (Book 2) now!

https://www.amazon.com/dp/B0GKCTCXFB/

About the Author

Virginia Ann is an IPPY Gold Medal-winning author of cozy mysteries including The Pooka Women's Club Mystery series set in a small town in the Midwest. She is a former consumer industry analyst whose decade of experience following financial mysteries now fuels her passion for crafting intricate whodunits. Her insights have been featured in *The Wall Street Journal, Forbes,* and *Reuters,* and she has appeared on CNBC's Squawk Box, BNN, and Bloomberg. A lifelong fan of small-town mysteries, she blends intrigue, humor, and strong female friendships in her writing. She lives in Wisconsin with her cocker spaniel, Millie.

Also by Virginia Ann

The Pooka Women's Club Mysteries

The Potter's Final Piece (Book 1)
Biddy Bramley never expected to return to Pooka. But after her husband's death, she's back in her hometown—grieving, restless, and drawn into a decades-old mystery involving her estranged sister and claims to a stolen pottery fortune. Buy on Amazon.

A Cryptic Death (Book 2)
For a year, Dymphna has tried to remember who she was before she arrived at the convent of Sacred Heart of the Woods: a woman with an unexplained fortune in her pockets, no memory of her past, and not one answer the doctors could give her. She's finally made peace with her unknown past. She's ready to take her vows and become a nun. But someone won't let her. Buy on Amazon.

The Thief of Traminette (Book 3)
Amelia Reagan has spent years holding her family together through hard times. But when her husband is arrested for murdering a wealthy vineyard owner, her world shatters overnight. Buy on Amazon.